Strange Relics

Other Handheld Classics

Strange Relics

Stories of Archaeology and the Supernatural,

1895–1954

edited by Amara Thornton and Katy Soar

Handheld Classic 28

This edition published in 2022 by Handheld Press
72 Warminster Road, Bath BA2 6RU, United Kingdom.
www.handheldpress.co.uk

Series design by Nadja Guggi and typeset in Adobe Caslon Pro
and Open Sans.

Contents

Acknowledgements

The editors would like to thank Elizabeth (Lisa) French and
Ann French for their permission to publish 'The Golden Ring',
and for their information about Alan Wace's life and work.

Amara Thornton is a historian of archaeology, and co-investigator
on the research project *Beyond Notability: Re-Evaluating Women's
Work in Archaeology, History and Heritage in Britain 1870–1950* at the
University of London. Her book *Archaeologists in Print: Publishing
for the People* was published in 2018.

Katy Soar is a Senior Lecturer in Classical Archaeology at the
University of Winchester. Her research interests are Greek
archaeology (especially the Bronze Age of the Aegean), and
the history and reception of archaeology. She is also a frequent
contributor to *Hellebore*.

Introduction

BY AMARA THORNTON AND KATY SOAR

M R James – author, medievalist and archaeologist – emphasised the importance of settings for ghost stories; that the best were set in the contemporary everyday world, into which horror moved ... slowly (James 1931). That everyday world, of course, includes the remains of the past in various forms – spaces and places which are the settings for what Tina Paphitis calls the 'haunting' potential of archaeology (Paphitis 2020, 343). Now considered one of the greatest ghost story authors of his age, James was noted by contemporaries for effectively pioneering 'the Archaeological Ghost Story' (Ellis 1926, 176). His antiquarian scholars' literal and metaphorical probings, leading to the unleashing of inevitable horrors, have become a byword for 'the archaeological uncanny' (Moshenka 2006, 92–93; 2012). It is perhaps less well known that in the 1920s James's tales, as well as those of E F Benson and Algernon Blackwood, were designated as 'magic' stories, encapsulating aspects of inexplicable phenomena not necessarily attached to ghosts (Swift et al 1923, 147). Similarly the French critic Évelyne Caron refers to Arthur Machen's work, particularly that of the late 1890s and one of the stories included here, as 'archaeological'. A translation of her definition is worth quoting in full as it gives scope to some of the ways 'archaeological' is meant in this anthology: 'Machen's "fantastic" is archaeological in nature. Beneath the surface of everyday life lie historic depths. Its characteristic is simultaneity; everything that has been and will be exists at the same time' (Caron 1972, 38; trans Katy Soar). 'Le fantastique' is a French literary and cinematic genre which incorporates elements of science fiction, horror and fantasy and introduces a malevolent phenomenon into everyday reality (Swoboda 2020, 207). It has been defined as 'a break in the acknowledged order, an intrusion of the inadmissible within the changeless everyday legality' (Caillois 1965, quoted in Todorov 1975, 26).

With this anthology we hope to move 'the Archaeological Ghost Story' beyond the discovery-led trope in which a naive (white male) scholar/excavator brings to light that-which-should-be-left-buried. Instead the stories presented here capture 'fantastic', one might say magical, encounters with the material remains of the past, whether movable or immovable, in the contemporary world – contemporary to the stories' original publication, at least. Through these encounters the barrier between the present and the past becomes thin, and strange happenings result. There are few explicit ghosts in this volume, and no 'traditional' mummies. Archaeologists, defined as persons who study, curate, or excavate the past, are present, but rather than being unwitting victims here they are either obsessive villains or specialists who *know* when to leave well alone. Specialism is key: some the archaeologists and antiquarians featured here are practitioners or students of the occult.

Contexts

In *Strange Relics* the settings are significant and add immeasurably to the eerieness of these tales. The historical context of the period in which these stories were written is important too as the framework for the settings featured here. From the late nineteenth century archaeologists from Europe and North America regularly excavated overseas, particularly in Egypt and Greece (see Gill 2011). The British School at Athens was established during this period; each year students arrived in Greece to travel, excavate and study artefacts in museums in the region. Among them were M R James, E F Benson, and Alan Wace, whose story 'The Golden Ring' (1954) in this volume reflects an archaeologist's experiences in the country. Egyptian legislation in place at this time made it possible for antiquities excavated by foreign teams to be exported to museums and private collections abroad, which included antiquities purchased from dealers (see Stevenson 2019). While the protagonist in Benson's 'The Ape' (1917) is a tourist, the story's setting reflects the seasonal migration of Western tourists and archaeologists to Egypt over the winter, and the market in antiquities that flourished in places like Luxor, the city across the Nile from the Valley of the Kings and Queens and adjacent to Karnak, where ancient temples and other buildings were located alongside a modern village. Large luxurious hotels dotted the riverbank at Luxor, built to accommodate this tourist traffic. The Egypt represented in 'The Ape' and 'The Curse of The Stillborn' (1925) is an Imperial space. Occupied by Britain from 1882, Egypt became a protectorate in the British Empire by the end of 1914 as the First World War was escalating. Benson's Egyptologist-occultist Rankin references this colonisation in 'The Ape', stating '[...] we have killed it [Egypt] with our board-schools and our steamers and our religion' (40).

War is also a context for some of the stories, particularly on the British home front and in the Mediterranean. In H D Everett's 'The Next Heir' (1920) and Algernon Blackwood's 'Roman Remains' (1948) the Roman sites of Britain's home front are places of supposed refuge – and horror – for traumatised and wounded soldiers, and expose the unsettled nature of home-at-war for these returning veterans. Many archaeologists joined the war effort in both world wars; some of those who had excavated in Greece, like Alan Wace, were tied to intelligence-gathering activities. In 'The Golden Ring', Wace introduces a narrator who is sent from the British front at Salonica to Athens in 1917 for 'special duty', a code for intelligence work. The parallel between his narrator's role and Wace's own wartime activities gives the story an authenticity that only increases its weirdness.

All but one of the authors in this volume called Britain home. The visible and invisible remains of Britain's past were also being researched, mapped and excavated during this period. Many local archaeological and historical societies were involved in or reported on investigations of Britain's Roman remains, and the Society for the Promotion of Roman Studies was founded in London in 1910. Arthur Machen's interest in archaeology was awoken early through the antiquarian activities of his grandfather, the Reverend Daniel Jones, in Caerleon in south Wales as well as other excavations in this area during his youth. He explicitly makes clear the debt he owes to these archaeological experiences in his autobiography *Far Off Things*. First he notes the setting: 'Down the valley in the distance was Caerleon-on-Usk; over the hill, somewhere in the lower slopes of the forest, Caerwent, also a Roman city, was buried in the earth, and gave up now and again strange relics'. Then he ponders whether he can 'invent a story which would recreate those vague impressions of wonder and awe and mystery that I myself had received from the form and shape of the land of my boyhood and youth' (Machen 1922, 19–20). Arthur Conan Doyle's 'Through the Veil' (1911) is set among the exposed remains, still under excavation, of the Roman fort at Newstead (Trimontium), near Melrose in the Scottish Borders. Located in a farmer's field where new drains were to be laid, Newstead had been excavated under the aegis of the Society of Antiquaries of Scotland between 1905 and 1910, with solicitor-turned-archaeologist James Curle as director of the work (Richie 2002). Doyle gives a dedicated spiritualist's interpretation of the power of archaeological excavation for reincarnating and resurrecting the ancient past at Trimontium.

Archaeologists of the early twentieth century, contemporary with M R James, were aware of the power of archaeological sites, artefacts, and the process of excavation for inspiring narratives of supernatural occurrences. Egyptologists Arthur Weigall and Margaret Murray both discussed this in print; Murray acknowledging that due to the nature of their work, archaeologists were essentially *assumed* to have supernatural encounters (see Weigall 1912; Murray 1963, 175; and Sheppard 2013, Ch 7). Weekly or monthly pulp and story magazines of the late nineteenth and early twentieth centuries were significant in circulating eerie archaeological tales, and archaeologists wrote supernatural short fiction. The American pulp magazine *Weird Tales* gives us a unique insight into the popular reception of archaeology in the early to mid-twentieth century. Advertising itself as 'A sensational departure from the beaten track', the magazine was first issued in March 1923, just months after the discovery of Tutankhamun's tomb. Stories and poems with archaeological settings, themes or set in the ancient past were regularly published. The first issue contained a story set in 'the Stone Age' – R T M Scott's 'Nimba, the Cave Girl'. Issue 2, from April 1923, includes a brief note 'Has "Tut"'s Tomb Really Been Found?' next to Hamilton Craigie's 'The Incubus', a tale of revenge set amidst Aztec tombs. Over 100 stories and poems published in *Weird Tales* are associated with archaeology or ancient history or feature archaeologists or ancient artefacts. Two in this anthology – Algernon Blackwood's 'Roman Remains' and Dorothy Quick's 'Cracks of Time' – were published in *Weird Tales* in 1948. Selected short notes on archaeological news and discoveries were frequently published, covering many geographical areas and ancient civilisations.

During the period in which many of these stories were set there was interest in psychical research, spiritualism and the occult. The Society of Psychical Research was founded in 1882 with the aim of gathering evidence of phenomena and conducting experiments. Members worked with mediums who were central to the continuing interest in spiritualism, extant since the mid-nineteenth century, for evidence of fraudulent activity (see Salter 1950). Many intellectuals across different disciplines were interested in psychical research.

The most famous and influential of the later nineteenth-century occult societies was the Hermetic Order of the Golden Dawn, founded in Britain in 1888 by three Freemasons, William Robert Woodman, William Wynn Westcott and Samuel Liddell Macgregor Mathers. Drawing on traditions such as Rosicrucianism,

Judeo-Christian mysticism, and the 'Egyptian' esotericism of Hermes Trismegistus (Owen 2004, 3), the society was designed as a place where the occult could be practiced, not just studied (Gilbert 2015, 237), and where, at the higher levels, one could learn how to control and influence the invisible forces of nature (Owen 2004, 4). Many members were from the literary and artistic world, and several authors in this anthology were members, including Arthur Machen, although he left after a year and was generally dismissive of the society in his later autobiographical works. Algernon Blackwood joined the order in 1900 after being introduced by W B Yeats. Over the next two years he progressed to the highest level of the First Order, but decided not to continue further (Ashley 2019, 193).

We chose the stories in this volume with a few parameters in mind. We deliberately excluded stories that explicitly featured mummies, as 'mummy stories' are widely available in many other collections. We also looked specifically for women authors whose stories incorporated archaeology and the supernatural. Our last main parameter was to avoid racism and forms of 'othering'. Stories written by white European and North American authors during this period that feature archaeologists or the discovery of archaeological artefacts and sites, particularly when the settings are outside Europe, are often suffused with racism. We have not been able to avoid it entirely in the stories we have included. Furthermore, in 'The Cure' and 'Roman Remains' physical and intellectual impairments are associated with disturbing elements. Future anthologies of archaeological supernatural stories could showcase more diverse writers and narratives than we were able to find.

Themes

Throughout this anthology several themes reoccur connected to the cause or agent of the supernatural. The common thread that links them is Caron's notion that the disruption or intrusion into quotidian experience, which brings forth the 'fantastic', is related in some way to archaeology.

The idea of the survival is a common theme. During the period when many of these stories were written, the anthropological idea of the 'survival' had an important hold on the academic and popular imagination. Promoted by scholars such as Edward Tylor and James Frazer, survivals were defined as earlier practices, ideas or customs which had, by some means, continued into the present, although in their contemporary context they appeared meaningless or nonsensical. While anthropologists of this period saw these as evidence of society moving in an evolutionary manner from simple to more complex, fiction writers saw the potential for survivals to act as catalysts of fear and horror. Evidence that had been considered, in academic circles, as remnants of earlier beliefs and practices was transmuted into stories of still-active cults practicing ancient and barbaric rites, which threaten to overwhelm those who encounter them. Thus we see the survival of ancient religious cults as a theme underpinning several stories. In the settings of 'The Next Heir', 'The Cure', 'Roman Remains', 'Whitewash', and 'The Ape' material evidence of ancient burial or temple sites indicate the presence of sacred spaces which during the course of the stories are re-used in a modern context.

Survivals are not just practices and beliefs but can also be physical, material artefacts from an earlier society which, as remnants, have the power to destabilise the present. In Quick's 'Cracks of Time' the artefact is a portal through which ancient beings can move. In Benson's 'The Ape' and Scott's 'The Cure', however, artefacts are powerfully transformative, enabling revenge or forcing characters towards an inevitable sacrifice. M R James presents a different survival through human remains, in 'The View from A Hill', in which a macabre relic enables the past and present to merge. In many of the stories in this collection, the survival is even more literal and physical – a mythical being from the past which has somehow survived into the present, as in Blackwood's 'Roman Remains', Quick's 'Cracks of Time', Everett's 'The Next Heir' and Wace's 'The Golden Ring'. In the case of Machen's 'The Shining Pyramid' the survival is an earlier race of humans, sometimes referred to as pygmies or fairies, who had survived into the present after being driven into hidden places in the landscape following the arrival of the iron-bearing Aryans (Card 2019, 46). This destablisation of the past and the present, the continuation of practices long since thought extinct, or the physical presence of artefacts or even beings from earlier civilisations, is the cause of many of the horrors which follow. The archaeological survival from the past is the 'brutal intrusion of mystery into the context of real life' which brings about the sense of horror (Castex 1951, in Todorov 1975, 26). The 'past' in these stories cannot be controlled or contained in the present. In Blackwood's 'Roman Remains' and Quick's 'Cracks of Time' the survivals are horrible, yet are also seductive.

At other times it is not a physical but a psychic connection with the past which produces the horror. Some ancient or historic settings of the stories are imbued with what has been called the 'Stone Tape' effect. This idea takes its name from Nigel Kneale's 1972 film *The Stone Tape* but its main proponent was T C Lethbridge, an archaeologist turned parapsychologist who argued in several works published in the 1960s that intense emotions can be impressed on the electromagnetic field of a given place, and these captured or recorded emotions or thoughts are later replayed when someone with the appropriate psychic sensitivities encounters the specific environment (see Lethbridge 1961 and 1965). However, this idea predates Lethbridge's work; Sir William Barrett, Professor of Experimental Physics at the Royal College of Science for Ireland as well as one of the founders of the Society for Psychical Research wrote in 1911 that:

> some kind of local imprint on material structures or places has been left by some past events occurring to certain persons, who, when on earth, lived or were

closely connected with that particular locality; an echo or phantom of these events becoming perceptible to those now living who happen to be endowed with some special psychic sensitiveness (Barrett 1911, 197)

In John Buchan's 'Ho! The Merry Masons' medieval pagan rites have soaked into the very framework of the medieval house in which our unsuspecting protagonist spends his nights. Similarly, in 'The Next Heir', overlapping histories, ancient and more recent, have been imprinted on the rooms and grounds of a contemporary mansion built to reference the Roman architecture that once stood there. Clement Quinton, its antiquarian proprietor with a penchant for paganism (and the occult), declares that this contemporary building was created 'to – call back to into life [...] associations from the dead past of an earlier period still' (81). In 'Whitewash', past atrocities are brought to terrifying life by a tourist who suffers psychic re-enactments in the Mediterranean cave and passageway where the original acts took place. This 'Stone Tape' effect can trigger memories of past lives too, as Arthur Conan Doyle explores in his story 'Through the Veil'. In all these stories the key element of horror is the blurring of the divide between the past and the present. The natural order of things, the onward march of both time and progress, has been disturbed.

These stories give us something more than the 'traditional' horror associated with the controlled excavation of ancient remains – an activity which most readers are unlikely to have experienced. Rather, it is when we are at home, or on holiday, during our trip to an archaeological site or historic property, our walk among the barrows, our swim in the sea, or even by treading on some very old tiles, that we may encounter a 'strange relic', out of time ...

Works cited

Ashley, Mike, 'The Blackwood-Derleth Correspondence' in *August Derleth Society Newsletter* 6:2 (1983), 1–6.

Ashley, Mike, *Starlight Man. The Extraordinary Life of Algernon Blackwood*. Eureka, CA: Stark House Press, 2019.

Bailey, K V, 'On Conan Doyle', *Foundation* 28 (1983), 78–80.

Barrett, W F, *Psychical* Research (London: Williams and Norgate, 1911).

Bennison, Deborah (ed), *Ghost Writings: A Ghost Story Guide* (Bennison Books, 2014).

Benson, E F, *Our Family Affairs, 1867–1896* (New York: George H Doran Co, 1921).

Blackwood, Algernon, *Episodes Before Thirty* (London: Cassell and Co, 1923).

Boyd, Kathleen, 'Dorothy Quick, Versatile Writer Wields Facile Pen in Many Fields', *Central New Jersey Home News* (22 June 1941), 3.

British School at Athens, 'War Service of Students of the School', *Bulletin of the British School at Athens* 23: viii–xiii (1918/19).

Card, Jeb J, 'Witches and Aliens: How an Archaeologist Inspired Two New Religious Movements', *Nova Religio*, 22: 4 (2019), 44–59.

Caron, Évelyne, 'Structures et organisation de quelques thèmes dans les œuvres d›Arthur Machen', *Littérature* 8 (1972), 36–40.

Clogg, Richard, 'Academics at War: the British School at Athens during the First World War', in Michael Llewellyn Smith, Paschalis M Kitromilides, Eleni Calligas (eds.) *Scholars, Travels, Archives: Greek History and Culture through the British School at Athens* (London: The British School at Athens, 2009), 163–178.

Conley, Greg, 'The Uncrossable Evolutionary Gulfs of Algernon Blackwood', *Journal of the Fantastic in the Arts*, 24: 3 (2013), 426–445.

Dalby, Richard, 'Afterword', in Eleanor Scott, *Randall's Round* (Cambridge: Oleander Press, 2010), 169–175.

Dalby, Richard, 'Introduction', in Margery Lawrence, *Nights of the Round Table* (Ashcroft: Ash-Tree Press, 2013a), np.

Dalby, Richard, 'Introduction', in Margery Lawrence, *Terraces of Night* (Ashcroft: Ash-Tree Press, 2013b), np.

Davin, Eric Leif, *Partners in Wonder: Women and the Birth of Science Fiction 1926–1965* (Lanham: Lexington Books, 2006).

Doyle, Arthur Conan, *The Last Galley: Impressions and Tales* (London: Smith, Elder & Co, 1911).

Edmundson, Melissa, 'The Cataclysm We All Remember': Haunting and Spectral Trauma in the First World War Supernatural Stories of H D Everett', *Women's Writing* 24: 1 (2017), 53–65.

Edmundson, Melissa, *Women's Colonial Gothic Writing 1850–1930: Haunted Empire* (London: Palgrave Macmillan, 2018).

Edmundson, Melissa, 'The Pagan in My Blood', *Hellebore* 2 (2020), 35–41.

Ellis, S M, 'Ghost Stories', *The Bookman* 71: 423 (1926), 176.

Gilbert, Robert A, 'The Hermetic Order of the Golden Dawn', in Christopher Partridge (ed) *The Occult World* (Oxford: Routledge, 2015), 237–246.

Gill, David W J, *Sifting the Soil of Greece: The Early Years of the British School at Athens* (London: Institute of Classical Studies, 2011).

Haining, Peter (ed), *The Supernatural Tales of Sir Arthur Conan Doyle* (W Foulsham & Co Ltd, 1987).

Haslett, Michael and Isobel, 'Buchan and the Classics', in Kate Macdonald (ed), *Reassessing John Buchan. Beyond The Thirty-Nine Steps* (London: Pickering & Chatto, 2016), 17–28.

Illustrated London News, Advertisements, 30 Dec 1950, 1091.

James, Montague Rhodes, 'Some Remarks on Ghost Stories' *The Bookman* December 1929, reprinted in Deborah Bennison (ed), *Ghost Writings: A Ghost Story Guide*, 2014, np.

James, Montague Rhodes, 'Ghosts, Treat Them Gently!', *London Evening News,* 17 April 1931. Reprinted in *M R James Curious Warnings. The Great Ghost Stories of M R James* (London: Jo Fletcher Books, 2012), 1–4.

Jones, Stephen, 'Afterword. The Stony Grin of Unearthly Malice', in M R James *Curious Stories. The Great Ghost Stories of M R James* (London: Jo Fletcher Books, 2012), 605–652.

Kerr, D W F, 'John Buchan, Myth and Modernism', in Kate Macdonald and Nathan Waddell (eds), *John Buchan and the Idea of Modernity* (London: Pickering & Chatto, 2013), 141–154.

Lawrence, Margery, 'Must a Wife Be A Housekeeper?' *Dundee Courier and Advertiser*, 24 July 1935, 6.

LeFanu, Sarah, *Rose Macaulay: A Writer's Life* (London: Virago Press, 2003).

Lethbridge, T C, *Ghost and Ghoul* (London: Routledge and Kegan Paul, 1961).

Lethbridge, T C, *Ghost and Divining Rod* (London: Routledge and Kegan Paul, 1965).

Machen, Arthur, *Far Off Things* (London: Martin Secker Ltd, 1922).

Mantrant, Sophie, 'Textual Secrecy: Arthur Machen and "The True Literature of Occultism"', *Volupté: Interdisciplinary Journal of Decadence Studies*, 1.2 (2018), 81–96.

Margree, Victoria, *British Women's Short Supernatural Fiction, 1860–1930: Our Own Ghostliness* (London: Palgrave Macmillan, 2019).

McCarthy, Julia, 'Miss Quick's Horror Tales Scare Her Too', *Daily News*, 24 March 1939, 44.

Moshenska, Gabriel, 'The Archaeological Uncanny', *Public Archaeology* 5: 2 (2006), 91–9.

Moshenska, Gabriel, *Key Concepts in Public Archaeology* (London: UCL Press, 2017).

Moshenska, Gabriel, 'M R James and the Archaeological Uncanny', *Antiquity* 86: 334 (2012), 1192–1201.

Murray, Margaret, *My First Hundred Years* (London: William Kimber, 1963).

Owen, Alex, *The Place of Enchantment: British Occultism and the Culture of the Modern* (London: University of Chicago Press, 2004).

Paphitis, Tina, 'Haunted landscapes: place, past and presence', *Time and Mind* 13: 4 (2020), 341–9.

Salter, Walter H, *The Society for Psychical Research: An Outline of Its History* (Society for Psychical Research, 1950).

Richie, J Graham, 'James Curle (1862–1944) and Alexander Ormiston Curle (1866–1955): pillars of the establishment', *Proceedings of the Society of Antiquaries of Scotland* 132 (2002), 19–41.

Savage, Elizabeth, 'Challenging Challenger: The Fallout between Sir Arthur Conan Doyle and the Society for Psychical Research' (4 April 2019),

Cambridge University Library Special Collections https://specialcollections-blog.lib.cam.ac.uk/?p=17548 (accessed 28 December 2021).

Scott, Eleanor, *Randall's Round* (1929). (Cambridge: Oleander Press, 2010).

Sheppard, Kathleen, *The Life of Margaret Alice Murray: A Woman's Work in Archaeology* (Langham, MD: Lexington Books, 2013).

Staffordshire Advertiser, 'Funeral of Mrs Everett, at Weston-On-Trent. Gifted Authoress and Philanthropist', 29 September 1923, 5.

Stevenson, Alice, *Scattered Finds: Archaeology, Egyptology and Museums* (London: UCL Press, 2019).

Swift, Benjamin, et al, 'Dreams, Ghosts and Fairies', *The Bookman* 65: 387 (1923), 142–49.

Swoboda, Anna, 'Fantastic Hesitation, Phenomena and the Male Character in Marie Ndiaye's *Three Strong Women*', *Romanica Cracoviensia* 4 (2020), 207–216.

Thornton, Amara, *Archaeologists in Print: Publishing for the People* (London: UCL Press, 2018).

Todorov, Tzevtan, *The Fantastic: A Structural Approach to a Literary Genre*, trans Richard Howard (Ithaca: Cornell University Press, 1975).

Wace, Alan J B, *Greece Untrodden* (Athens: privately published, 1964).

Weigall, Arthur E B P, 'Ghosts in the Valley of the Tombs of the Queens', *Pall Mall Magazine* 49: 230 (1912), 753–66.

Wills, David, 'The Salonica Campaign of the First World War from an Archaeologist's Perspective: Alan J B Wace's Greece Untrodden' (1964). *Balkan Studies* 50 (2015), 139–158.

Biographies

Edward Frederic Benson (1870-1940) attended the University of Cambridge where he studied Classics at King's College and counted 'Monty James' (M R James) among his friends. Benson was admitted to the British School at Athens (BSA) for three consecutive sessions between 1891 and 1895 (Gill 2011, 303-304). In addition to research in Athens he took part in the School's excavations at Megalopolis, the site of an ancient city in Arcadia where, he noted, 'All the plums had already been picked out' (Benson 1921, 286). In 1894 he set out with his sister Margaret Benson for Greece and Egypt; he later wrote they had 'a Tremendous Time' (op cit, 302). Once in Egypt Benson took part in preliminary surveying and excavations at Alexandria and assisted 'Maggie' at Karnak, close to Luxor, where she had begun her own excavations at the Temple of Mut (this temple is explicitly referenced in 'The Ape'). In contrast to Greece, his land of light, for Benson Egypt was a land of darkness, death and nightmares. 'The Ape' was published in 1917, when Benson was working on propaganda for the war effort (British School at Athens 1918/19, ix).

Alongside his short Weird stories 'The Ape' and 'Monkeys', Benson's supernatural novel *Image in the Sand* (1905) was another product of his Egyptian sojourn. Benson's short stories appeared in a number of different magazines, including *Weird Tales*, and anthologies of his stories were published during his lifetime and after his death. A number of his short stories focus on Spiritualism, which is also the topic of his book *Across the Stream* (1919). Among the other stories Benson wrote with archaeological themes are 'Gavon's Eve', 'The Temple', and 'The Flint Knife'.

Algernon Blackwood (1869-1951) Before publishing his first collection of short stories in 1906, Blackwood had led an eventful life. Born into a strict Calvinist family in Kent, he studied psychiatric medicine in Germany, and later founded an unsuccessful dairy farm in Canada. He then ran a hotel, before disappearing into the Canadian wilderness for a summer. After several years in New York, where he became a reporter for *The New York Times*, he returned to England in 1899. In 1906 his first collection, *The Empty House and Other Ghost Stories*, was published by Eveleigh Nash, shortly followed by a series of novels featuring John Silence, a psychic detective and 'physician extraordinary'. Blackwood then moved to Switzerland, where he lived from 1908 to 1914. His visits from there to the Caucasus Mountains produced the novel *The Centaur* (1910), and after visits to Egypt he wrote 'The Sand', 'A Descent in Egypt', and 'The Wave'. After serving in British Military Intelligence in the First World War, Blackwood returned to England, where he continued to write. In 1934, he was invited to read ghost stories on BBC radio, and in 1947 appeared on television.

His travels, time spent in the Canadian wilderness, interest in theosophical works, investigation of haunted houses for the Society of Psychical Research, and membership of the Golden Dawn (Conley 2013, 428), all manifest themselves in his work, in which animistic views of nature dominate. He believed that 'everything was alive, a dim sense that some kind of consciousness struggled through every form, even that a sort of inarticulate communication with this "other life" was possible, could I but discover the way' (Blackwood 1923, 32–33), and this comes through strongly in some of his most famous works, such as 'The Willows' (1907). 'Roman Remains' (1948) was the last story Blackwood published and combines these ideas of old gods and Nature. He sent his only copy to August Derleth, whom he thanked for placing 'my somewhat questionable story' (which he now hoped to develop 'into something really worthwhile' at a later date) into *Weird Tales* magazine (Ashley 1893, 5).

John Buchan (1875–1940) studied Classics at the University of Glasgow and then at Brasenose College, Oxford, where he received a first in Literae Humaniores, while also winning the Newdigate

Prize for poetry, becoming President of the Oxford Union, and publishing his first novel (*Sir Quixote of the Moors*) in 1895. He then read law and was called to the Bar in 1901, the same year he moved to South Africa as private secretary to the High Commissioner. His subsequent career involved journalism, publishing, and writing as a historian and war correspondent during the First World War. He served as a Member of Parliament, Lord High Commissioner to the General Assembly of the Church of Scotland, and, in 1935, as Governor General of Canada. He had a lifelong friendship with his Classics professor Gilbert Murray, who wrote extensively on Greek tragedy and religion. He published over 100 books, many of them the novels and short stories for which he is best known.

Although most famous for the spy thriller *The Thirty Nine Steps* (1915), Buchan's works often involved landscape and ancient history. His travels to Greece (Haslett and Haslett 2016, 23) and knowledge of ancient Greek religion (particularly as discussed by Cambridge Ritualists such as Jane Ellen Harrison, as well as his friend and mentor Murray) resulted in the short story 'Basilissa' in 1914, which in 1926 was expanded into the novel *The Dancing Floor* (Kerr 2013, 142). His interest in pre-Christian cults also appeared in 'The Grove of Ashtaroth' (1910) and in his novel *Witch Wood* (1927). The Roman and pre-Roman history of Britain are featured in his novella 'No Man's Land' (1899) and in the story 'The Wind in the Portico' (1928).

Arthur Conan Doyle (1859–1930) was born in Edinburgh and received his medical degree from the University of Edinburgh in 1881, by which time he had already begun writing short stories (Haining 1987). He is known primarily as the creator of the detective Sherlock Holmes and his assistant Dr Watson. However, his writing shows a strong engagement with history and archaeology, dating to the early years of his writing career with 'A Silver Hatchet' (1883) in which a mysterious murder follows the donation of medieval weapons to a University museum. The burial of an ancient Egyptian mummified woman underpins his story of the undead set in the Louvre Museum, 'The Ring of Thoth' (1890), while his much-anthologised short story 'Lot No 249' (1892), features an obsessive student-Egyptologist's experiments in resurrection at Oxford. In 'Burger's Secret' (1898), set in Rome, Doyle returned to the idea of an obsessive archaeologist. During the 1890s he also became a member of the Society for Psychical Research (see Savage 2019).

Conan Doyle was a firm proponent of Spiritualism, and was famously supportive of the existence of fairies as photographed at Cottingley in 1917, later shown to be a hoax. In *The Last Galley*, the anthology in which 'Through the Veil Appears' appears, Doyle brings together several tales that are set in an ancient past. He conceived of these stories 'as trial flights' for longer works that would bring out 'the actual drama' of life in the past. It was recorded that he valued these stories more than any others he wrote (Doyle 1911, v–vi; Bailey 1983, 78).

Henrietta Dorothy (Huskisson) Everett (1851–1923) Everett's life as an author began in the 1890s. Married at 18, according to the Census she was mother to three children, with a household including six servants by the time her first novel, *A Bride Elect*, was published in 1896. Writing mainly under her pseudonym 'Theo Douglas', Everett established herself as a popular author of supernatural stories, including a vampire novel, *Malevola* (1914). Her second novel *Iras: A Mystery* (1897) involved an Egyptian mummified woman smuggled out of Egypt in a box of Turkish sponges, who comes back to life.

Some of Everett's work appeared in serial form and her short stories were published in a wide variety of periodicals. The *Death Mask and other Ghosts* (1920), in which 'The Next Heir' appears, was Everett's only anthology during her long and successful career (see Edmundson 2017). A few years after her death, M R James wrote a chronological overview of ghostly fiction short stories for *The Bookman* in which he praised Everett for the potency of her tales in *Death Mask* (James 1929 in Bennison 2014: 44, see also 181–182).

Some measure of her life beyond writing may be found in the fact that, at her death, H D Everett was noted for her work in instituting University Extension lectures in Stafford, the town where she lived for many years (*Staffordshire Advertiser*, 1923).

Montague Rhodes James (1862–1936) was born in the Kent village of Goodnestone. 'Monty' as he liked to be called, was the fourth and youngest child of a clergyman. He attended Eton before studying at King's College Cambridge in 1882, where he gained a double first in Classics, becoming a fellow in 1887, and a Provost in 1905. He also became director of the Fitzwilliam Museum in 1893, after unsuccessfully applying for the Disney Professorship of Archaeology in 1892. He became Provost of Eton in 1918, where he remained until his death in 1936.

James was a noted medievalist and antiquarian, whose specialism was in Apocryphal Books of the Bible and western medieval manuscripts. He catalogued every medieval manuscript in the Cambridge college libraries between 1895 and 1914. He also took part in archaeological excavations; as a student of the British School at Athens he excavated on Cyprus at the temple of Aphrodite at Old Paphos, where he focused on deciphering the inscriptions (Moshenka 2012, 1194). However, this would be the limit of his involvement in both classical scholarship and archaeology, as he turned instead towards his main interests of philology and medieval studies (Moshenka 2017, 163). He also took part in the excavations at the chapterhouse of Bury St Edmunds between 1902–3, where due to his study of medieval manuscripts he discovered the burial places of the medieval abbots (ibid).

Both medieval antiquities and the antiquarians interested in them loom large in James' work, and his interests in these topics clearly fed into his ghost stories, which were originally read aloud in college at Christmas meetings of the Chit-Chat Society – whose members also included E F Benson (Jones 2012, 607). The first collection of these was published in 1890 in magazine form, and then in 1904 as *Ghost Stories of an Antiquary*. Further short collections appeared until 1925, and in 1931 came a collected edition by Edward Arnold entitled *The Collected Ghost Stories of M R James*.

Margery Harriet Lawrence (1889–1969) began her professional life as an artist, publishing her first book in her early twenties. She quickly became a successful and popular author, with a few of her novels being made into films (see Dalby 2013a, Dalby 2013b, Edmundson 2018). She was outspoken in her views that women should continue with professional careers after marriage (she married hotelier Arthur Towle in 1927). Homemaking was not for Lawrence (see Lawrence 1935) – she travelled frequently, was a highly visible public figure, and wrote until her death.

In the 1920s, she wrote several short stories for *Hutchinson's Mystery Story Magazine*, including 'The Curse of the Stillborn'. A firm believer in re-incarnation and a committed Spiritualist from an early age, Lawrence described her experience reliving the past as triggered by a Roman road and encampment in Wales in her memoir *Ferry Over Jordan* (1944). History, archaeology, folklore and the occult feature in a number of Lawrence's works, both short fiction and novels. She wrote a biographical novel of the famous ancient Egyptian queen Hatshepsut in *Daughter of the Nile* (1956), and her novel *The Gate of Yesterday* (1960) is set in ancient Greece. Her short story 'Robin's Rath' plays with the idea of Pan/the Green Man (see Edmundson 2020a).

The themes of re-incarnation and parallel lives in the past can be found in 'The Case of the Bronze Door' and 'The Case of Ella McLeod' from Lawrence's 1969 anthology *Number Seven Queer Street,* and in *The Rent in the Veil* (1951). As well as the Egyptologist narrator Frith in 'Curse of the Stillborn', archaeologists appear in other Lawrence works as characters, including in *The Rent in the Veil* and *Bride of Darkness* (1967; see Thornton 2018, Ch 9).

(Emilie) Rose Macaulay (1881–1958) read modern history at Somerville College, Oxford, from 1900 to 1903. During this period she formed a firm friendship with Margerie Venables Taylor, who would become an esteemed archaeologist of Roman Britain (LeFanu 2003, 49). Alongside her many novels, Macaulay wrote regularly for newspapers and magazines as a columnist and reviewer, and she was a regular commentator, panel member, and programme presenter on BBC radio.

Macaulay travelled abroad frequently from an early age – during her childhood her family lived near Genoa, Italy for nearly ten years. Her journey to Greece on a Hellenic cruise in 1912 provided inspiration for another of her ghost stories, 'The Empty Berth' (LeFanu 2003, 100). Later on she contributed to British European Airways' 1950 promotional pamphlet *Sunshine Holidays now* (*Illustrated London News*, 30 December 1950). 'Whitewash', set in Capri, was published in Cynthia Asquith's *Third Ghost Book* in 1954. In *Pleasure of Ruins* (1953), Macaulay ruminates on archaeological remains through histories of travel, exploration, and excavations. Her chapter 'Ghostly Streets' in this work includes a section on Italy's various abandoned Roman towns.

Arthur Machen (1863–1947), the pen-name of Arthur Llewellyn Jones, was born in Caerleon-on-Usk and between then and his death in Beaconsfield in 1947 he had a varied career. Never wealthy, he worked as a cataloguer, translator, teacher, actor and journalist at the London Evening News – all jobs which supported his writing. He published multiple stories and novels between 1890 and 1936, as well as two autobiographies and numerous essays. His works from the period between 1890 and 1900 are the most clearly supernatural. Many of these feature ancient relics and the survival of ancient rites, which are often related to the presence of the 'little people', primitive humans who still lived on the edges of the civilised world.

Machen was interested in mysticism and spiritualism – he was briefly a member of the Golden Dawn after the death of his first wife in 1899, and during the 1880s he worked as a cataloguer of occult books for bookseller and publisher George Redway, producing the annotated catalogue *The Literature of Occultism and Archaeology*. Later in his life he also discussed humanity's – and his own – attraction to secret societies and rituals in the article 'The Cult of the Secret' (1926) (Mantrant 2018, 81).

Archaeological excavations in his native Caerleon certainly inspired many of Machen's stories. Similar artefacts appear in his works, and he explicitly makes clear the debt he owes to this background in his autobiography *Far Off Things*.

Dorothy Quick (1896–1962) was born in New York, and achieved early press attention due to her childhood friendship with American author Mark Twain, who encouraged her to write, giving her critical feedback on her drafts. Her memoir of this friendship, *Enchantment: A Little Girl's Friendship with Mark Twain*, was published in 1961. She had a long-standing interest in history which filters through her many short stories and poems. She spent time in Europe during her childhood, and frequently travelled there as an adult. Quick dated her beginnings as a writer of horror stories for pulp magazines to the mid 1930s, following an injury that kept her temporarily bed-ridden (McCarthy 1939). She saw pulp magazines as a worthy – if de-valued – literary venue (Boyd 1941).

Dorothy Quick was among the most frequently published women authors in *Weird Tales*, from 1932 when her poem 'Candles' was published until the year the magazine folded in 1954 (see Davin 2006, 353, 359, 399). Many of her *Weird Tales* stories are either set in the past, feature historic artefacts or houses, or involve the resurrection of ancient gods. Settings include a Hollywood film set, an ancient temple in Mexico, a restored Tudor farmhouse in England, a medieval castle in France, and a river in Ceylon (Sri Lanka).

Alongside her poetry, which was published both in magazines and in anthologies, Quick also had a column, 'Quick Look at Things', for literary and film reviews. She also wrote detective fiction.

Eleanor Scott (1892–1965) was the nom de plume of Helen Madeline Leys from Hampton Hill, Middlesex. She was surrounded by writing from an early age: her father John Kirkwood Leys was a popular novelist in the late nineteenth and early twentieth centuries, and after his sudden death, Helen's mother Ellen turned to writing stories and novelettes to pay the bills (Dalby 2010, 170). Helen attended St Hilda's College, Oxford, and after the First World War she began teaching, eventually becoming principal of a teacher training college. Her first work, 'The Room', was published under her own name in 1923, after which she published under Eleanor Scott. She would write several novels and prize-winning non-fiction works between 1928 and 1939.

Randall's Round, published in 1929, was her only collection of supernatural fiction. Its stories draw on her lifelong interest in history, and references to pagan ritual and Roman antiquities, as well as allusions to James George Frazer's *The Golden Bough*, were no doubt inspired by her undergraduate studies (Margree 2019, 156). The influence of M R James is also notable. However, a key inspiration for these tales are her own nightmares. In the foreword to *Randall's Round*, she notes that these stories 'have all had their origins in dreams' (Scott 2010, 7). It is possible that in writing these down she was able to exorcise her nightmares, as it seems she never again wrote a supernatural story. However, Richard Dalby suggests that she may have published several supernatural stories in the *Creeps* anthologies published by Philip Allen and Co. between 1932 and 1936, under the name N Dennet. A D Marks, the director of Philip Allen and Co, had previously been the director of Ernest Benn, which had published *Randall's Round*, and the stories by Dennett are very similar in style. This connection between Dennett and Scott however remains unproven (Dalby 2010, 173).

Alan Wace (1879–1957) graduated from Pembroke College Cambridge in 1902, with a first-class degree in both parts of the classical tripos. Between then and 1912, when he became a lecturer in Ancient History and Archaeology at the University of St Andrews, he was a student at the British School at Athens (Gill 2011, 61–2). In total, he spent nine sessions at the School, and became its Director in 1914. With the outbreak of the First World War, Wace was seconded to the British legation at Athens between 1915–19 as Director of Relief for the British Refugees from Turkey (a role that he himself later admitted was 'merely camouflage for Intelligence'; Clogg 2009, 168). He took up the directorship again in 1920, a post he held until 1923.

His first and most famous project as Director was at Mycenae, and he excavated there intermittently between 1920 and 1955. Wace's years at Mycenae and his familiarity with its material culture meant that he was one of the first to argue against Arthur Evans's theory that the origin of Mycenaean civilisation lay with the Minoans, who predate the Mycenaeans in regard to their development in the Aegean. The controversy surrounding these arguments can be seen in his story 'The Golden Ring'.

Storytelling was an important element of the field experience on Wace's excavations. After the evening meals, rather than sing or play cards, Wace and his friends would tell stories, many of which were created at the time, while others would be based on folk tales of the Vlachs; all of them were designed to 'capture something of the intangible character of Greece' (Wace 1964, 8). These stories were collected together and published posthumously by his wife in 1964 as Greece Untrodden, and several of them, including the story included in this volume, feature the fictional archaeologist George Evesham (Wills 2015, 152).

1 The Shining Pyramid (1895)

ARTHUR MACHEN

1 The Arrow-head Character

'Haunted, you said?'

'Yes, haunted. Don't you remember, when I saw you three years ago, you told me about your place in the west with the ancient woods hanging all about it, and the wild, domed hills, and the ragged land? It has always remained a sort of enchanted picture in my mind as I sit at my desk and hear the traffic rattling in the street in the midst of whirling London. But when did you come up?'

'The fact is, Dyson, I have only just got out of the train. I drove to the station early this morning and caught the 10.45.'

'Well, I am very glad you looked in on me. How have you been getting on since we last met? There is no Mrs Vaughan, I suppose?'

'No,' said Vaughan, 'I am still a hermit, like yourself. I have done nothing but loaf about.'

Vaughn had lit his pipe and sat in the elbow chair, fidgeting and glancing about him in a somewhat dazed and restless manner. Dyson had wheeled round his chair when his visitor entered and sat with one arm fondly reclining on the desk of his bureau, and touching the litter of manuscript.

'And you are still engaged in the old task?' said Vaughan, pointing to the pile of papers and the teeming pigeon-holes.

'Yes, the vain pursuit of literature, as idle as alchemy, and as entrancing. But you have come to town for some time I suppose; what shall we do to-night?'

'Well, I rather wanted you to try a few days with me down in the west. It would do you a lot of good. I'm sure.'

'You are very kind, Vaughan, but London in September is hard to leave. Doré could not have designed anything more wonderful and mystic than Oxford Street as I saw it the other evening; the sunset flaming, the blue haze transmuting the plain street into a road "far in the spiritual city".'

'I should like you to come down though. You would enjoy roaming over our hills. Does this racket go on all day and night? It quite bewilders me; I wonder how you can work through it. I am sure you would revel in the great peace of my old home among the woods.'

Vaughan lit his pipe again, and looked anxiously at Dyson to see if his inducements had had any effect, but the man of letters shook his head, smiling, and vowed in his heart a firm allegiance to the streets.

'You cannot tempt me,' he said.

'Well, you may be right. Perhaps, after all, I was wrong to speak of the peace of the country. There, when a tragedy does occur, it is like a stone thrown into a pond; the circles of disturbance keep on widening, and it seems as if the water would never be still again.'

'Have you ever any tragedies where you are?'

'I can hardly say that. But I was a good deal disturbed about a month ago by something that happened; it may or may not have been a tragedy in the usual sense of the word.'

'What was the occurrence?'

'Well, the fact is a girl disappeared in a way which seems highly mysterious. Her parents, people of the name of Trevor, are well-to-do farmers, and their eldest daughter Annie was a sort of village beauty; she was really remarkably handsome. One afternoon she thought she would go and see her aunt, a widow who farms her own land, and as the two houses are only about five or six miles apart, she started off, telling her parents she would take the short cut over the hills. She never got to her aunt's, and she never was seen again. That's putting it in a few words.'

'What an extraordinary thing! I suppose there are no disused mines, are there, on the hills? I don't think you quite run to anything so formidable as a precipice?'

'No; the path the girl must have taken had no pitfalls of any description; it is just a track over wild, bare hillside, far, even from a byroad. One may walk for miles without meeting a soul, but it is perfectly safe.'

'And what do people say about it?'

'Oh, they talk nonsense – among themselves. You have no notion as to how superstitious English cottagers are in out-of-the-way parts like mine. They are as bad as the Irish, every whit, and even more secretive.'

'But what do they say?'

'Oh, the poor girl is supposed to have "gone with the fairies", or to have been "taken by the fairies". Such stuff!' he went on, 'one would laugh if it were not for the real tragedy of the case.'

Dyson looked somewhat interested.

'Yes,' he said, '"fairies" certainly strike a little curiously on the ear in these days. But what do the police say? I presume they do not accept the fairy-tale hypothesis?'

'No; but they seem quite at fault. What I am afraid of is that Annie Trevor must have fallen in with some scoundrels on her way. Castletown is a large seaport, you know, and some of the worst of the foreign sailors occasionally desert their ships and go on the tramp up and down the country. Not many years ago a Spanish sailor named Garcia murdered a whole family for the sake of plunder that was not worth sixpence. They are hardly human, some of these fellows, and I am dreadfully afraid the poor girl must have come to an awful end.'

'But no foreign sailor was seen by anyone about the country?'

'No; there is certainly that; and of course country people

are quick to notice anyone whose appearance and dress are a little out of the common. Still it seems as if my theory were the only possible explanation.'

'There are no data to go upon,' said Dyson, thoughtfully. 'There was no question of a love affair, or anything of the kind, I suppose?'

'Oh, no, not a hint of such a thing. I am sure if Annie were alive she would have contrived to let her mother know of her safety.'

'No doubt, no doubt. Still it is barely possible that she is alive and yet unable to communicate with her friends. But all this must have disturbed you a good deal.'

'Yes, it did; I hate a mystery, and especially a mystery which is probably the veil of horror. But frankly, Dyson, I want to make a clean breast of it; I did not come here to tell you all this.'

'Of course not,' said Dyson, a little surprised at Vaughan's uneasy manner. 'You came to have a chat on more cheerful topics.'

'No, I did not. What I have been telling you about happened a month ago, but something which seems likely to affect me more personally has taken place within the last few days, and to be quite plain, I came up to town with the idea that you might be able to help me. You recollect that curious case you spoke to me about on our last meeting; something about a spectacle-maker.'

'Oh, yes, I remember that. I know I was quite proud of my acumen at the time; even to this day the police have no idea why those peculiar yellow spectacles were wanted. But, Vaughan, you really look quite put out; I hope there is nothing serious?'

'No, I think I have been exaggerating, and I want you to reassure me. But what has happened is very odd.'

'And what has happened?'

'I am sure that you will laugh at me, but this is the story. You must know there is a path, a right of way, that goes through my land, and to be precise, close to the wall of the kitchen garden. It is not used by many people; a woodman now and again finds it useful, and five or six children who go to school in the village pass twice a day. Well, a few days ago I was taking a walk about the place before breakfast, and I happened to stop to fill my pipe just by the large doors in the garden wall. The wood, I must tell you, comes to within a few feet of the wall, and the track I spoke of runs right in the shadow of the trees. I thought the shelter from a brisk wind that was blowing rather pleasant, and I stood there smoking with my eyes on the ground. Then something caught my attention. Just under the wall, on the short grass; a number of small flints were arranged in a pattern; something like this': and Mr Vaughan caught at a pencil and piece of paper, and dotted down a few strokes.

'You see,' he went on, 'there were, I should think, twelve little stones neatly arranged in lines, and spaced at equal distances, as I have shown it on the paper. They were pointed stones, and the points were very carefully directed one way.'

'Yes,' said Dyson, without much interest, 'no doubt the children you have mentioned had been playing there on their way from school. Children, as you know, are very fond of making such devices with oyster shells or flints or flowers, or with whatever comes in their way.'

'So I thought; I just noticed these flints were arranged in a sort of pattern and then went on. But the next morning I was taking the same round, which, as a matter of fact, is habitual with me, and again I saw at the same spot a device in flints. This time it was really a curious pattern; something like the spokes of a wheel, all meeting at a common centre, and this centre formed by a device which looked like a bowl; all, you understand done in flints.'

'You are right,' said Dyson, 'that seems odd enough. Still it is reasonable that your half-a-dozen school children are responsible for these fantasies in stone.'

'Well, I thought I would set the matter at rest. The children pass the gate every evening at half-past five, and I walked by at six, and found the device just as I had left it in the morning. The next day I was up and about at a quarter to seven, and I found the whole thing had been changed. There was a pyramid outlined in flints upon the grass. The children I saw going by an hour and a half later, and they ran past the spot without glancing to right or left. In the evening I watched them going home, and this morning when I got to the gate at six o'clock there was a thing like a half moon waiting for me.'

'So then the series runs thus: firstly ordered lines, then, the device of the spokes and the bowl, then the pyramid, and finally, this morning, the half moon. That is the order, isn't it?'

'Yes; that is right. But do you know it has made me feel very uneasy? I suppose it seems absurd, but I can't help thinking that some kind of signalling is going on under my nose, and that sort of thing is disquieting.'

'But what have you to dread? You have no enemies?'

'No; but I have some very valuable old plate.'

'You are thinking of burglars then?' said Dyson, with an accent of considerable interest, 'but you must know your neighbours. Are there any suspicious characters about?'

'Not that I am aware of. But you remember what I told you of the sailors.'

'Can you trust your servants?'

'Oh, perfectly. The plate is preserved in a strong room; the butler, an old family servant, alone knows where the key is kept. There is nothing wrong there. Still, everybody is aware that I have a lot of old silver, and all country folks are given to gossip. In that way information may have got abroad in very undesirable quarters.'

'Yes, but I confess there seems something a little unsatisfactory in the burglar theory. Who is signalling to whom? I cannot see my way to accepting such an explanation. What put the plate into your head in connection with these flint signs, or whatever one may call them?'

'It was the figure of the Bowl,' said Vaughan. 'I happen to possess a very large and very valuable Charles II punch-bowl. The chasing is really exquisite, and the thing is worth a lot of money. The sign I described to you was exactly the same shape as my punch-bowl.'

'A queer coincidence certainly. But the other figures or devices: you have nothing shaped like a pyramid?'

'Ah, you will think that queerer. As it happens, this punch-bowl of mine, together with a set of rare old ladles, is kept in a mahogany chest of a pyramidal shape. The four sides slope upwards, the narrow towards the top.'

'I confess all this interests me a good deal,' said Dyson. 'let us go on then. What about the other figures; how about the Army, as we may call the first sign, and the Crescent or Half Moon?'

'Ah, there is no reference that I can make out of these two. Still, you see I have some excuse for curiosity at all events. I should be very vexed to lose any of the old plate; nearly all the pieces have been in the family for generations. And I cannot get it out of my head that some scoundrels mean to rob me, and are communicating with one another every night.'

'Frankly,' said Dyson, 'I can make nothing of it; I am as much in the dark as yourself. Your theory seems certainly the only possible explanation, and yet the difficulties are immense.'

He leaned back in his chair, and the two men faced each other, frowning, and perplexed by so bizarre a problem.

'By the way,' said Dyson, after a long pause, 'what is your geological formation down there?'

Mr Vaughan looked up, a good deal surprised by the question.

'Old red sandstone and limestone, I believe,' he said. 'We are just beyond the coal measures, you know.'

'But surely there are no flints either in the sandstone or the limestone?'

'No, I never see any flints in the fields. I confess that did strike me as a little curious.'

'I should think so! It is very important. By the way, what size were the flints used in making these devices?'

'I happen to have brought one with me; I took it this morning.'

'From the Half Moon?'

'Exactly. Here it is.'

He handed over a small flint, tapering to a point, and about three inches in length.

Dyson's face blazed up with excitement as he took the thing from Vaughan.

'Certainly,' he said, after a moment's pause, 'you have some curious neighbours in your country. I hardly think they can harbour any designs on your punch-bowl. Do you know this is a flint arrowhead of vast antiquity, and not only that, but an arrow-head of a unique kind? I have seen specimens from all parts of the world, but there are features about this thing that are quite peculiar.' He laid down his pipe, and took out a book from a drawer.

'We shall just have time to catch the 5.45 to Castletown,' he said.

2 The Eyes on the Wall

Mr Dyson drew in a long breath of the air of the hills and felt all the enchantment of the scene about him. It was very early morning, and he stood on the terrace in the front of the house.

Vaughan's ancestor had built on the lower slope of a great hill, in the shelter of a deep and ancient wood that gathered on three sides about the house, and on the fourth side, the southwest, the land fell gently away and sank to the valley, where a brook wound in and out in mystic esses, and the dark and gleaming alders tracked the stream's course to the eye. On the terrace in the sheltered place no wind blew, and far beyond, the trees were still. Only one sound broke in upon the silence, and Dyson heard the noise of the brook singing far below, the song of clear and shining water rippling over the stones, whispering and murmuring as it sank to dark deep pools.

Across the stream, just below the house, rose a grey stone bridge, vaulted and buttressed, a fragment of the Middle Ages, and then beyond the bridge the hills rose again, vast and rounded like bastions, covered here and there with dark woods and thickets of undergrowth, but the heights were all bare of trees, showing only grey turf and patches of bracken, touched here and there with the gold of fading fronds; Dyson looked to the north and south, and still he saw the wall of the hills, and the ancient woods, and the stream drawn in and out between them; all grey and dim with morning mist beneath a grey sky in a hushed and haunted air.

Mr Vaughan's voice broke in upon the silence.

'I thought you would be too tired to be about so early,' he said. 'I see you are admiring the view. It is very pretty, isn't it, though I suppose old Meyrick Vaughan didn't think much about the scenery when he built the house. A queer grey, old place, isn't it?'

'Yes, and how it fits into the surroundings; it seems of a piece with the grey hills and the grey bridge below.'

'I am afraid I have brought you down on false pretences, Dyson,' said Vaughan, as they began to walk up and down the terrace. 'I have been to the place, and there is not a sign of anything this morning.'

'Ah, indeed. Well, suppose we go round together.'

They walked across the lawn and went by a path through the ilex shrubbery to the back of the house. There Vaughan pointed out the track leading down to the valley and up to the heights above the wood, and presently they stood beneath the garden wall, by the door.

'Here, you see, it was,' said Vaughan, pointing to a spot on the turf. 'I was standing just where you are now that morning I first saw the flints.'

'Yes, quite so. That morning it was the Army, as I call it; then the Bowl, then the Pyramid, and, yesterday, the Half Moon. What a queer old stone that is,' he went on, pointing to a block of limestone rising out of the turf just beneath the wall. 'It looks like a sort of dwarf pillar, but I suppose it is natural.'

'Oh, yes, I think so. I imagine it was brought here, though, as we stand on the red sandstone. No doubt it was used as a foundation stone for some older building.'

'Very likely,' Dyson was peering about him attentively, looking from the ground to the wall, and from the wall to the deep wood that hung almost over the garden and made the place dark even in the morning.

'Look here,' said Dyson at length, 'it is certainly a case of children this time. Look at that.' He was bending down and staring at the dull red surface of the mellowed bricks of the wall.

Vaughan came up and looked hard where Dyson's finger was pointing, and could scarcely distinguish a faint mark in deeper red.

'What is it?' he said. 'I can make nothing of it.'

'Look a little more closely. Don't you see it is an attempt to draw the human eye?'

'Ah, now I see what you mean. My sight is not very sharp. Yes, so it is, it is meant for an eye, no doubt, as you say. I thought the children learnt drawing at school.'

'Well, it is an odd eye enough. Do you notice the peculiar almond shape; almost like the eye of a Chinaman?'

Dyson looked meditatively at the work of the undeveloped artist, and scanned the wall again, going down on his knees in the minuteness of his inquisition.

'I should like very much,' he said at length, 'to know how a child in this out of the way place could have any idea of the shape of the Mongolian eye. You see the average child has a very distinct impression of the subject; he draws a circle, or something like a circle, and put a dot in the centre. I don't think any child imagines that the eye is really made like that; it's just a convention of infantile art. But this almond-shaped thing puzzles me extremely. Perhaps it may be derived from a gilt Chinaman on a tea-canister in the grocer's shop. Still that's hardly likely.'

'But why are you so sure it was done by a child?'

'Why! Look at the height. These old-fashioned bricks are little more than two inches thick; there are twenty courses from the ground to the sketch if we call it so; that gives a height of three and a half feet. Now, just imagine you are going to draw something on this wall. Exactly; your pencil, if you had one, would touch the wall somewhere on the level with your eyes, that is, more than five feet from the ground. It seems, therefore, a very simple deduction to conclude that this eye on the wall was drawn by a child about ten years old.'

'Yes, I had not thought of that. Of course one of the children must have done it.'

'I suppose so; and yet as I said, there is something singularly unchildlike about those two lines, and the eyeball itself, you see, is almost an oval. To my mind, the thing has an odd, ancient air; and a touch that is not altogether pleasant. I cannot help fancying that if we could see a whole face from the same hand it would not be altogether agreeable. However, that is nonsense, after all, and we are not getting farther in our investigations. It is odd that the flint series has come to such an abrupt end.'

The two men walked away towards the house, and as they went in at the porch there was a break in the grey sky, and a gleam of sunshine on the grey hill before them.

All the day Dyson prowled meditatively about the fields and woods surrounding the house. He was thoroughly and completely puzzled by the trivial circumstances he proposed to elucidate, and now he again took the flint arrow-head from his pocket, turning it over and examining it with deep attention. There was something about the thing that was altogether different from the specimens he had seen at the museums and private collections; the shape was of a distinct type, and around the edge there was a line of little punctured dots, apparently a suggestion of ornament. Who, thought Dyson, could possess such things in so remote a place; and who, possessing the flints, could have put them to the fantastic use of designing meaningless figures under Vaughan's garden wall? The rank absurdity of the whole affair offended him unutterably; and as one theory after another rose in his mind only to be rejected, he felt strongly tempted to take the next train back to town. He had seen the silver plate which Vaughan treasured, and had inspected the punch-bowl, the gem of the collection, with close attention; and what he saw and his interview with the butler convinced him that a plot to rob the strong box was out of the limits of enquiry. The chest in which the bowl was kept, a heavy piece of mahogany, evidently dating from the beginning of the century, was certainly strongly suggestive of a pyramid, and Dyson was at first inclined to the inept manoeuvres of the detective, but a little sober thought convinced him of the impossibility of the burglary hypothesis, and he cast wildly about for something more satisfying. He asked Vaughan if there were any gipsies in the neighbourhood, and heard that the Romany had not been seen for years. This dashed him a good deal, as he knew the gipsy habit of leaving queer hieroglyphics on the line of march, and had been much elated when the thought occurred to him. He was facing Vaughan by the old-fashioned hearth when he put the question, and leaned back in his chair in disgust at the destruction of his theory.

'It is odd,' said Vaughan, 'but the gipsies never trouble us here. Now and then the farmers find traces of fires in the wildest part of the hills, but nobody seems to know who the fire-lighters are.'

'Surely that looks like gipsies?'

'No, not in such places as those. Tinkers and gipsies and wanderers of all sorts stick to the roads and don't go very far from the farmhouses.'

'Well, I can make nothing of it. I saw the children going by this afternoon, and, as you say, they ran straight on. So we shall have no more eyes on the wall at all events.'

'No, I must waylay them one of these days and find out who is the artist.'

The next morning when Vaughan strolled in his usual course from the lawn to the back of the house he found Dyson already awaiting him by the garden door, and evidently in a state of high excitement, for he beckoned furiously with his hand, and gesticulated violently.

'What is it?' asked Vaughan. 'The flints again?'

'No; but look here, look at the wall. There; don't you see it?'

'There's another of those eyes!'

'Exactly. Drawn, you see, at a little distance from the first, almost on the same level, but slightly lower.'

'What on earth is one to make of it? It couldn't have been done by the children; it wasn't there last night, and they won't pass for another hour. What can it mean?'

'I think the very devil is at the bottom of all this,' said Dyson. 'Of course, one cannot resist the conclusion that these infernal almond eyes are to be set down to the same agency as the devices in the arrow-heads; and where that conclusion is to lead us is more than I can tell. For my part, I have to put a strong check on my imagination, or it would run wild.'

'Vaughan,' he said, as they turned away from the wall, 'has it struck you that there is one point – a very curious point – in common between the figures done in flints and the eyes drawn on the wall?'

'What is that?' asked Vaughan, on whose face there had fallen a certain shadow of indefinite dread.

'It is this. We know that the signs of the Army, the Bowl, the Pyramid, and the Half Moon must have been done at night. Presumably they were meant to be seen at night. Well, precisely the same reasoning applies to those eyes on the wall.'

'I do not quite see your point.'

'Oh, surely. The nights are dark just now, and have been very cloudy, I know, since I came down. Moreover, those overhanging trees would throw that wall into deep shadow even on a clear night.'

'Well?'

'What struck me was this. What very peculiarly sharp eyesight, they, whoever 'they' are, must have to be able to arrange arrow-heads in intricate order in the blackest shadow of the wood, and then draw the eyes on the wall without a trace of bungling, or a false line.'

'I have read of persons confined in dungeons for many years who have been able to see quite well in the dark,' said Vaughan.

'Yes,' said Dyson, 'there was the abbé in *Monte Cristo*. But it is a singular point.'

3 The Search for the Bowl

'Who was that old man that touched his hat to you just now?' said Dyson, as they came to the bend of the lane near the house.

'Oh, that was old Trevor. He looks very broken, poor old fellow.'

'Who is Trevor?'

'Don't you remember? I told you the story that afternoon I came to your rooms – about a girl named Annie Trevor, who disappeared in the most inexplicable manner about five weeks ago. That was her father.'

'Yes, yes, I recollect now. To tell the truth I had forgotten all about it. And nothing has been heard of the girl?'

'Nothing whatever. The police are quite at fault.'

'I am afraid I did not pay very much attention to the details you gave me. Which way did the girl go?'

'Her path would take her right across those wild hills above the house: the nearest point in the track must be about two miles from here.'

'Is it near that little hamlet I saw yesterday?'

'You mean Croesyceiliog, where the children came from? No; it goes more to the north.'

'Ah, I have never been that way.'

They went into the house, and Dyson shut himself up in his room, sunk deep in doubtful thought, but yet with the shadow of a suspicion growing within him that for a while haunted his brain, all vague and fantastic, refusing to take definite form. He was sitting by the open window and looking out on the valley and saw, as if in a picture, the intricate winding of the brook, the grey bridge, and the vast hills rising beyond; all still and without a breath of wind to stir the mystic hanging woods, and the evening sunshine glowed warm on the bracken, and down below a faint mist, pure white, began to rise from the stream. Dyson sat by the window as the day darkened and the huge bastioned hills loomed vast and vague, and the woods became dim and more shadowy: and the fancy that had seized him no longer appeared altogether impossible. He passed the rest of the evening in a reverie, hardly hearing what Vaughan said; and when he took his candle in the hall, he paused a moment before bidding his friend good-night.

'I want a good rest,' he said. 'I have got some work to do tomorrow.'

'Some writing, you mean?'

'No. I am going to look for the Bowl.'

'The Bowl! If you mean my punch-bowl, that is safe in the chest.'

'I don't mean the punch-bowl. You may take my word for it that your plate has never been threatened. No; I will not bother you with any suppositions. We shall in all probability have something much stronger than suppositions before long. Good-night, Vaughan.'

The next morning Dyson set off after breakfast. He took the path by the garden wall, and noted that there were now eight of the weird almond eyes dimly outlined on the brick.

'Six days more,' he said to himself, but as he thought over the theory he had formed, he shrank, in spite of strong conviction, from such a wildly incredible fancy. He struck up through the dense shadows of the wood, and at length came out on the bare hillside, and climbed higher and higher over the slippery turf, keeping well to the north, and following the indications given him by Vaughan. As he went on, he seemed to mount ever higher above the world of human life and customary things; to his right he looked at a fringe of orchard and saw a faint blue smoke rising like a pillar; there was the hamlet from which the children came to school, and there the only sign of life, for the woods embowered and concealed Vaughan's old grey house. As he reached what seemed the summit of the hill, he realized for the first time the desolate loneliness and strangeness of the land; there was nothing but grey sky and grey hill, a high, vast plain that seemed to stretch on for ever and ever, and a faint glimpse of a blue-peaked mountain far away and to the north. At length he came to the path, a slight track scarcely noticeable, and from its position and by what Vaughan had told him he knew that it was the way the lost girl, Annie Trevor, must have taken. He followed the path on the bare hill-top, noticing the great limestone rocks that cropped out of the turf, grim and hideous, and of an aspect as forbidding as an idol of the South Seas; and suddenly he halted, astonished, although he had found what he searched for.

Almost without warning the ground shelved suddenly away on all sides, and Dyson looked down into a circular depression, which might well have been a Roman amphitheatre, and the ugly crags of limestone rimmed it round as if with a broken wall. Dyson walked round the hollow, and noted the position of the stones, and then turned on his way home.

'This,' he thought to himself, 'is more than curious. The Bowl is discovered, but where is the Pyramid?'

'My dear Vaughan,' he said, when he got back, 'I may tell you that I have found the Bowl, and that is all I shall tell you for the present. We have six days of absolute inaction before us; there is really nothing to be done.'

4 The Secret of the Pyramid

'I have just been round the garden,' said Vaughan one morning.
'I have been counting those infernal eyes, and I find there are
fourteen of them. For heaven's sake, Dyson, tell me what the
meaning of it all is.'

'I should be very sorry to attempt to do so. I may have
guessed this or that, but I always make it a principle to keep
my guesses to myself. Besides, it is really not worth while
anticipating events; you will remember my telling you that
we had six days of inaction before us? Well, this is the sixth
day, and the last of idleness. To-night, I propose we take a
stroll.'

'A stroll! Is that all the action you mean to take?'

'Well, it may show you some very curious things. To be
plain, I want you to start with me at nine o'clock this evening
for the hills. We may have to be out all night, so you had
better wrap up well, and bring some of that brandy.'

'Is it a joke?' asked Vaughan, who was bewildered with
strange events and strange surmises.

'No, I don't think there is much joke in it. Unless I am
much mistaken we shall find a very serious explanation of
the puzzle. You will come with me, I am sure?'

'Very good. Which way do you want to go?'

'By the path you told me of; the path Annie Trevor is
supposed to have taken.'

Vaughan looked white at the mention of the girl's name.

'I did not think you were on that track,' he said. 'I thought it
was the affair of those devices in flint and of the eyes on the
wall that you were engaged on. It's no good saying any more,
but I will go with you.'

At a quarter to nine that evening the two men set out,
taking the path through the wood, and up the hill-side. It
was a dark and heavy night, the sky was thick with clouds,

and the valley full of mist, and all the way they seemed to walk in a world of shadow and gloom, hardly speaking, and afraid to break the haunted silence. They came out at last on the steep hill-side, and instead of the oppression of the wood there was the long, dim sweep of the turf, and higher, the fantastic limestone rocks hinted horror through the darkness, and the wind sighed as it passed across the mountain to the sea, and in its passage beat chill about their hearts. They seemed to walk on and on for hours, and the dim outline of the hill still stretched before them, and the haggard rocks still loomed through the darkness, when suddenly Dyson whispered, drawing his breath quickly, and coming close to his companion:

'Here,' he said, 'we will lie down. I do not think there is anything yet.'

'I know the place,' said Vaughan, after a moment. 'I have often been by in the daytime. The country people are afraid to come here, I believe; it is supposed to be a fairies' castle, or something of the kind. But why on earth have we come here?'

'Speak a little lower,' said Dyson. 'It might not do us any good if we are overheard.'

'Overheard here! There is not a soul within three miles of us.'

'Possibly not; indeed, I should say certainly not. But there might be a body somewhat nearer.'

'I don't understand you in the least,' said Vaughan, whispering to humour Dyson, 'but why have we come here?'

'Well, you see this hollow before us is the Bowl. I think we had better not talk even in whispers.'

They lay full length upon the turf; the rock between their faces and the Bowl, and now and again, Dyson, slouching his dark, soft hat over his forehead, put out the glint of an eye, and in a moment drew back, not daring to take a prolonged view. Again he laid an ear to the ground and listened, and the hours went by, and the darkness seemed to blacken, and the faint sigh of the wind was the only sound.

Vaughan grew impatient with this heaviness of silence, this watching for indefinite terror; for to him there was no shape or form of apprehension, and he began to think the whole vigil a dreary farce.

'How much longer is this to last?' he whispered to Dyson, and Dyson who had been holding his breath in the agony of attention put his mouth to Vaughan's ear and said:

'Will you listen?' with pauses between each syllable, and in the voice with which the priest pronounces the awful words.

Vaughan caught the ground with his hands, and stretched forward, wondering what he was to hear. At first there was nothing, and then a low and gentle noise came very softly from the Bowl, a faint sound, almost indescribable, but as if one held the tongue against the roof of the mouth and expelled the breath. He listened eagerly and presently the noise grew louder, and became a strident and horrible hissing as if the pit beneath boiled with fervent heat, and Vaughan, unable to remain in suspense any longer, drew his cap half over his face in imitation of Dyson, and looked down to the hollow below.

It did, in truth, stir and seethe like an infernal caldron. The whole of the sides and bottom tossed and writhed with vague and restless forms that passed to and fro without the sound of feet, and gathered thick here and there and seemed to speak to one another in those tones of horrible sibilance, like the hissing of snakes, that he had heard. It was as if the sweet turf and the cleanly earth had suddenly become quickened with some foul writhing growth. Vaughan could not draw back his face, though he felt Dyson's finger touch him, but he peered into the quaking mass and saw faintly that there were things like faces and human limbs, and yet he felt his inmost soul chill with the sure belief that no fellow soul or human thing stirred in all that tossing and hissing host. He looked aghast, choking back sobs of horror, and at length the loathsome forms gathered thickest about some vague object in the middle of the hollow, and the hissing of their speech grew more venomous, and he saw in the uncertain light the abominable limbs, vague and yet too plainly seen, writhe and intertwine, and he thought he heard, very faint, a low human moan striking through the noise of speech that was not of man. At his heart something seemed to whisper ever 'the worm of corruption, the worm that dieth not,' and grotesquely the image was pictured to his imagination of a piece of putrid offal stirring through and through with bloated and horrible creeping things. The writhing of the dusky limbs continued, they seemed clustered round the dark form in the middle of the hollow, and the sweat dripped and poured off Vaughan's forehead, and fell cold on his hand beneath his face.

Then, it seemed done in an instant, the loathsome mass melted and fell away to the sides of the Bowl, and for a moment Vaughan saw in the middle of the hollow the tossing of human arms.

But a spark gleamed beneath, a fire kindled, and as the voice of a woman cried out loud in a shrill scream of utter anguish and terror, a great pyramid of flame spired up like a bursting of a pent fountain, and threw a blaze of light upon the whole mountain. In that instant Vaughan saw the myriads beneath; the things made in the form of men but stunted like children hideously deformed, the faces with the almond eyes burning with evil and unspeakable lusts; the ghastly yellow of the mass of naked flesh and then as if by magic the place was empty, while the fire roared and crackled, and the flames shone abroad.

'You have seen the Pyramid,' said Dyson in his ear, 'the Pyramid of fire.'

5 The Little People

'Then you recognize the thing?'

'Certainly. It is a brooch that Annie Trevor used to wear on Sundays; I remember the pattern. But where did you find it? You don't mean to say that you have discovered the girl?'

'My dear Vaughan, I wonder you have not guessed where I found the brooch. You have not forgotten last night already?'

'Dyson,' said the other, speaking very seriously, 'I have been turning it over in my mind this morning while you have been out. I have thought about what I saw, or perhaps I should say about what I thought I saw, and the only conclusion I can come to is this, that the thing won't bear recollection. As men live, I have lived soberly and honestly, in the fear of God, all my days, and all I can do is believe that I suffered from some monstrous delusion, from some phantasmagoria of the bewildered senses. You know we went home together in silence, not a word passed between us as to what I fancied I saw; had we not better agree to keep silence on the subject? When I took my walk in the peaceful morning sunshine, I thought all the earth seemed full of praise, and passing by that wall I noticed there were no more signs recorded, and I blotted out those that remained. The mystery is over, and we can live quietly again. I think some poison has been working for the last few weeks; I have trod on the verge of madness, but I am sane now.'

Mr Vaughan had spoken earnestly, and bent forward in his chair and glanced at Dyson with something of entreaty.

'My dear Vaughan,' said the other, after a pause, 'what's the use of this? It is much too late to take that tone; we have gone too deep. Besides you know as well as I that there is no delusion in the case; I wish there were with all my heart. No, in justice to myself I must tell you the whole story, so far as I know it.'

'Very good,' said Vaughan with a sigh, 'if you must, you must.'

'Then,' said Dyson, 'we will begin with the end if you please. I found this brooch you have just identified in the place we have called the Bowl. There was a heap of grey ashes, as if a fire had been burning, indeed, the embers were still hot, and this brooch was lying on the ground, just outside the range of the flame. It must have dropped accidentally from the dress of the person who was wearing it. No, don't interrupt me; we can pass now to the beginning, as we have had the end. Let us go back to that day you came to see me in my rooms in London. So far as I can remember, soon after you came in you mentioned, in a somewhat casual manner, that an unfortunate and mysterious incident had occurred in your part of the country; a girl named Annie Trevor had gone to see a relative, and had disappeared. I confess freely that what you said did not greatly interest me; there are so many reasons which may make it extremely convenient for a man and more especially a woman to vanish from the circle of their relations and friends. I suppose, if we were to consult the police, one would find that in London somebody disappears mysteriously every other week, and the officers would, no doubt, shrug their shoulders, and tell you that by the law of averages it could not be otherwise. So I was very culpably careless to your story, and besides, here is another reason for my lack of interest; your tale was inexplicable. You could only suggest a blackguard sailor on the tramp, but I discarded the explanation immediately.

'For many reasons, but chiefly because the occasional criminal, the amateur in brutal crime, is always found out, especially if he selects the country as the scene of his operations. You will remember the case of that Garcia you mentioned; he strolled into a railway station the day after the murder, his trousers covered with blood, and the works of the Dutch clock, his loot, tied in a neat parcel. So rejecting this, your only suggestion, the whole tale became, as I say, inexplicable, and, therefore, profoundly uninteresting. Yes, *therefore*, it is a perfectly valid conclusion. Do you ever trouble your head about problems which you know to be insoluble? Did you ever bestow much thought on the old puzzle of Achilles and the tortoise? Of course not, because you knew it was a hopeless quest, and so when you told me the story of a country girl who had disappeared I simply placed the whole thing down in the category of the insoluble, and thought no more about the matter. I was mistaken, so it has turned out; but if you remember, you immediately passed on to an affair which interested you more intensely, because personally, I need not go over the very singular narrative of the flint signs, at first I thought it all trivial, probably some children's game, and if not that a hoax of some sort; but your showing me the arrow-head awoke my acute interest. Here, I saw, there was something widely removed from the commonplace, and matter of real curiosity; and as soon as I came here I set to work to find the solution, repeating to myself again and again the signs you had described. First came the sign we have agreed to call the Army; a number of serried lines of flints, all pointing in the same way. Then the lines, like the spokes of a wheel, all converging towards the figure of a Bowl, then the triangle or Pyramid, and last of all the Half moon. I confess that I exhausted conjecture in my efforts to unveil this mystery, and as you will understand it was a duplex or rather triplex problem. For I had not merely to ask myself: what do these figures mean? but also, who can possibly be responsible for the designing of them? And again, who can possibly possess such valuable things, and knowing their value thus throw them down by the wayside? This line of thought led me to suppose that the person or persons in question did not know the value of unique flint arrow-heads, and yet this did not lead me far, for a well-educated man might easily be ignorant on such a subject. Then came the complication of the eye on the wall, and you remember that we could not avoid the conclusion that in the two cases the same agency was at work. The peculiar position of these eyes on the wall made me inquire if there was such a thing as a dwarf anywhere in the neighbourhood, but I found that there was not, and I knew that the children who pass by every day had nothing to do with the matter. Yet I felt convinced that whoever drew the eyes must be from three and a half to four feet high, since, as I pointed out at the time, anyone who draws on a perpendicular surface chooses by instinct a spot about level with his face. Then again, there was the question of the peculiar shape of the eyes; that marked Mongolian character of which the English countryman could have no conception, and for a final cause of confusion the obvious fact that the designer or designers must be able practically to see in the dark. As you remarked, a man who has been confined for many years in an extremely dark cell or dungeon might acquire that power; but since the days of Edmond Dantès, where would such a prison be found in Europe? A sailor, who had been immured for a considerable period in some horrible Chinese *oubliette*, seemed the individual I was in search of, and though it looked improbable, it was not absolutely impossible that a sailor or, let us say, a man employed on shipboard, should be a dwarf. But how to account for my imaginary sailor being in possession of prehistoric arrow-heads? And the possession granted, what was the meaning and object of these mysterious signs of flint, and the almond-shaped eyes? Your theory of a contemplated burglary I saw, nearly from the first, to be quite untenable, and I confess I was utterly at a loss for a working hypothesis. It was a mere accident which put me on the track; we passed poor old Trevor, and your mention of his name and of the disappearance of his daughter, recalled the story which I had forgotten, or which remained unheeded. Here, then, I said to myself, is another problem, uninteresting, it is true, by itself; but what if it prove to be in relation with all these enigmas which torture me? I shut myself in my room, and endeavoured to dismiss all prejudice from my mind, and I went over everything *de novo*, assuming for theory's sake that the disappearance of Annie Trevor had some connection with the flint signs and the eyes on the wall. This assumption did not lead me very far, and I was on the point of giving the whole problem up in despair, when a possible significance of the Bowl struck me. As you know there is a 'Devil's Punch-bowl' in Surrey, and I saw that the symbol might refer to some feature in the country. Putting the two extremes together, I determined to look for the Bowl near the path which the lost girl had taken, and you know how I found it. I interpreted the sign by what I knew, and read the first, the Army, thus:

'there is to be a gathering or assembly at the Bowl in a fortnight (that is the Half Moon) to see the Pyramid, or to build the Pyramid.'

The eyes, drawn one by one, day by day, evidently checked off the days, and I knew that there would be fourteen and no more. Thus far the way seemed pretty plain; I would not trouble myself to inquire as to the nature of the assembly, or as to who was to assemble in the loneliest and most dreaded place among these lonely hills. In Ireland or China or the West of America the question would have been easily answered; a muster of the disaffected, the meeting of a secret society; vigilantes summoned to report: the thing would be simplicity itself; but in this quiet corner of England, inhabited by quiet folk, no such suppositions were possible for a moment. But I knew that I should have an opportunity of seeing and watching the assembly, and I did not care to perplex myself with hopeless research; and in place of reasoning a wild fancy entered into judgment: I remembered what people had said about Annie Trevor's disappearance, that she had been "taken by the fairies". I tell you, Vaughan, I am a sane man as you are, my brain is not, I trust, mere vacant space to let to any wild improbability, and I tried my best to thrust the fantasy away. And the hint came of the old name of fairies, "the little people", and the very probable belief that they represent a tradition of the prehistoric Turanian inhabitants of the country, who were cave dwellers: and then I realized with a shock that I was looking for a being under four feet in height, accustomed to live in darkness, possessing stone instruments, and familiar with the Mongolian cast of features! I say this, Vaughan, that I should be ashamed to hint at such visionary stuff to you, if it were not for that which you saw with your very eyes last night, and I say that I might doubt the evidence of my senses, if they were not confirmed by yours. But you and I cannot look each other in the face and pretend delusion; as you lay on the turf beside me I felt your flesh shrink and quiver, and I saw your eyes in the light of the flame. And so I tell you without any shame what was in my mind last night as we went through the wood and climbed the hill, and lay hidden beneath the rock.

'There was one thing that should have been most evident that puzzled me to the very last. I told you how I read the sign of the Pyramid; the assembly was to see a pyramid, and the true meaning of the symbol escaped me to the last moment. The old derivation from πυρ, fire, though false, should have set me on the track, but it never occurred to me.

'I think I need say very little more. You know we were quite helpless, even if we had foreseen what was to come. Ah, the particular place where these signs were displayed? Yes, that is a curious question. But this house is, so far as I can judge, in a pretty central situation amongst the hills; and possibly, who can say yes or no, that queer, old limestone pillar by your garden wall was a place of meeting before the Celt set foot in Britain. But there is one thing I must add: I don't regret our inability to rescue the wretched girl. You saw the appearance of those things that gathered thick and writhed in the Bowl; you may be sure that what lay bound in the midst of them was no longer fit for earth.'

'So?' said Vaughan.

'So she passed in the Pyramid of Fire,' said Dyson, 'and they passed again to the underworld, to the places beneath the hills.'

2 Through the Veil (1911)

ARTHUR CONAN DOYLE

He was a great shock-headed, freckle-faced Borderer, the lineal descendant of a cattle-thieving clan in Liddesdale. In spite of his ancestry he was as solid and sober a citizen as one would wish to see, a town councillor of Melrose, an elder of the Church, and the chairman of the local branch of the Young Men's Christian Association. Brown was his name – and you saw it printed up as 'Brown and Handiside' over the great grocery stores in the High Street. His wife, Maggie Brown, was an Armstrong before her marriage, and came from an old farming stock in the wilds of Teviothead. She was small, swarthy, and dark-eyed, with a strangely nervous temperament for a Scotch woman. No greater contrast could be found than the big tawny man and the dark little woman; but both were of the soil as far back as any memory could extend.

One day – it was the first anniversary of their wedding – they had driven over together to see the excavations of the Roman Fort at Newstead. It was not a particularly picturesque spot. From the northern bank of the Tweed, just where the river forms a loop, there extends a gentle slope of arable land. Across it run the trenches of the excavators, with here and there an exposure of old stonework to show the foundations of the ancient walls. It had been a huge place, for the camp was fifty acres in extent, and the fort fifteen. However, it was all made easy for them since Mr Brown knew the farmer to whom the land belonged. Under his guidance they spent a long summer evening inspecting the trenches, the pits, the ramparts, and all the strange variety of objects which were waiting to be transported to the Edinburgh Museum of Antiquities. The buckle of a woman's belt had been dug up that very day, and the farmer was discoursing upon it when his eyes fell upon Mrs Brown's face.

'Your good leddy's tired,' said he. 'Maybe you'd best rest a wee before we gang further.'

Brown looked at his wife. She was certainly very pale, and her dark eyes were bright and wild.

'What is it, Maggie? I've wearied you. I'm thinkin' it's time we went back.'

'No, no, John, let us go on. It's wonderful! It's like a dreamland place. It all seems so close and so near to me. How long were the Romans here, Mr Cunningham?'

'A fair time, mam. If you saw the kitchen midden-pits you would guess it took a long time to fill them.'

'And why did they leave?'

'Well, mam, by all accounts they left because they had to. The folk round could thole them no longer, so they just up and burned the fort aboot their lugs. You can see the fire marks on the stanes.'

The woman gave a quick little shudder. 'A wild night – a fearsome night,' said she. 'The sky must have been red that night – and these grey stones, they may have been red also.'

'Aye, I think they were red,' said her husband. 'It's a queer thing, Maggie, and it may be your words that have done it; but I seem to see that business aboot as clear as ever I saw anything in my life. The light shone on the water.'

'Aye, the light shone on the water. And the smoke gripped you by the throat. And all the savages were yelling.'

The old farmer began to laugh. 'The leddy will be writin' a story aboot the old fort,' said he. 'I've shown many a one over it, but I never heard it put so clear afore. Some folk have the gift.'

They had strolled along the edge of the foss, and a pit yawned upon the right of them.

'That pit was fourteen foot deep,' said the farmer. 'What d'ye think we dug oot from the bottom o't? Weel, it was just the skeleton of a man wi' a spear by his side. I'm thinkin' he was grippin' it when he died. Now, how cam' a man wi' a spear doon a hole fourteen foot deep? He wasna' buried there, for they aye burned their dead. What make ye o' that, mam?'

'He sprang doon to get clear of the savages,' said the woman.

'Weel, it's likely enough, and a' the professors from Edinburgh couldna gie a better reason. I wish you were aye here, mam, to answer a' oor deefficulties sae readily. Now, here's the altar that we foond last week. There's an inscreeption. They tell me it's Latin, and it means that the men o' this fort give thanks to God for their safety.'

They examined the old worn stone. There was a large deeply-cut 'VV' upon the top of it.

'What does "VV" stand for?' asked Brown.

'Naebody kens,' the guide answered.

'*Valeria Victrix*,' said the lady softly. Her face was paler than ever, her eyes far away, as one who peers down the dim aisles of overarching centuries.

'What's that?' asked her husband sharply.

She started as one who wakes from sleep. 'What were we talking about?' she asked.

'About this "VV" upon the stone.'

'No doubt it was just the name of the Legion which put the altar up.'

'Aye, but you gave some special name.'

'Did I? How absurd! How should I ken what the name was?'

'You said something – "*Victrix*", I think.'

'I suppose I was guessing. It gives me the queerest feeling, this place, as if I were not myself, but someone else.'

'Aye, it's an uncanny place,' said her husband, looking round with an expression almost of fear in his bold grey eyes. 'I feel it mysel'. I think we'll just be wishin' you good evenin', Mr Cunningham, and get back to Melrose before the dark sets in.'

Neither of them could shake off the strange impression which had been left upon them by their visit to the excavations. It was as if some miasma had risen from those damp trenches and passed into their blood. All the evening they were silent and thoughtful, but such remarks as they did make showed that the same subject was in the minds of each. Brown had a restless night, in which he dreamed a strange connected dream, so vivid that he woke sweating and shivering like a frightened horse. He tried to convey it all to his wife as they sat together at breakfast in the morning.

'It was the clearest thing, Maggie,' said he. 'Nothing that has ever come to me in my waking life has been more clear than that. I feel as if these hands were sticky with blood.'

'Tell me of it – tell me slow,' said she.

'When it began, I was oot on a braeside. I was laying flat on the ground. It was rough, and there were clumps of heather. All round me was just darkness, but I could hear the rustle and the breathin' of men. There seemed a great multitude on every side of me, but I could see no one. There was a low chink of steel sometimes, and then a number of voices would whisper "Hush!" I had a ragged club in my hand, and it had spikes o' iron near the end of it. My heart was beatin' quickly, and I felt that a moment of great danger and excitement was at hand. Once I dropped my club, and again from all round me the voices in the darkness cried, "Hush!" I put oot my hand, and it touched the foot of another man lying in front of me. There was someone at my very elbow on either side. But they said nothin'.

'Then we all began to move. The whole braeside seemed to be crawlin' downwards. There was a river at the bottom and a high-arched wooden bridge. Beyond the bridge were many lights – torches on a wall. The creepin' men all flowed towards the bridge. There had been no sound of any kind, just a velvet stillness. And then there was a cry in the darkness, the cry of a man who has been stabbed suddenly to the hairt. That one cry swelled out for a moment, and then the roar of a thoosand furious voices. I was runnin'. Every one was runnin'. A bright red light shone out, and the river was a scarlet streak. I could see my companions now. They were more like devils than men, wild figures clad in skins, with their hair and beards streamin'. They were all mad with rage, jumpin' as they ran, their mouths open, their arms wavin', the red light beatin' on their faces. I ran, too, and yelled out curses like the rest. Then I heard a great cracklin' of wood, and I knew that the palisades were doon. There was a loud whistlin' in my ears, and I was aware that arrows were flyin' past me. I got to the bottom of a dyke, and I saw a hand stretched doon from above. I took it, and was dragged to the top. We looked doon, and there were silver men beneath us holdin' up their spears. Some of our folk sprang on to the spears. Then we others followed, and we killed the soldiers before they could draw the spears oot again. They shouted loud in some foreign tongue, but no mercy was shown them. We went ower them like a wave, and trampled them doon into the mud, for they were few, and there was no end to our numbers.

'I found myself among buildings, and one of them was on fire. I saw the flames spoutin' through the roof. I ran on, and then I was alone among the buildings. Someone ran across in front o' me. It was a woman. I caught her by the arm, and I took her chin and turned her face so as the light of the fire would strike it. Whom think you that it was, Maggie?'

His wife moistened her dry lips. 'It was I,' she said.

He looked at her in surprise. 'That's a good guess,' said he. 'Yes, it was just you. Not merely like you, you understand. It was you – you yourself. I saw the same soul in your frightened eyes. You looked white and bonny and wonderful in the firelight. I had just one thought in my head – to get you awa' with me; to keep you all to mysel' in my own home somewhere beyond the hills. You clawed at my face with your nails. I heaved you over my shoulder, and I tried to find a way oot of the light of the burning hoose and back into the darkness.

'Then came the thing that I mind best of all. You're ill, Maggie. Shall I stop? My God! You have the very look on your face that you had last night in my dream. You screamed. He came runnin' in the firelight. His head was bare; his hair was black and curled; he had a naked sword in his hand, short and broad, little more than a dagger. He stabbed at me, but he tripped and fell. I held you with one hand, and with the other –'

His wife had sprung to her feet with writhing features.

'Marcus!' she cried. 'My beautiful Marcus! Oh, you brute! you brute! you brute!' There was a clatter of tea-cups as she fell forward senseless upon the table.

They never talk about that strange isolated incident in their married life. For an instant the curtain of the past had swung aside, and some strange glimpse of a forgotten life had come to them. But it closed down, never to open again. They live their narrow round – he in his shop, she in her household – and yet new and wider horizons have vaguely formed themselves around them since that summer evening by the crumbling Roman fort.

3 The Ape (1917)

E F BENSON

Hugh Marsham had spent the day, as a good tourist should, in visiting the temples and the tombs of the kings across the river, and the magic of the hour of sunset flamed over earth and heaven as he crossed the Nile again to Luxor in his felucca. It seemed as if the whole world had been suddenly transferred into the heart of an opal, and burned with a myriad fiery colours. The river itself was of the green that beech trees are clad in at spring-time; the columns of the temple that stood close to its banks glowed as if lit from within by the flame of some perpetual evening sacrifice; the cloudless sky was dusky blue in the east, the blue of turquoise overhead, and melted into aquamarine above the line of desert where the sun had just sunk. All along the bank which he was fast approaching under the press of the cool wind from the north were crowds of Arabs, padding softly home in the dust from their work, and chattering as sparrows chatter among the bushes in the long English twilights. Even the dust that hovered and hung and was dispersed again by the wind was rainbowed; it caught the hues from the river and the sky and the orange-flaming temple, and those who walked in it were clad in brightness.

Here in the South no long English twilight lingered, and as he walked up the dusky fragrant tunnel of mimosa that led to the hotel, night thickened, and in the sky a million stars leaped into being, while the soft gathering darkness sponged out the glories of the flaming hour. On the hotel steps the vendors of carpets and Arabian hangings, of incense and filigree work, of suspicious turquoises and more than suspicious scarabs were already packing up their wares, and probably recounting to each other in their shrill incomprehensible gabble the iniquitous bargains they had made with the gullible Americans and English, who so innocently purchased the wares of Manchester. Only in his accustomed corner old Abdul still squatted, for he was of a class above the ordinary vendors, a substantial dealer in antiques, who had a shop in the village, where archaeologists resorted, and bought, *sub rosa*, pieces that eventually found their way into European museums. He was in his shop all day, but evening found him, when serious business hours were over, on the steps of the hotel, where he sold undoubted antiquities to tourists who wanted something genuine.

The day had been very hot, and Hugh felt himself disposed to linger outside the hotel in this cool dusk, and turn over the tray of scarabs which Abdul Hamid presented to his notice. He was a wrinkled, dried-up husk of a man, loquacious and ingratiating in manner, and welcomed Hugh as an old customer.

'See, sir,' he said, 'here are two more scroll-scarabs like those you bought from me before the week. You should have these; they are very fine and very cheap, because I do no business this year. Mr Rankin, you know him? of the British Museum, he give me two pounds each last year for scroll-scarabs not so fine, and to-day I sell them at a pound and a half each. Take them; they are yours. Scroll-scarabs of the twelfth dynasty; if Mr Rankin were here he pay me two pounds each, and be sorry I not ask more.'

Hugh laughed.

'You may sell them to Mr Rankin then,' he said. 'He comes here tomorrow.'

The old man, utterly unabashed, grinned and shook his head.

'No; I promised you them for pound and a half,' he said. 'I am not cheat-dealer. They are yours – pound and a half. Take them, take them.'

Hugh resisted this unparalleled offer, and, turning over the contents of the tray, picked out of it and examined carefully a broken fragment of blue glaze, about an inch in height. This represented the head and shoulders of an ape, and the fracture had occurred half-way down the back, so that the lower part of the trunk, the forearms which apparently hung by its sides, and the hind legs were missing. On the back there was an inscription in hieroglyphics, also broken. Presumably the missing piece contained the remainder of the letters. It was modelled with extreme care and minuteness, and the face wore an expression of grotesque malevolence.

'What's this broken bit of a monkey?' asked Hugh carelessly.

Abdul, looking much like a monkey himself, put his eyes close to it.

'Ah, that's the rarest thing in Egypt,' he said, 'so Mr Rankin he tell me, if only the monkey not broken. See the back? There it says: "He of whom this is, let him call on me thrice—" and then some son of a dog broke it. If the rest was here, I would not take a hundred pounds for it; but now ten years have I kept half-monkey, and never comes half-monkey to it. It is yours, sir, for a pound it is yours. Half-monkey nothing to me; it is fool-monkey only being half-monkey. I let it go – I give it you, and you give me pound.'

Hugh Marsham felt in one pocket, then in another, with no appearance of hurry or eagerness.

'There's your pound,' he said casually.

Abdul peered at him in the dusk. It was very odd that Hugh did not offer him half what he asked, instead of paying up without bargaining. He regretted extremely that he had not asked more. But the little blue fragment was now in Hugh's pocket, and the sovereign glistened very pleasantly in his own palm.

'And what was the rest of the hieroglyphic, do you think?' Hugh asked.

'Eh, Allah only knows the wickedness and the power of the monkeys,' said Abdul. 'Once there were such in Egypt, and in the temple of Mut in Karnak, which the English dug up, you shall see a chamber with just such monkeys sitting round it, four of them, all carved in sandstone. But on them there is no writing; I have looked at them behind and before; they not master-monkeys. Perhaps the monkey promised that whoso called on him thrice, if he were owner of the blue image of which gentleman has the half, would be his master, and that monkey would do his bidding. Who knows? It is of the old wickedness of the world, the old Egyptian blackness.'

Hugh got up. He had been out in the sun all day, and felt at this moment a little intimate shiver, which warned him that it was wiser to go indoors till the chill of sunset had passed.

'I expect you've tried it on with the half-monkey, haven't you?' he said.

Abdul burst out into a toothless cackle of laughter.

'Yes, effendi,' he said. 'I have tried it a hundred times, and nothing happens. Else I would not have sold it you. Half-monkey is no monkey at all. I have tried to make boy with the ink-mirror see something about monkeys, but nothing comes, except the clouds and the man who sweeps. No monkey.'

Hugh nodded to him.

'Good-night, you old sorcerer,' he said pleasantly.

As he walked up the broad flagged passage to his room, carrying the half-monkey in his hand, Hugh felt with a disengaged thumb in his waistcoat pocket for something he had picked up that day in the valley of the tombs of the kings. He had eaten his lunch there, after an inspection of the carved and reeking corridors, and, as he sat idly smoking, had reached out a lazy hand to where this thing had glittered among the pebbles. Now, entering his room, he turned up the electric light, and, standing under it with his back to the window, that opened, door fashion, on to the three steps that led into the hotel garden, he fitted the fragment he had found to the fragment he had just purchased. They joined on to each other with the most absolute accuracy, not a chip was missing. There was the complete ape, and down its back ran the complete legend.

The window was open, and at this moment he heard a sudden noise as of some scampering beast in the garden outside. His light streamed out in an oblong on to the sandy path, and, laying the two pieces of the image on the table, he looked out. But there was nothing irregular to be seen; the palm trees waved and clashed in the wind, and the rose bushes stirred and scattered their fragrance. Only right down the middle of the sandy path that ran between the beds, the ground was curiously disturbed, as by some animal, heavily frolicking, scooping and spurning the light soil as it ran.

The midday train from Cairo next day brought Mr Rankin, the eminent Egyptologist and student of occult lore, a huge red man with a complete mastery of colloquial Arabic. He had but a day to spend in Luxor, for he was *en route* for Merawi, where lately some important finds had been made; but Hugh took occasion to show him the figure of the ape as they sat over their coffee in the garden just outside his bedroom after lunch.

'I found the lower half yesterday outside one of the tombs of the kings,' he said, 'and the top half by the utmost luck among old Abdul's things. He told me you said that if it was complete it would be of the greatest rarity. He lied, I suppose?'

Rankin gave one gasp of amazed surprise as he looked at it and read the inscription on the back. Marsham thought that his great red face suddenly paled.

'Good Lord!' he said. 'Here, take it!' And he held out the two pieces to him.

Hugh laughed.

'Why in such a hurry?' he said.

'Because there comes a breaking-point to every man's honesty, and I might keep it, and swear that I had given it back to you. My dear fellow, do you know what you've got?'

'Indeed I don't. I want to be told,' said Hugh.

'And to think that it was you who only a couple of months ago asked me what a scarab was! Well, you've got there what all Egyptologists, and even more keenly than Egyptologists all students of folklore and magic black and white – especially black – would give their eyes to have found. Good Lord! what's that?'

Hugh was sitting by his side in a deck-chair, idly fitting together the two halves of the broken image. He too heard what had startled Rankin; for it was the same noise as had startled him last night, namely, the scampering of some great frolicsome animal, somewhere close to them. As he jumped up, pulling his hands apart, the noise ceased.

'Funny,' he said, 'I heard that last night. There's nothing; it's some stray dog in the bushes. Do tell me what it is that I've got.'

Rankin, who had surged to his feet also, stood listening a moment. But there was nothing to be heard but the buzzing of bees in the bushes and the chiding of the remote kites overhead. He sat down again.

'Well, give me two minutes,' he said, 'and I can tell you all I know. Once upon a time, when this wonderful and secret land was alive and not dead – oh, we have killed it with our board-schools and our steamers and our religion – there was a whole hierarchy of gods, Isis, Osiris, and the rest, of whom we know a great deal. But below them there was a company of semi-divinities, demons if you will, of whom we know practically nothing. The cat was one, certain dwarfish creatures were others, but most potent of all were the cynocephali, the dog-faced apes. They were not divine, rather they were demons, of hideous power, *but*' – and he pointed a great hand at Hugh – 'they could be controlled. Men could control them, men could turn them into terrific servants, much as the genii in the *Arabian Nights* were controlled. But to do that you had to know the secret name of the demon, and had yourself to make an image of him, with the secret name inscribed thereon, and by that you could summon him and all the incarnate creatures of his species.

'So much we know from certain very guarded allusions in the Book of the Dead and other sources, for this was one of the great mysteries never openly spoken of. Here and there a priest in Karnak, or Abydos, or in Hieropolis, had had handed down to him one of those secret names, but in nine cases out of ten the knowledge died with him, for there was something dangerous and terrible about it all. Old Abdul here, for instance, believes that Moses had the secret names of frogs and lice, and made images of them with the secret name inscribed on them, and by those produced the plagues of Egypt. Think what you could do, think what he did, if infinite power over frog-nature were given you, so that the king's chamber swarmed with frogs at your word. Usually, as I said, the secret name was but sparingly passed on, but occasionally some very bold advanced spirit, such as Moses, made his image, and controlled –'

He paused a moment, and Hugh wondered if he was in some delirious dream. Here they were, taking coffee and cigarettes underneath the shadow of a modern hotel in the year AD 1912, and this great savant was talking to him about the spell that controlled the whole frog-nature in the universe. The gist, the moral of his discourse, was already perfectly clear.

'That's a good joke,' Hugh said. 'You told your story with extraordinary gravity. And what you mean is that those two blue bits I hold in my hand control the whole ape-nature of the world? Bravo, Rankin! For a moment, you and your impressiveness almost made me take it all seriously. Lord! You do tell a story well! And what's the secret name of the ape?'

Rankin turned to him with the shake of an impressive forefinger.

'My dear boy,' he said, 'you should never be disrespectful towards the things you know nothing of. Never say a thing is moonshine till you know what you are talking about. I know, at this moment, exactly as much as you do about your ape-image, except that I can translate its inscription, which I will do for you. On the top half is written, "He, of whom this is, let him call on me thrice" –'

Hugh interrupted.

'That's what Abdul read to me,' he said.

'Of course. Abdul knows hieroglyphics. But on the lower half is what nobody but you and I know. "Let him call on me thrice," says the top half, and then there speaks what you picked up in the valley of the tombs, "and I, Tahu-met, obey the order of the Master".'

'Tahu-met?' asked Hugh.

'Yes. Now in ten minutes I must be off to catch my train. What I have told you is all that is known about this particular affair by those who have studied folklore and magic, and Egyptology. If anything – if anything happens, do be kind enough to let me know. If you were not so abominably rich I would offer you what you liked for that little broken statue. But there's the way of the world!'

'Oh, it's not for sale,' said Hugh gaily. 'It's too interesting to sell. But what am I to do next with it? Tahu-met? Shall I say Tahu-met three times?'

Rankin leaned forward very hurriedly, and laid his fat hand on the young man's knee.

'No, for Heaven's sake! Just keep it by you,' he said. 'Be patient with it. See what happens. You might mend it, perhaps. Put a drop of gum-arabic on the break and make it whole. By the way, if it interests you at all, my niece Julia Draycott arrives here this evening, and will wait for me here till my return from Merawi. You met her in Cairo, I think.'

Certainly this piece of news interested Hugh more than all the possibilities of apes and super-apes. He thrust the two pieces of Tahu-met carelessly into his pocket.

'By Jove, is she really?' he said. 'That's splendid. She told me she might be coming up, but didn't feel at all sure. Must you really be off? I shall come down to the station with you.'

While Rankin went to gather up such small luggage as he had brought with him, Hugh wandered into the hotel bureau to ask for letters, and seeing there a gum-bottle, dabbed with gum the fractured edges of Tahu-met. The two pieces joined with absolute exactitude, and wrapping a piece of paper round them to keep the edges together, he went out through the garden with Rankin. At the hotel gate was the usual crowd of donkey-boys and beggars, and presently they were ambling down the village street on bored white donkeys. It was almost deserted at this hottest hour of the afternoon, but along it there moved an Arab leading a large grey ape, that tramped surlily in the dust. But just before they overtook it, the beast looked round, saw Hugh, and with chatterings of delight strained at his leash. Its owner cursed and pulled it away, for Hugh nearly rode over it, but it paid no attention to him, and fairly towed him along the road after the donkeys.

Rankin looked at his companion.

'That's odd,' he said. 'That's one of your servants. I've still a couple of minutes to spare. Do you mind stopping a moment?'

He shouted something in the vernacular to the Arab, who ran after them, with the beast still towing him on. When they came close the ape stopped and bent his head to the ground in front of Hugh.

'And that's odd,' said Rankin.

Hugh suddenly felt rather uncomfortable.

'Nonsense!' he said. 'That's just one of his tricks. He's been taught it to get *baksheesh* for his master. Look, there's your train coming in. We must get on.'

He threw a couple of piastres to the man, and they rode on. But when they got to the station, glancing down the road, he saw that the ape was still looking after them.

※

Julia Draycott's arrival that evening speedily put such antique imaginings as the lordship of apes out of Hugh's head. He chucked Tahu-met into the box where he kept his scarabs and ushapti figures, and devoted himself to this heartless and exquisite girl, whose mission in life appeared to be to make as miserable as possible the largest possible number of young men. Hugh had already been selected by her in Cairo as a decent victim, and now she proceeded to torture him. She had no intention whatever of marrying him, for poor Hugh was certainly ugly, with his broad, heavy face, and though rich, he was not nearly rich enough. But he had a couple of delightful Arab horses, and so, since there was no one else on hand to experiment with, she let him buy her a side-saddle, and be, with his horses, always at her disposal. She did not propose to use him for very long, for she expected young Lord Paterson (whom she did intend to marry) to follow her from Cairo within a week. She had beat a Parthian retreat from him, being convinced that he would soon find Cairo intolerable without her; and in the meantime Hugh was excellent practice. Besides, she adored riding.

They sat together one afternoon on the edge of the river opposite Karnak. She had treated him like a brute beast all morning, and had watched his capability for wretchedness with the purring egoism that distinguished her; and now, as a change, she was seeing how happy she could make him.

'You are such a dear,' she said. 'I don't know how I could have endured Luxor without you; and, thanks to you, it has been the loveliest week.'

She looked at him from below her long lashes, through which there gleamed the divinest violet, smiling like a child at her friend. 'And to-night? You made some delicious plan for to-night.'

'Yes; it's full moon to-night,' said he. 'We are going to ride out to Karnak after dinner.'

'That will be heavenly. And, Mr Marsham, do let us go alone. There's sure to be a mob from the hotel, so let's start late, when they've all cleared out. Karnak in the moonlight, just with you.'

That completely made Hugh's mind up. For the last three days he had been on the lookout for a moment that should furnish the great occasion; and now (all unconsciously, of course) she indicated it to him. This evening, then. And his heart leaped.

'Yes, yes,' he said. 'But why have I become Mr Marsham again?'

Again she looked at him, now with a penitent mouth.

'Oh, I was such a beast to you this morning,' she said. 'That was why. I didn't deserve that you should be Hugh. But will you be Hugh again? Do you forgive me?'

In spite of Hugh's fixing the great occasion for this evening, it might have come then, so bewitching was her penitence, had not the rest of their party on donkeys, whom they had outpaced, come streaming along the riverbank at this moment.

'Ah, those tiresome people,' she said. 'Hughie, what a bore everybody else is except you and me.'

They got back to the hotel about sunset, and as they passed into the hall the porter handed Julia a telegram which had been waiting some couple of hours. She gave a little exclamation of pleasure and surprise, and turned to Hugh.

'Come and have a turn in the garden, Hughie,' she said, 'and then I must go down for the arrival of the boat. When does it come in?'

'I should think it would be here immediately,' he said. 'Let's go down to the river.'

Even as he spoke the whistle of the approaching steamer was heard. The girl hesitated a moment.

'It's a shame to take up all your time in the way I'm doing,' she said. 'You told me you had letters to write. Write them now; then – then you'll be free after dinner.'

'Tomorrow will do,' he said. 'I'll come down with you to the boat.'

'No, you dear, I forbid it,' she said. 'Oh, do be good, and write your letters. I ask you to.'

Rather puzzled and vaguely uncomfortable, Hugh went into the hotel. It was true that he had told her he had letters that should have been written a week ago, but something at the back of his mind insisted that this was not the girl's real reason for wanting him to do his task now. She wanted to go and meet the boat alone, and on the moment an unfounded jealousy stirred like a coiled snake in him. He told himself that it might be some inconvenient aunt whom she was going to meet, but such a suggestion did not in the least satisfy him when he remembered the obvious pleasure with which she had read the telegram that no doubt announced this arrival. But he nailed himself to his writing-table till a couple of very tepid letters were finished, and then, with growing restlessness, went out through the hall into the warm, still night. Most of the hotel had gone indoors to dress for dinner, but sitting on the veranda with her back to him was Julia. A chair was drawn in front of her, and facing her was a young man, on whose face the light shone. He was looking eagerly at her, and his hand rested on her knee. Hugh turned abruptly and went back into the hotel.

He and Julia for these last three days had, with two other friends, made a very pleasant party of four at lunch and dinner. Tonight, when he entered the dining-room, he found that places were laid here for three only, and that at a far-distant table in the window were sitting Julia and the young man whom he had seen with her on the veranda. His identity was casually disclosed as dinner went on; one of his companions had seen Lord Paterson in Cairo. Hugh had only a wandering ear for table-talk, but a quick glancing eye, ever growing more sombre, for those in the window, and his heavy face, as he noted the tokens and signs of their intimacy, grew sullen and savage. Then, before dinner was over, they rose and passed out into the garden.

Jealousy can no more bear to lose sight of those to whom it owes its miseries than love can bear to be parted from the object of its adoration, and presently Hugh and his two friends went and sat, as was usual with them, on the veranda outside. Here and there about the garden were wandering couples, and in the light of the full moon, which was to be their lamp at Karnak to-night when the 'tiresome people' had gone, he soon identified Julia and Lord Paterson. They passed and repassed down a rose-embowered alley, hidden sometimes behind bushes and then appearing again for a few paces, and each sight of them, each vanishing of them again served but to confirm that which already needed no confirmation. And as his jealousy grew every moment more bitter, so every moment Hugh grew more and more dangerously enraged. Apparently Lord Paterson was not one of the 'tiresome people' whom Julia longed to get away from.

Presently his two companions left him, for they were

starting now to ride out to Karnak, and Hugh sat on, smoking and throwing away half consumed an endless series of cigarettes. He had ordered that his two horses, one with a side-saddle, should be ready at ten, and at ten he meant to go to the girl and remind her of her engagement. Till then he would wait here, wait and watch. If the veranda had been on fire, he felt he could not have left it to seek safety in some place where he was unable to see the bushy path where the two strolled. Then they emerged from that on to the broader walk that led straight to where he was sitting, and after a few whispered words, Lord Paterson left her there, and came quickly towards the hotel. He passed close by Hugh, gave him (so Hugh thought) a glance of amused derision, and went into the hotel.

Julia came quickly towards him when Lord Paterson had gone.

'Oh, Hughie,' she said. 'Will you be a tremendous angel? Lord Paterson – yes, he's just gone in, such a dear, you would delight in him – Lord Paterson's only here for one night, and he's dying to see Karnak by moonlight. So will you lend us your horses? He absolutely insists I should go out there with him.'

The amazing effrontery of this took Hugh's breath away, and in that moment's pause his rage flamed within him.

'I thought you were going out with me?' he said.

'I was. But, well, you see –'

She made the penitent mouth again, which had seemed so enchanting to him this afternoon.

'Oh, Hughie, don't you understand?' she said.

Hugh got up, feeling himself to be one shaking black jelly of wounded anger.

'I'm not sure if I do,' he said. 'But no doubt I soon shall. Anyhow, I want to ask you something. I want you to promise to marry me.'

She opened her great childlike eyes to their widest. Then they closed into mere slits again as she broke out into a laugh.

'Marry you?' she said. 'You silly, darling fellow! That is a good joke.'

Suddenly from the garden there sounded the jubilant scamper of running feet, and next moment a great grey ape sprang on to the veranda beside them, and looked eagerly, with keen dog's eyes, at Hugh, as if intent on obeying some yet unspoken command. Julia gave a little shriek of fright and clung to him.

'Oh, that horrible animal!' she cried. 'Hughie, take care of me!'

Some sudden ray of illumination came to Hugh. All the extraordinary fantastic things that Rankin had said to him became sober and real. And simultaneously the girl's clinging fingers on his arm became like the touch of some poisonous, preying thing, snake-coil, or suckers of an octopus, or hooked wings of a vampire bat. Something within him still shook and trembled like a quicksand, but his conscious mind was quite clear and collected.

'Go away,' he said to the ape, and pointed into the garden, and it scampered off, still gleefully spurning and kicking the soft sandy path. Then he quietly turned to the girl.

'There, it's gone,' he said. 'It was just some tame thing escaped. I saw it, or one like it, the other day on the end of a string. As for the horses, I shall be delighted to let you and Lord Paterson have them. It is ten now; they will be round.'

The girl had quite recovered from her fright.

'Ah, Hughie, you are a dear,' she said. 'And you do understand?'

'Yes, perfectly,' said he.

Julia went to dress herself for riding, and presently Hugh saw them off from the gate, with courteous wishes for a pleasant ride. Then he went back to his bedroom and opened the little box where he kept his scarabs.

※

An hour later he was walking out alone on the road to Karnak, and in his pocket was the image of Tahu-met. He had formed no clear idea of what he was meaning to do; the immediate reason for his expedition was that once again he could not bear to lose sight of Julia and her companion. The moon was high, the feathery outline of palm-groves was clearly and delicately etched on the dark velvet of the heavens, and stars sat among their branches like specks of golden fruit. The caressing scent of bean-flowers was wafted over the road, and often he had to stand aside to let pass a group of noisy tourists mounted on white donkeys, coming riotously home from the show-piece of Karnak by moonlight. Then, striking off the road, he passed beside the horseshoe lake, in the depths of whose black waters the stars burned unwaveringly, and by the entrance of the ruined temple of Mut. And then, with a stab of jealousy that screamed for its revenge, he saw, tied up to a pillar just within, his own horses. So they were here.

He gave the beasts a wide berth, lest, recognizing him, they should whinny and perhaps betray his presence, and, creeping in the shadow of the walls behind the row of great cat-headed statues, he stole into the inner court of the temple. Here for the first time he caught sight of the two at the far end of the enclosure, and as they turned, white-faced in the moonlight, he saw Paterson kiss the girl, and they stood there with neck and arms interlaced. Then they began walking towards him again, and he stepped into a dark chamber on his right to avoid meeting them.

It had that strange stale animal odour about it that hangs in Egyptian temples, and with a thrill of glee he saw, by a ray of moonlight that streamed in through the door, that by chance he had stepped into the shrine round which sit the dog-faced apes, whose secret name he knew, and whose controlling spell lay in his breast-pocket. Often he had felt the underworld horror that dwelt here, as a thing petrified and corpse-like; tonight it was petrified no longer, for the images seemed tense and quivering with the life that at any moment he could put into them. Their faces leered and hated and lusted, and all that demoniac power, which seemed to be flowing into him from them, was his to use as he wished. Rankin's fantastic tales were bursting with reality; he knew with the certainty with which the night-watcher waits for the day, that the lordship of the spirit of apes, incarnate and discarnate, would descend on him as on some anointed king the moment he thrice pronounced the secret name. He was going to do it too; he knew also that all he hesitated for now was to determine what orders their lord should give. It seemed that the image in his breast-pocket was aware, for it throbbed and vibrated against his chest like a boiling kettle.

He could not make up his mind what to do; but fed as with fuel by jealousy, and love, and hate, and revenge, his sense of the magical control he wielded could be resisted no longer, but boiled over, and he drew from his pocket the image where was engraven the secret name.

'Tahu-met, Tahu-met, Tahu-met,' he shouted aloud.

There was a moment's absolute stillness; then came a wild scream of fright from his horses, and he heard them gallop off madly into the night. Slowly, like a lamp turned down and then finally turned out, the blaze of the moon faded into utter darkness, and in that darkness, which whispered with a gradually increasing noise of scratchings and scamperings, he felt that the walls of the narrow chamber where he stood were, as in a dream, going farther and farther away from him, until, though still the darkness was impenetrable, he knew that he was standing in some immense space. One wall, he fancied, was still near him, close behind him, but the space which was full of he knew not what unseen presences, extended away and away to both sides of him and in front of him. Then he was aware that he was not standing, but sitting, for beneath his hands he could feel the arms as of some throne, of which the seat's edge pressed him just below his knees. The animal odour he had noticed before increased enormously in pungency, and he sniffed it in ecstatically, as if it had been the scent of beanfields, and mixed with it was the sweetness of incense and the savour as of roast meat. And at that the withdrawn light began to glow once more, only now it was not the whiteness of the moon, but a redder glow as of flames that aspired and sank again.

He saw where he was now. He was seated on a chair of pink granite, and a little in front of him was a huge altar, on which limbs smoked. Overhead was a low roof supported at intervals by painted pillars, and the whole of the vast floor was full of great grey apes, squatting in dense rows. Sometimes they all bowed their heads to the ground, sometimes, as by a signal, they raised them again, and myriads of obscene expectant eyes faced him. They glowed from within, as cats' eyes glow in the dusk, but with an infinity of hellish power. All that power was his to command, and he gloried in it.

'Bring them in,' he said, and no more. Indeed, he was not sure if he said it; it was just his thought. But as if he spoke the soundless language of animals, they understood, and they clambered and leaped over each other to do his bidding. Then a huddled wave of them surged up in front of where he sat, and as it broke in a foam of evil eyes and paws and switching tails, it disclosed the two whom he had ordered to be brought before him.

'And what shall I do with them?' he asked himself, cudgelling his monkey-brain for some infamous invention.

'Kiss each other,' he said at length, in order to inflame the brutality of his jealousy further, and he laughed shatteringly, as their white trembling lips met. He felt that all remnants of humanity were draining from him; there was but a little left in his whole nature that could be deemed to belong to a man. A hundred awful schemes ran about through his brain, as sparks of fire run through the charred ashes of burnt paper.

And then Julia turned her face towards him. In the hideous entry that she had made in that wave of apes her hair had fallen down and streamed over her shoulders. And at that, the sight of a woman's hair unbound, the remnant of his manhood, all that was not submerged in the foulness of his supreme apehood, made one tremendous appeal to him, like some final convulsion of the dying, and at the bidding of that impulse his hands came together and snapped the image in two.

Something screamed; the whole temple yelled with it, and mixed with it was a roaring in his ears as of great waters or hurricane winds. He stamped on the broken image, grinding it to powder below his heel, and felt the ground and the temple walls rocking round him.

Then he heard someone not far off speaking in human voice again, and no music could be so sweet.

'Let's get out of the place, darling,' it said. 'That was an earthquake, and the horses have bolted.'

He heard running steps outside, which gradually grew fainter. The moon shone whitely into the little chamber with the grotesque stone apes, and at his feet was the powdered blue glaze and baked white clay of the image he had ground to dust.

4 The Next Heir (1920)

H D EVERETT

1

Fryer and Fryer, solicitors, of Lincoln's Inn, the original firm and their successors, have for the past hundred years acted as guardians of the interests of the landed gentry, buying and selling portions of estates, proving wills, drawing up marriage settlements and the like. And a glance at the japanned deed-boxes in their somewhat shabby office would discover among the inscriptions sundry names of note.

The original Fryers have long been dead and gone, but there is still a Fryer at the head of the firm. And on a certain day of spring, this ruling Fryer was alone in his private office-room, when his clerk brought in a message.

'Mr Richard Quinton to see you, sir. He has no card to send up, but he says you will know his name and his business, as he has called to answer an advertisement.'

Without doubt Mr Fryer did know the name of Quinton, as it was legibly painted on a deed-box full in view, but something in his countenance expressed surprise. He signified his willingness to see Mr Richard Quinton, and presently the visitor entered, a pleasant-faced youngish man, brown of attire, and indeed altogether a brown man, except for the whitish patch where his forehead had been screened from the sun. Bronzed of skin, brown of short cut hair, and opening on the world a frank pair of hazel eyes, which looked as if they had been used to regard the wide spaces of wastelands, and were not fully used to the pressure and hurry and strenuousness of our over-civilised older world.

'I have called, sir, about an advertisement inserted by Fryer and Fryer in a Montreal paper. I have it here to show you.

It was posted to me at the London hospital, where I have been since my wound. I see that the representative of Richard Morley Quinton, who emigrated to Canada in 1827, will hear on applying to you of something to his advantage.'

'*May* hear of something,' corrected the man of law. 'Are you the representative in this generation?'

'I am, sir. Richard Morley Quinton was my grandfather.'

'Great-grandfather, surely? You are under thirty, and he was twenty-six years old when he left England.'

'No: grandfather. He had a hard struggle in his first years on the other side. His English brother was not the sort to help him, and he never asked for help: he would not. He did not marry until late in life, and my old dad was the only son who survived infancy. There was a daughter who married and had children. But I don't suppose you want to know about her.'

'We want the male heir. Or at least to know where he might be found.'

'My dad married earlier, but he had no children by his first wife. He was well over fifty when he married my mother, and I am their only child. I can put you in the way of getting all the certificates you want, and vouchers from responsible people who have known the family. And now, tell me. Why am I advertised for? Is it an inheritance?'

'Not at the present moment, but it may be.'

'Of Quinton and Quinton Verney – is that so? My dad would have been pleased. He thought much of Quinton, hearing about it from his father, who was born at the Court.'

'If the present Mr Quinton, your second cousin, makes no will, the Quinton property goes to the heir-male of your mutual great-grandfather. But he has the power of willing the whole where he pleases – to a hospital, or to a beggar in the street. You can count on no certain inheritance. You understand?'

'Then why –?'

'We advertised because Mr Quinton wished to ascertain who represented the Canadian branch of the family, and also to make your personal acquaintance. We can give you no certainty, but I gather from what he has written, that, if your cousin likes you, and if you agree to certain stipulations respecting the property, he intends to make you his heir. When the particulars you give me are verified, you will have to go down to Quinton, but he will reimburse any expense you may be put to, through loss of time and detention in England. You can hold yourself at our disposal?'

'If military orders do not interfere – yes, gladly, for the sake of a look at old Quinton Court, even with nothing to come after. But perhaps Mr Quinton may prefer to meet me in London.'

'You will have to go down there. Mr Quinton is a complete invalid, and keeps a resident doctor: he is still under sixty, but most unlikely, I should say, to marry. His father was killed in the hunting-field; he had not been long married, but his wife, who was one of the Pengwyns, gave birth to twin sons, posthumous children. This Clement was the younger of the two, but his elder brother died at nineteen, also from an accident. There you have the family history in a nutshell. Give me an address, where a letter will certainly find you when I have looked into this.'

✕

Richard had not long to wait for the expected letter. Mr Clement Quinton seemed disposed to take his young kinsman on trust, without holding aloof till his story was verified. Mr Fryer was still in correspondence with Canada when the summons came for Richard to present himself at Quinton Verney. The young Canadian was prompt in obeying, and on the day following he took train for the nearest railway point. No day or time had been named for arrival, so, after changing at the junction and alighting at a small wayside station, no conveyance was there to meet him. Nor, on enquiry, was any trap to be hired. His portmanteau could be sent by a returning cart in the course of a couple of hours, but for himself there was no alternative. He would have to walk the four miles, or rather more, which separated the station from Mount Verney. Mount Verney, these people styled Mr Quinton's dwelling, and not Quinton Court as he expected; the Quinton Court his old father used to talk of, told by the grandfather reminiscent of his youth. Why had the original name been changed? – that should be a first question when the time for putting questions came. Meanwhile he was not ill-pleased to be approaching Quinton on foot and alone, and a walk of four miles and over was but a light matter.

Four miles of lovely country verdant with the early green of spring, hill and dale unfolding wooded glimpses here and there, and the ancient Roman road stretching its white line before him, enduring still after all these centuries. He could hardly mistake the way, but after a while he thought it better to ask direction. There were iron gates and an avenue leading to Mount Verney, so he was told, and when he came to the iron gates he must turn in.

Gates and an avenue! His father had spoken of no such appendage to Quinton Court, but no doubt they were additions of a later time. He had his father much in mind during that walk, and the interest he would have felt in this possible – nay, probable – inheritance for his son. His grandfather too; the grandfather who died before his birth: it was as if the two old men went beside him along the green-fenced way, made fair by the sunshine of late April. And he had another person in mind, one who up to now has not been named. Nan, his girl, who waited for him far off across the Atlantic, full of love and faith. If this succession truly came to pass, if it were even an assured future to him and to his heirs, marriage would be no longer an imprudence, it might be entered into at once on his return, released from war-service. That hope was enough to gild the sunshine, and spread the pastures with a brighter green. And then he came to the gates, and they stood open.

Mount Verney did not boast a lodge, though the drive was a long one. The avenue had been closely planted with ilex and pine, too closely for the good of the trees, and it was consequently dark in shadow: as he turned in he was conscious of a certain chill.

The open gates were hung on stone pillars, and the ornamentation of these uprights caught his eye. On either side, inwards and outwards, a face was carved in relief, but a face that was not human: the mask of a satyr, with pricked animal ears and sprouting horns, and an evil leering grin. Richard had seen nothing of this sort in his backwoods experience, though possibly other things that were starker and grimmer. The leering faces filled him with repugnance; they should not remain there, he thought, to watch over the comings and goings of the house, did ever that house become his own.

The dark avenue had a bend in it; he could not see to the end, but he thought he knew well what he would find there, the old Quinton homestead had been so often described to him. The grey stone house, with its gables and mullioned windows, diamond-paned; the steep roof, up and down which the pigeons strutted and plumed themselves; the paved courtyard with its breast-high wall and mounted urns. He had a clear picture of it in his mind, and this was what at the turn of the avenue he expected to see. But when the turn was reached, his joyful anticipations fell dead. This was quite another place. Had he been misdirected after all?

What lay before him was a white stuccoed villa, spreading over much ground, but so pierced with big window-spaces that it presented to the beholder scant solidity of wall. This was the entrance side; towards the valley the walls rounded themselves into two semi-circles with a flat central division, and here again were the big sash windows of plate-glass, overlooking the view. But there was no mistake. This was Mount Verney.

A grave-looking elderly manservant answered the bell, and it became evident the Canadian visitor had arrived too soon. Mr Richard Quinton was expected, yes certainly, but the day had not been named, and Mr Quinton was at present out in the car, and Dr Lindsay with him. If Mr Richard would step into the library, tea should be brought to him – unless he preferred sherry. His room had been so far prepared that it could be quickly made ready; he, Peters, would tell the housekeeper. And would Mr Richard come this way?

So tea was served to Richard in the library, and his first meal under the Mount Verney roof was taken in solitude, as the master of the house did not return. The library possessed one of the wide bows overlooking the valley, but in spite of the tall sash windows the room was a dark one. They were, it is true, heavily draped with crimson curtains, and the furniture was also heavy, and of an inartistic period. He tried to picture Nan in these surroundings, sitting in the opposite big chair (it would have swallowed her up entirely unless she perched on the arm) and pouring out for him from the huge old teapot, but the effort was in vain. The fancy portrait of his little love would not fit into this frame, but doubtless the frame could be altered: like the grinning masks on the gates, there was much it would be possible to change. Meanwhile hurrying footsteps were heard on the floor overhead, housemaids were busy there; and presently Peters came again to ask if he should conduct the guest to his room.

Richard left the dull library with a sensation of relief. The chamber immediately above had been prepared for him, of equal size, and with windows commanding the view. Richard made some appreciative comment, which seemed to please the old servant.

'Yes, sir,' he said, 'this is the best bedroom, it has the finest look-out. Mr Quinton himself gave orders for it to be yours. It used to be Lady Anna Quinton's.'

'Lady Anna Quinton!' Richard repeated the name in his surprise. 'I did not know Mr Quinton had ever been married.'

'No, sir, and he never was. Her ladyship was his mother. She went away to France and died there; it is getting on for thirty years ago, but Mr Quinton couldn't bear to take the room to be his, though it is the best in the house. I'll send up your portmanteau, sir, directly it arrives.' And with that, Peters withdrew.

Here Richard was certainly well lodged. He stood at the middle window which had been set open, and looked out over a wide prospect. The sun was now beginning to decline, and the first flush of rosy cloud was reflected in the chain of pools which filled the valley to the right, widened out almost to the dimensions of a lake – no doubt artificially formed by damning up the natural stream, which rushed over a weir out of sight. In the middle distance, between the house and the water, was a grove of young oaks, not thickly set like the planting of the avenue, but high-trimmed and rising tall and bare-stemmed out of evergreen undergrowth. The shimmer of water was visible through them in the background, not wholly concealed, though it might be when leafage was full.

The name of Quinton Verney was familiar, cherished

among those legends of the importance of the family which the Canadian branch had preserved and handed down; but the lake was to Richard another innovation and surprise. Was it good fishing water, he wondered, and would rainbow trout flourish and breed there? As he stood looking, a boat shot out from the headland to the right, and, crossing the field of view, was lost behind the grove: it was only after it had disappeared that Richard began to wonder what had been the motive power. He could not recall any flash of oars or figures of rowers, or indeed any occupier of the boat.

This might have puzzled him still more, but his attention was diverted by the sound of an arrival below. A car had drawn up at the entrance, voices were now heard in the hall, footsteps on the stairs. After a brief interval, a sharp, rather authoritative knock came at his door and a man entered, a man still on the younger side of middle-age, reddish-haired and short of stature, with a close-trimmed bristly moustache.

'Mr Quinton?' Richard exclaimed, coming forward. If this was his host, he was quite unlike the fancy picture he had formed. But then at Mount Verney everything was unlike and unexpected.

'No – My name's Lindsay – I'm the doctor. Mr Quinton is sorry you were not met, but he had not understood you were arriving to-day.'

'I hope my coming has not been inconvenient?'

'Not at all – not at all, unless to yourself. But I do not suppose you minded the walk from the station; it is pretty country, and you came here especially to acquaint yourself with the place and its surroundings. One thing more. I have to ask you to excuse Mr Quinton for this evening, and put up with my company only. Mr Quinton is, as you know, an invalid, and I have been with him to-day to his dentist for some extractions under an anaesthetic. He is a wreck in consequence' – here the little reddish man shrugged his shoulders – 'and will not leave his own rooms again to-night. You are comfortable here, I hope?' – this after Richard had expressed concern at his host's condition. Now it was necessary he should praise his quarters, which he did without stint.

'Mr Quinton would have it that Lady Anna's room should be made ready for the heir, and we were all surprised, as it has been long out of use. Well, adieu for the present: come down as soon as you are ready. Dinner is at seven: we keep early hours here in the country. What! your portmanteau not come? Then never mind about dressing; we will not stand on ceremony for to-night.'

With that, Lindsay the doctor took himself off. But, after he had closed the door, some of his last words kept repeating in Richard's mind. *Made ready for the heir!* That was taking intention for granted in a way for which he was not prepared; and, suddenly, he felt strangely doubtful of his own wish in the matter. Did he really desire to be the owner of the Quinton property, and, if not, from what hidden root did disinclination spring?

Presently a gong sounded from below, and he went down to find the dining-room lighted up, though it was scarcely more than dusk without, and the window-screens were still undrawn. The table was set out with some fine old silver and an abundance of flowers, the service of the meal was faultless, and Lindsay made an excellent deputy host. Good food has a cheering influence, and the causeless depression which had threatened to engulf Richard's spirit was lifted, at least for the time.

'I hope you will like Quinton Verney,' Lindsay was saying with apparent heartiness. 'Mr Quinton is particularly anxious that you should like the place, and take an interest in his hobbies. He will explain better than I can what they are. But be prepared to hear a great deal about Roman remains in Britain, and to be cross-questioned about your knowledge.'

'Then I can only avow ignorance. It is a study that has not come in my way, but I am at least ready to be interested.'

'Ah, well, interest won't be difficult in what has been discovered on your own land, for that is his especial pride. A fine tessellated pavement down there by the pools, and an altar in what is now the grove. I am a duffer myself in these matters, but Mr Quinton is a downright enthusiast about the old pagans and their times. It was he who replanted the grove where it is supposed that a sacred one existed, and set up in the midst of it a statue of Pan copied from the antique. I chaff him sometimes about it, and tell him I believe there is nothing he would like better than to revive the Lupercalia, and convert the entire neighbourhood. That's an exaggeration, of course, but the element of mystery appeals to him. As you will discover.'

Following this touch of personal revelation, Richard remarked: 'You know Mr Quinton very well. I suppose you have been with him a long time?'

'Eighteen months – no less, no more. But you can get to know a man pretty well in that time, especially when you happen to be his doctor as well as his house-mate. He has been an invalid for many years – since boyhood in fact: a sad case: you'll know more about it after a while. I was at the war before that: got knocked out, and when free of hospital could only take on a soft job, and fate or luck sent me here. Quinton and I have got on well together. Indeed I may tell you in confidence that he offered to leave me all he possessed, provided I would bind myself by his conditions.'

So the Quinton inheritance had been offered and refused elsewhere. Here was a matter that might well give Richard food for thought.

'And why did you not –?' he began impulsively.

'Why didn't I grasp at such a chance? Well, I allow it was tempting enough, to a man who is a damaged article – a damage that will be life-long. But I couldn't consent to bind myself as he would have me bound; and there was another reason. I would have been suspected of using my position here to exercise undue influence, and that I couldn't stomach. It was I who suggested to Mr Quinton that he should seek out his next of kin – eh, what; what is the matter?' The query was to Peters, who was whispering at his elbow.

'Pray excuse me. I am sorry, but my patient is not so well.' And the little doctor hurried away.

Peters brought in the next course. 'Dr Lindsay hopes you will go on with the dinner, sir, and not wait for him. He may be detained some time.'

For the rest of the meal Richard was solitary. He declined after-dinner wine and dessert, so Peters, who felt himself responsible towards the guest, suggested that he might like to smoke in the library, and coffee would be brought to him there. Richard rose from the table, and, as he did so, turned towards the unscreened window behind his chair, and experienced the shock of a surprise. There stood a strange-looking figure, gazing in at him and at the room, with face pressed against the glass. His exclamation recalled Peters, who was in the act of carrying out a tray; but by the time the old butler returned, the figure had disappeared. Who, or what was it? But Peters could not tell.

'I'll have it inquired into, sir. No one had any call to be there. These windows look into the enclosed garden, that is always kept private. A man, did you say, sir? Like a tramp?'

'A man,' Richard assented, but he did not add in what likeness. Surely it must have been some freak of fancy that suggested those lineaments, the white leering face which resembled the bestial masks at the gate of the avenue, with their pricked ears and budding horns; and suggested also the naked torso, of which a glimpse was afforded by the light.

Peters brought word with the coffee that no one was found in the garden, but he meant to be extra careful in locking up, 'lest it should be somebody after the plate.' And indeed, were ill characters about, the unscreened window was likely to bring danger, as the display of silver on sideboard and table might well excite the cupidity of a looker-in.

Dr Lindsay came down an hour later, but it was only to ask whether Richard had all he wanted for comfort and for the night.

'I shall be sitting up with Mr Quinton,' he explained. 'Unluckily, haemorrhage has followed these extractions, and he is morbidly affected by the sight and taste of blood. No, not a sufficient loss to be alarming: it will be subdued by tomorrow I don't doubt: it is serious only as it affects his special case. You'll give Peters your orders, will you not, and tell him when you wish to be called, and all that. I understand your portmanteau has arrived.'

So Richard found himself back again in the best bedroom at an early hour, with the night before him, and his luggage unpacked, and despatch-case set on the writing-table. Now was the time for the letter he had promised Nan, with his first impressions of Quinton Verney, about which she was naturally curious; the old homestead he had described to her, which might some day be his home and hers. But when he spread paper before him, he felt an overmastering reluctance to write that letter. What could he say if he told her the truth – and surely nothing less than the truth and the whole truth was due to Nan, however much it might disappoint and puzzle her. Could he tell her, with no reason to allege, of the distaste he felt for this place, for the house and all that it contained? – a distaste which began with the first sight of those leering masks at the avenue gate: how tell her of that other living face which resembled them, seen peering into the lighted dining-room, pressed against the glass of the shut window a couple of hours ago? Better delay, than that he should fill a letter with maunderings such as these, when another day's experience, or a personal interview with the invisible cousin, might bring about an altered mind.

He was tired and out of spirits, and though he rejected with scorn the suggestion that a walk of less than five miles could have fatigued him, he was only lately out of hospital, and it was long since so much pedestrian exercise had come his way. And there had been throughout a certain excitement of highly strung expectation, from which no doubt reaction played its part. No, he would not attempt to write to Nan; the letter should be postponed until the morrow. And he would betake himself at once to bed.

2

It has been said that the chamber allotted to him was spacious and well-appointed, a private bathroom opened from it, and with one notable exception, it fulfilled every modern requirement. The rest of the house had been wired, and electric light installed, but here there were no means of illumination but candles, and, though these had been abundantly supplied on toilet and mantelpiece, and also at the bedside, the result was curiously dull. It was as if the walls and hangings of the apartment absorbed and did not reflect the light; a room of ordinary size would have been as well illuminated by a farthing dip. One of the windows was opened down a hand's breadth behind the curtains, and they stirred faintly in the air. Richard drew them apart to push up the lower sash, and then was struck by the beauty of the scene below. The valley had put on a veil of silvery mist, so delicate as hardly to obscure, and away to the left the moon was rising, a full yellow moon, magnified by its nearness to the horizon.

How still it all was. He had been used of late to the roar of a great city, audible even through hospital walls; before that to the thudding of great guns, and the scream of shell. How silent, and how peaceful: but presently not completely silent, for music broke into the stillness.

Somebody down below was playing on the flute, long-drawn notes and a simple air, but of enthralling sweetness. The music was difficult to locate; sometimes it seemed to come from near the house, sometimes from the grove of trees, and now to be a mere echo from a greater distance still. Could some rustic lover be serenading a housemaid? but no, that seemed impossible. Richard was himself no musician, but he knew enough to appreciate the rare quality of the performer. And then the final notes died away, and silence reigned under the rising moon.

He dropped the curtain over the window, leaving it open, and now applied himself quickly to prepare for bed. Tired as he was, he expected to sleep as soon as his head touched the pillow: such was his custom in high health, and the habit had served him in good stead when recruiting strength. But on this first night at Mount Verney sleep and he were to be strangers. No doubt there was some excitement of nerve or brain, the cause of which might be looked for entirely in himself. This at first; but by-and-bye there was something external, something more, though it was nameless and undefined.

A change had set in: this was no restlessness of his own that he was suffering, it was the misery and torture of another; a misery all the greater that it could not be expressed. It seemed to him that he was divided; he recognised that he was lying on the bed, but he was also walking the room from wall to wall, with tossed arms, with hands clenched and threatening, and then spread open; gestures foreign to his nature under any extreme of passion. He, or the entity which absorbed him, did not weep: no tears came to the relief of this distress, and his own voice was dumb in his throat; there could be no cry of appeal. Whether the passion which tore him was fury solely, or grief solely, he could not tell; or whether in its extreme anguish it combined the two.

For a while he was completely paralysed by this strange experience: he was walking the room with the sufferer; he was the sufferer: and then again he knew the personality and the agony were not his own; that his real self was stretched upon the bed, though he could neither lift a finger nor move a limb. How long did this endure in its alternations?

Keen as was his after memory, he could not tell: moments count as hours when under torture, and in an experience so abnormal time does not exist, even as we are told it will be effaced for us hereafter. One fragment of knowledge informed his brain; how he knew cannot be told, for no voice spoke. The entity was a woman. It was no man's agony into the vortex of which he had been drawn; this was a woman who knew both love and hate, a mother who had possessed and also lost.

Then, in a moment, the strain upon him snapped: he could move again, he had the government of his limbs, he was in his own body and not that other, if the other was a body indeed. Candles – the means of striking a light – were at his hand; in less time than it takes to write, both flames were kindled: the whole room was plain to see, and there was nothing, nothing but empty air. And yet he knew, he knew that the woman was still there – that she was pacing up and down from wall to wall – that she was still torn with fury, from the vortex of which his own spirit was scarcely yet set free, as consciousness of it remained.

This would have been a staggering experience, even to one versed in psychic marvels, but of such matters Richard Quinton was completely ignorant. To him the ordeal he had passed through was as unique as it was unaccountable – a horror to have so penetrated another's being, and also in a way a thing of shame, to be covered up shuddering from the light of day. He leapt out of bed; he must seek the window, the free air, if he would not choke and die. In his rush forward it seemed as if he encountered and passed through the frantic figure that yet was invisible and disembodied; but the collision, if it was collision, affected neither: roused as he was, the grip of individuality was too strong. He tore the curtains apart, and there at last was the cool night, the serene moon, the wafting of free air, in which, behind him in the room, the lighted candles flared.

The moon was now high in heaven, the scene was bathed in white light, the shadows, where shadows fell, were black and sharply defined. The silvery mist of the earlier evening had disappeared, the light veil of it withdrawn, rolled up and swept away before that stirring of air. There was a path of reflected light across the quiet water of the pool, the headland stood out dark. And, strange to relate, from behind it again shot out the mysterious boat, the boat he had seen before, but now there were two men on board. He saw, or thought he saw, one man attack the other; for a dozen seconds they were locked together struggling. Then the rocking boat capsized and sank, and the men also disappeared.

Richard saw this, and yet in some dim way he realised that he had witnessed no actual disaster for which he need give the alarm: it was a scene projected into his mind from the mind of another. It did not even occur to him that there, within a bowshot of the house, were men drowning who might be saved. The moon-path on the water was smooth again now, undisturbed by even a ripple, the night utterly still. But a moment later the silence was broken by the same flute music which had discoursed so sweetly earlier in the night. It was, however, tuned to a livelier measure this second time, one that might accompany dancing feet. It sounded from the grove, and underneath the clear light Richard could distinguish moving figures, leaping among the trees.

There were five or six of them apparently, men or boys, and the figures looked as if naked above the waist. And the dance was not solely a dance, for they seemed to be chasing, or driving before them, some large animal which fled with leaps through the undergrowth, a goat possibly, or a sheep. The animal and the pursuing figures disappeared among the trees, and then appeared again as if they had made a circuit of the grove; the goat (if it was a goat) leaping in front, and the others pursuing. This was the end; a cloud drifted over the moon, and when it passed there was no more sign of movement in the grove, and the jocund fluting had ceased.

Richard turned back into the room, and now his perception of that fury and distress, if not wholly effaced, was dulled as if here, too, was the shadowing of a merciful cloud. But stretch himself on that bed he could not, nor address himself to sleep, lest it should be renewed with all the former horror. He would keep the lights burning, if only he had a book he would occupy himself with reading, but literature had formed no part of his light luggage.

He might seek one in the library below, treading softly in stocking-soles so as not to disturb the sleeping house.

But as he issued forth, candle in hand, he found a burner switched on on the landing, and the dressing-gowned small doctor crossing over from an opposite door. Lindsay at once accosted him.

'Can I do anything: what is the matter? – oh, can't sleep, and want a book: is that it? I can find you one close at hand,

and mine are livelier than the fossils in the library. Come this way.'

Lindsay's room opened over the entrance, next to Mr Quinton's bedchamber. A set of bookshelves filled a recess.

'Help yourself. The yellow-backs on the top shelf are French – I daresay you read French. But you'll find English ones below, and perhaps they are more likely to put you asleep.' He snapped on an extra light, and then turned for a fuller scrutiny of his companion. 'You look pretty bad,' was his remark. 'Does a sleepless night always knock you up like this? I'm doctor to the establishment you know, and I prescribe a peg. Whisky or brandy will you have? Both of them are here, and so is a syphon. Sit down while I get it ready. Three fingers – two – one? Good: you do well to be moderate. Get outside that, and you'll feel better. And then you can pick your book.'

Lindsay did not question further as to the cause of disturbance, though he looked inquisitive, as if suspicions were aroused. Richard for his part remained tongue-tied, time was needed to digest and try to understand his experience: he might speak of it later on, but not now, while still his nerves were vibrating from the strain. The human companionship was, however, reassuring, and by the time the prescribed dose was swallowed, he felt altogether more normal. He inquired for Mr Quinton, sat for a while conversing on indifferent subjects, and then departed with a book.

He did not venture again to lie down, but installed himself in a deep chair, the candles burning at his elbow. The effect of the novel may have been soporific, though he was an inattentive reader. After a long interval he fell asleep, and waked to find morning already brightening in the east.

The night was over, its perplexities and distresses had sunk into the past, and a new day had begun. It was refreshing to spirit as well as body to wash and re-clothe, to undo the bolts and chains which guarded the front door, and find himself in the free air. Though it was still the air which breathed over Mount Verney, he was delivered from the evil shadow of that roof. He retraced his steps of the day before, down the dark curving drive, out through the satyr-headed gates, to the highroad which was free to all, the road traversed by Roman legions in centuries that were past. He turned to the right, with the eastern sky behind him, and walked on, without object, but steeping himself in the freshness of the newly awakened world.

At first he appeared to be the only person astir and observant, but presently an old man of the labouring class pushed open a gate some way ahead and came towards him, a shepherd accompanied by his dog. Richard would have liked to exchange ideas with an English working man, but felt too suddenly shy to venture on more than a good-morning as they drew abreast. The man, however, stopped and accosted him.

'Beg pardon, master, but as you came along, did you mebbe happen on a straying sheep? A ewe she is, and has taken her lamb with her, one getting on in size, as it was dropped early. Me and the dog have been after her since first it was light.'

Richard had no information to give; he had not seen the ewe and her lamb. And then he bethought him.

'I stayed last night at Mount Verney, and, looking out in the moonlight, I saw a sheep leaping about in the grove, the coppice of oaks by the water. Would that be the one you have lost?'

The man shook his head.

'No, sir, that would be Mr Quinton's sheep. I drove it down myself, a prime wether, only a day ago; and my heart was sore for the poor thing. It seemed as if the dog here was sorry too, for he didna like the job. Mr Quinton he buys one at the spring full moon, and again at harvest, of my master or one of the other breeders, always to be driven into the coppice and left there, and I doubt if ever the creatures live as much as two days. What he wants them for 'tis beyond me to say. Seems a waste of good meat and good wool, for it is just a hole in the field and dig them under, so I am told, and not a soul the better. Some folks will eat braxy mutton, meat being dear as it is; but not one of them would touch a sheep that had died up there in the wood, poisoned as like as not. 'Tis just a mystery to all of us. But I've no call to be passing remarks, seeing you know Mr Quinton, and are staying at Mount Verney.'

Richard might have replied with truth that he did not know Mr Quinton, their acquaintance was still to make. But he asked instead for direction, and was told to cross a stile to the right into a certain field-path, which would bring him out opposite the house, by the bridge over the water.

The bridge was a rustic affair of planks and a hand-rail, and beyond it the way diverged to right and left, the path on the left entering the grove, barred only by a light iron turnstile. Was it curiosity, or another sort of attraction which drew Richard thither, to see by daylight the spot on which he had looked down under the moon the night before? Now it seemed ordinary enough; the paths cut through it were grassed over and green, but here and there, where the turf was soft, he noticed they were trampled by divided hoofs, larger than those of sheep. The trees, young and slender, shorn of their lower branches, were now faintly green with unexpanded leafage; the undergrowth, which was chiefly rhododendron, was here and there breaking into purple and pinkish flower.

While still some way from it, he could distinguish among the trees the statue of which Lindsay had spoken. It was mounted on a pedestal, and was, as he said, a modern copy of the antique. Pan with his pipes in bronze, an abhorrent half-animal figure; the brooding face less repulsive perhaps than those of the satyrs at the gate, but the regard it appeared to bend on the observer who approached, had a keener expression of intelligence and evil power. Richard as he drew near, his attention riveted on that face and crouching figure, almost stumbled over an object lying at the foot of the column.

It was the dead sheep. Had it been dragged thither with a purpose, or hunted till it fell exhausted where it lay? There was no mark upon it that he could see, of the knife of the executioner, but the swollen tongue protruded from the half open jaws, and thick blood had flowed from both nostrils, staining the ground.

Truly Mount Verney was a spot where there were strange happenings. The shudder of the night again passed over Richard, and he had now no least desire to linger in the grove, or to make further discoveries. Passing through another gate he gained a steep slope of lawn, leading up to the gravelled terrace on which the windows of the library opened. His approach had been observed, and here was Lindsay waving him a cheerful greeting, with the intelligence of waiting breakfast.

3

'Been for an early ramble? – that was well done. Mr Quinton wants you to see as much as possible of the place before he speaks to you of the future. A lovely morning. And this house stands well, does it not, above the valley? Gives you a first rate view.'

Richard assented. And then put the question he had been meditating.

'Was this house built on the site of another, do you know? The house my father used to speak about was called Quinton

Court. It was built long before his father's time, and was of stone; it had a walled courtyard and mullioned windows. I don't suppose it was ever a grand mansion. But that was what I expected to find in coming down here.'

'Quinton Court is still in existence; the man lives there who has the farm. It is a fine-looking old place, but I expect it has gone a long way downhill since it was given up as the family residence. You will find it about a mile from here, on the other side of the hill.'

'I should like to see it. I should greatly like to see it –!'

'Make it the object of your next walk. Go the length of the lake to the head water, and through the field beyond, and you will come upon a cart-road. I would show you the way, but I may have difficulty in leaving. And perhaps you would rather go alone.'

That he would prefer to make the visit alone was so true that Richard left the suggestion uncontested. Lindsay passed lightly to another subject; one on which he was not improbably curious.

'I hope the novel and the "peg" helped you to sleep? I hate to lie awake myself, but sometimes a strange bed –! There is fish, I think, under that cover. Or do you prefer bacon?'

'I am a good sleeper usually, in any sort of bed, strange or familiar. Dr Lindsay, I am sorry to be a troublesome guest, but can I change my room? And, if you will allow me, I will do so before to-night.'

'You can, without doubt. There are other guest-rooms, though with fewer advantages than the bow-room, as we call it. I will see about the exchange. But – may I be so indiscreet as to ask why? Because Mr Quinton will put the question to me, and I had better be prepared to answer him.'

'Then perhaps I may put a question on my side. I understand that bedroom has been long out of use. I know nothing about ghosts, and have never believed in them, but – it is not like other rooms. Is it supposed to be haunted? And, if so, why was it chosen for me?'

'I can't tell you much about it; remember I only came here eighteen months ago. As for why it was chosen, you must ask Mr Quinton: it was his doing, not mine. I never heard of any ghost being seen there. The only queer thing said about the room sounds like illusion, and could not disturb a sleeper. Nor would it, I suppose, be visible at night. But perhaps you, as a Quinton, would be more sensitive than a stranger.'

'What is the queer thing?'

'Why it seems absurd, but they say whoever looks through that window sees a boat on the lake. I saw something like it myself on one occasion, but I expect it is a flaw in the glass. Was there a ghost last night?'

'No ghost in the sense you mean, but such an impression of misery – and not misery only, anger – that I found sleep impossible. That is all I have to tell. If Mr Quinton is affronted by my wish to change, I must find quarters elsewhere till he is ready to speak to me.'

'Nonsense: he won't be affronted, it would be absurd. I doubt if you will see him to-day, but he is decidedly better, and I shall not need to sit up another night. You'll like him, I think. He has his eccentricities, that must be allowed. But you would be sorry for him from your heart if you knew all.'

'He is eccentric? I heard a strange story about him this morning, from an old shepherd I met in the road. Is it true that he purchases a sheep twice a year, and that it is driven into the grove to die? There is one lying dead there now, at the foot of the statue of Pan.'

Lindsay shrugged his shoulders.

'I told you he was half a pagan, and I don't defend the sheep business. That sacrifice is one of the things he wants continued, and makes a condition; but I told him straight out that no successor would pledge himself to a thing so out of reason, and you had better be firm about it when he speaks. Of course it is natural he should wish Mount Verney kept up as the residence of the owner; there one can be in sympathy. His grandfather built it, and his father planned the grounds, and the ornamental water and all that. Odd about the lake, seeing what happened after. Why, don't you know? The elder son was drowned there. Mr Quinton's twin brother. Archibald, his name was. He was the Quinton heir.'

Richard saw again, in a flash of memory, the two figures struggling in the boat and disappearing under water; but where was the good of taking Lindsay into confidence? He had said enough, and made it plain he would occupy the room no more, nor look from it over the lake: he did not care to what sort of apartment he was transferred; it would serve him for the time, however mean.

The doctor hurried away as soon as they had breakfasted, apologising for his enforced absence, but Richard was well content to be alone. He wanted to think out the warning again given about conditions. That which concerned the sheep was unthinkable, and could hardly be pressed; but evidently there were others, by reason of which Lindsay had refused the offered heirship. If he was required to live at Mount Verney in the future, and make it his home and his wife's home – what then? In one way the prospect of the inheritance was tempting enough to him, and would be to any man – an inheritance that would at once convert him into a person of importance, with a stake in the country as the saying is; a good position to offer his wife, ample means, provision for the children that might be born to them.

But if what he began dimly to suspect was fact; if the place had somehow fallen under a curse, in pagan times or now – such a curse as affected inanimate building, and tainted the very ground – it would be no fit home for her. And Nan was not covetous of riches – she would not mind struggling on with him and being poor; she would approve, so he justly thought, of a refusal made for the sake of right.

There was nothing to detain him indoors, so with these cogitations in mind, he set out in the direction Lindsay had indicated, following the north shore of the artificial lake, and crossing the headland which, viewed from above, had been the departure point of the mysterious boat. On the western side of the headland, furthest from the house and half hidden by the bank, were the remains of what certainly had been a boathouse; but in these days no boat sheltered there, and the timbers of the roof had rotted and fallen in decay. He passed through the gate by the headwater, a clear and fast running stream; found and followed the cart-road, which after a while was merged in a superior approach, now well nigh as worn and deeply rutted as the other.

He came upon the old Court suddenly, round a fold of the hill, and there he stood for a while, his heart moved by a mysterious feeling of kinship – if not utterly fantastic to suppose flesh and blood can feel itself akin to walls of stone. The old homestead had fallen from its first estate, but there was a dignity about it still, the dignity of fine proportion and high quality, differing widely from the jerrybuilding of to-day. The grey gables were there as of old, the roof of slabbed stone, the panes of diamond lattice; there the flagged courtyard with its breast-high boundary wall, and five of the six urns mounted in place; the sixth had fallen, and lay broken at the foot.

The front door was fast shut, an oak door studded with iron, but Richard drew near and knocked, treading the very stones the footsteps of the dead had worn. Why, why had the later degenerates forsaken this dear place, and fixed their abode at Mount Verney?

A neatly-dressed young woman opened to him, and looked inquiringly at the stranger.

'I'm sorry, sir, my father is not in, if so be as you come seeking him.'

No, Richard said, that was not his errand; but might he be allowed to see inside the house, if only a couple of the rooms?

'Why certainly, if you are thinking of taking the place. I didn't know as it had got about that we are leaving, but news do fly apace. But we shall not be out until September.'

'My name is Quinton, and I am from Canada. My great-grandfather lived here, and it was here that my grandfather was born. I am anxious to see the Court now I am in England. If you would be so good as to allow –'

'Come in, sir, and look where you like; you are kindly welcome. My father would make you so I know, for he is the oldest tenant on the estate. We have no fault to find with the place, but the farm is too big for father now he has no son with him, and the house too large for us too. I am the only one at home, and mother is laid by with the rheumatics. These long stone passages take a lot of cleaning, to say nothing of the many rooms, though more than half of them we shut away.'

So upon this invitation Richard had his wish, and saw over the house upstairs and down. In some of the rooms put out of use there were still pieces of old furniture, Quinton property, his guide told him: an oak chest or two, corner cupboards with carven doors, a worm-eaten dresser, chairs in the last stage of decrepitude. They were let with the house, having been thought unworthy of removal to Mount Verney. In the best parlour sacks of grain were stored, and on the threshold of two of the empty bedrooms he was warned to step warily, as the floors were thought to be unsafe.

Quinton Court had fallen from its first estate, but it was still lovely in the eyes of this late descended son. It had been cleanly kept, however roughly, and there was an air of purity about its homeliness, of open casements and scents of lavender and apples. He could picture his Nan here, a happy house-mistress under the ancient roof of his forefathers; but not as the chatelaine of Mount Verney with all its wealth: never at Mount Verney. Ah, if only Mr Quinton would make this place his bequest to the next heir, the old Court and the surrounding farm which he might work for a living; and leave Quinton Verney and his accumulated thousands, where else and to whom else he pleased!

4

Such were Richard's thoughts as he walked back along the green shores of the lake, and under the mid-day sun. He and the doctor were again tête-a-tête at luncheon; but he was told Mr Quinton desired to see him that afternoon in his private room above stairs; also that he intended to dine with them, being greatly better than the day before. So the first interview with his host came about earlier than he had been led to expect.

The appearance of his elderly cousin took him by surprise. Mr Clement Quinton was strikingly handsome, though older-looking than his two and fifty years. He might have been taken for a man advanced in the seventies, though his tall thin figure was still upright. He owned a thick thatch of grey hair, a close-cut white beard, and bushy grey eyebrows above eyes of steely blue, rather unnaturally wide open. He welcomed Richard cordially, shaking him by the hand: a cold hand, his was, and yet the younger man felt uncomfortably, the instant they were palm to palm, that he touched something sticky and moist. Mr Quinton's left hand was gloved, and Richard remembered after that he held a dark silk handkerchief in the other while they talked together.

There was nothing embarrassing or note-worthy about the earlier conversation. Mr Quinton appeared kindly interested in Richard's past history, asking about his father and home, how he had been educated and where, and also the details of his military service. They had been talking together for half an hour, before any reference was made to the future.

'I want you to be interested in this place,' he said with emphasis. 'I want you to be particularly interested. For there are various things I am bound to leave to the doing of others, and much will depend on their punctual carrying on. It will smooth my pillow – as the saying is – if I may be assured of the co-operation of my successor.'

This was not very easy to answer, as Richard could not assume successorship on a hint so vague. So he struck out into an account of his visit to Quinton Court, and pleasure over the discovery that the old house of which his grandfather had spoken with affection, was still solidly existent.

'I was afraid it had been pulled down, and Mount Verney built on its site.'

'No, we destroyed nothing. My respect for antiquity is too great. As I will show you later, it has been my great desire to – call back into life, I may say – associations from the dead past of an earlier period still. Traces of what had been, were thick on the ground hereabouts: you shall have the complete history of how, and why, and what. You will find it remarkable indeed. I will tell you frankly, my young cousin, it is here and on Mount Verney I want your interest focussed. This place dates back to the Roman occupation of Britain, and in comparison with the relics here, Quinton Court is but a thing of yesterday.'

'Dr Lindsay told me Roman remains had been unearthed. I think he said some portions of a pavement.'

'There was a villa here, on this very spot; baths in the valley, with the water running through them; and an altar where you see the grove, which was once a dense thicket of wood. I have other means of knowing, besides conclusions drawn from the fragments that remain, and these communications the excavations have strikingly confirmed. I was directed where to dig. There was a special cult connected with this place. The worship of Pan.'

'I observed the statue in the grove.'

'It marks the site of the old altar. Pan is a deity about whom little has been known and much mistaken. From the sources of information at my command, I have compiled a treatise. And that is one thing I require of my successor. If unpublished at the time of my decease, I wish it given to the world.'

The posthumous publication of a treatise! It would be well if other conditions were no more formidable than this.

'Some writers have made the mistake of confounding Pan with Faunus; surely an extraordinary error. My theory is entirely different. Cain was his prototype. Cain.'

Here the recluse seemed to be stirred by some inward excitement, and he got up to pace the room.

'Cain!' he repeated. 'Of course you know the scriptural narrative, and probably little else about that founder of an early race. There are mistakes in that account – it is libellous, the fabrication of an enemy. Eve put about unworthy slanders. If Cain did truly kill his brother, it was in self-defence, or in a fury of panic anger: I say if, for I do not allow it to be the truth. Abel, the favourite, was a sneak and a coward, and he knew whatever lie he set up, so long as it was against the other, would stand as unassailable truth. He was better blotted out, than left to be the father of a degenerate race. Cain was at least a man – And it is said the Lord put a mark on him. What did that mean, think you?'

'I have not the least idea. Does anybody know?'

'I know this much, that it was the curse of the partly animal form. Cain was crippled into that likeness, and some of his sons took after him. Not the daughters, for they were in the likeness of Eve. And it is on record that they were beautiful. The sons of God saw the daughters of men that they were fair. But that does not come into the argument, nor concern us now. It was because of the mark set on him that Pan loved solitary places, the cool depths of caves and the shadow of woods. It was he in the beginning, and not Abel, who was the keeper of flocks. Abel did nothing but laze in the sun and watch the fruits ripen, and then gather them for an offering. I told you that the record lied. Do you wonder how I know all this?'

Richard could do nothing but assent.

'I will tell you – show you. I wish to instruct you in my methods, that they may be yours hereafter. It is not all who have the gift of sight. Lindsay is psychically blind. But something tells me you have it, or will have it. Come here with me.'

He opened a door and showed an inner, smaller room, probably intended as a dressing-closet in the original design of the house. There was a writing-table and chair in the sole window, but the only other furniture was a high stand, on which was some object covered over with black velvet drapery. Mr Quinton turned back part of the covering, and directed Richard to seat himself before it. The lifted flap revealed the smooth and shining surface of a large crystal, or ball of glass, set into a frame.

'You know what this is, and what its use? I want to test whether I can make a scryer of you. The black cloth is used only to prevent confusing lights. Now look steadily into the crystal, and tell me what you see.'

Richard looked, in some amusement and complete incredulity.

'I see the reflection of my own face,' he said presently. 'Nothing more. Except – yes – something which looks like smoke.'

'Go on looking, and be patient. There will be more.'

As Richard gazed, his own reflection disappeared, the

smoke cleared away, and there were the gates of the avenue with the leering faces, exactly as he saw them the day before. Then the cloud of smoke returned, blotting them out; cleared again, and showed the spy of the evening, peering in at the window of the dining-room. Succeeding this, came the scene of the grove by moonlight, with the figures leaping among the trees, and driving the doomed sheep.

'I am seeing a procession of scenes,' he replied to a further question. 'But only what are in my mind and memory. Nothing new.'

'Go on looking,' was again the command. 'What is new will come.'

The next scene was, as Richard half expected, the grove as he entered it that morning, with the statue of Pan on its pedestal, and the sheep before it lying dead. This persisted, not small as dwarfed within the limits of the ball, but now as if a window opened before him on the actual scene. But a change was taking place in the figure of the god. The bronze seemed to soften and warm into flesh, the terrible, wise face was no longer serene and meditative, the eyes looked into his, and now there was mockery in them, revelling in his surprise. The thing was alive, moving, surely about to descend.

But no. The figure, without leaving its pedestal, stretched out one hairy ape-like arm, and clutched the body of the sheep, drawing it up to rest on his crossed hocks, while the mocking face bent closer, as if to snuff or lick the blood. Was the monstrous creature about to tear the victim open, ready to devour? The action of the hands looked like it.

Richard could look no longer. A sweat of horror broke out over him, and stood in beads on his forehead; he started up gasping for air.

'Let me go,' he cried out wildly: 'let me go!'

Mr Quinton replaced the velvet covering. 'That is enough for to-day,' he said. 'I am sufficiently answered. You can see.'

Richard hardly knew how he got out of the room, whether it was by Mr Quinton's dismissal or his own will. Or how long a time elapsed before, finding himself alone, he happened to look at the palm of his right hand, which had felt curiously sticky after contact with Mr Quinton's. The smear on it was dry and easily effaced by washing, but without doubt what he had touched was blood.

Mr Quinton seemed to have been in no way affronted by Richard's abrupt withdrawal. He was in a genial mood when he joined the two younger men at dinner, now with his loose wrapping gown put off, and faultlessly attired in evening dress. A handsome man; and Richard noticed that his hands were beautifully shaped and white. But, to the guest's vision, there was one striking peculiarity about his appearance, a peculiarity which seemed to increase as the meal went forward. Perhaps the opening of Richard's clairvoyance, artificially induced some hours before, had not wholly closed. For doubtless what he now perceived, would not have been visible to ordinary sight.

Most of us in these later days have heard of the existence of auras, a species of halo which is supposed to emanate from every mortal, indicative of spiritual values and degrees of power; but it is doubtful whether our backwoodsman was aware. What he saw, however, was an aura, though formed of shadow and not light. It encompassed the seated figure of his host with a surrounding of grey haze, spreading to a yard or more from either shoulder, and equally above the head; not obstructing the view of the room behind him, but dimming it, as might a stretched veil of grey crape. It was curious to see Peters waiting on him and passing through this, evidently unaware; his hand and the bottle advancing into the full light as he filled Mr Quinton's glass, and then withdrawing to leave the veil as perfect as before.

Mr Quinton made an excellent dinner, and chaffed Richard

on his want of appetite; he also drank freely of the wines Peters was handing round, and pressed them on his guests. The glasses were particularly elegant, of Venetian pattern, slender stemmed and fragile. Peters had just replenished his master's glass, when Mr Quinton in the course of argument, lifted and brought it down sharply on the table with the result of breakage. The accident attracted little notice; Peters cleared away the fragments and mopped up the spilt wine, and another glass was set in its place and filled. But as Mr Quinton raised the fresh glass to his lips, Richard noticed that blood was dripping from his right hand in heavy spots, staining his shirt-cuff and the cloth.

'I am afraid, sir, you have cut yourself,' he exclaimed impulsively; and almost at the same instant Peters appeared at his master's elbow offering a dark silk handkerchief.

Mr Quinton did not answer, but uttered an exclamation of annoyance, and abruptly rose from table and left the room. Lindsay followed him, but presently returned, looking unusually grave. Richard inquired if the cut was serious.

'Mr Quinton did not cut his hand,' Lindsay answered. 'I am charged to tell you what is the matter. Though it is as far as possible kept secret, he thinks it better you should know.'

The gravity of Lindsay's countenance did not relax. He poured out half a glass of wine and drank it, as if to nerve himself for the telling of the tale.

'When I came here as resident doctor eighteen months ago, I heard the story: it was, of course, necessary I should be informed as I had to treat his case. I shall have to go a long way back to make you understand. Lady Anna, Quinton's mother, had twin sons, born shortly after her husband's death. She must have been a strange woman. They were her only children, but almost from infancy she made a difference between them, setting all her affection on Archibald, the elder, and treating the other, Clement, with coldness and every evidence of dislike. Quinton says he can never remember his mother caressing him, or even speaking kindly. He was always the one held to blame for any childish fault or mischief, and pushed into the background, while everything was for Archibald the heir. We cannot wonder that this folly of hers led to bad feeling between the lads. It was active in their school days, though they were educated at different schools, and met only in the holidays. Whenever they met they fought. What the last quarrel was about I cannot say, but Archibald was entering an expensive regiment, and the army could not be afforded for Clement, though it was his great desire: he owns to having been very sore. They were in a boat on the lake, and they fought there, and the boat capsized.

'It was said that Archibald hadn't a chance; he had been stunned by a blow on the head, or else had struck his head in falling. They both could swim a little, but he went down like a stone, and Clement reached the shore: the distance could not have been great, nor could one have expected such an accident to result in anything worse than a ducking. The horrible part of it was that Lady Anna saw what happened from her window in the bow room.'

'Ah –!'

'Yes, the room you had, and where you were disturbed last night. She saw the fight and the struggle, and was convinced of Clement's guilt: that he had plotted the occasion and killed Archibald, so that he might take his place. She wanted to have the boy tried for murder; ay, and would have had her way, had it not been for her brother, Lord Pengwyn, who was guardian to both the lads. He got the thing passed over as an accident, as no doubt it was. But the point I am coming to, though I've been long about it, is this. When Clement was drawn from the water, and brought in, sick and dazed, Lady Anna met him in a fury of passion. He was Cain over again, the first murderer who slew his brother: I wonder, did Eve do the like! 'Your brother's blood,' she said, 'will be upon your hands for ever.' Quinton says he would not have cared, after that, if they had hung him then and there. He had an illness, and the palms of his hands began to bleed – from the pores as it were, without a wound – and they have continued to bleed at intervals from that day to this. You saw what happened to-night.'

'It sounds like a miracle. Is there no cure?'

'Everything has been tried – styptics, hypnotism even. Sometimes the symptom remits for two or three weeks, and the bleeding is generally early in the day; he thought himself safe this evening. Miracle? no, unless the power of the mind over the body is held to be miraculous. You have read of the stigmatists – women, ay and men too – on whom the wounds of Christ have broken out, to bleed always on Fridays?'

'I have heard of them – certainly. But I set it down as a fraud – a monkish trick.'

'It is as well vouched for as any other physical phenomenon. And this case of Quinton's is nearly allied, though horror created it in his case, and not saintly adoration. It has spoiled his life; for over thirty years he has been an invalid, and will so continue to the end. His aberration of mind has all arisen from this root: his queer fancies about Cain and Pan, blood-sacrifices to Pagan gods – satyrs and fauns and hobgoblins, and I know not what!'

'You speak of aberration, and yet assert that he is sane?'

'He is sane enough for all practical purposes – a good man of business even, with a sharp eye to the main chance. Take him apart from these cranks of his, I like him – I can't help liking him. You'll like him too, when you know him better. You have seen the least attractive side of him, coming down like this, with the misgiving he is driving you into a corner. I'd have you stand up to him and speak your mind about what you will and will not do. And I believe he will hear reason in the end.'

✻

Next morning's post brought Richard a letter, forwarded on from London: a notice requiring his appearance before a certain Medical Board, and obliging his return to town. He sent a message to Mr Quinton by Lindsay, explaining his abrupt departure, but saying he was willing to return if desired. The reply message requested an interview, in the same upstairs room as before.

It proved to be a long one. Lindsay, waiting in the hall for the car to come round, wondered what was the delay, and what was passing between the two. At last a door in the upper regions opened and shut, and Richard came down the stairs. He was white as chalk, staggering like a man dizzy or blind, and a cold sweat stood in beads on his forehead, as happened after the scrying of the day before. Lindsay sprang forward to meet him, and propped him with a hand under his arm. He leaned against the wall, and gasped out:

'It's all over – I've refused – you were right to refuse too. The thing he asks is impossible. This house is full of devils – of devils, I tell you – and they come out of Quinton's crystal. He made me look again – against my will, and I saw – what I can't speak of – what I never can forget!'

'Come into the dining-room with me, and I'll give you a dram. You have been upset; you may think differently when you are calm.'

'No – no. Never this place for me. He is beyond reason: he is given over to the fiend. I told him I would thank him for ever for just Quinton Court and a farm, but he would not part the property. It had to be all or nothing. And not even to gain Quinton Court would I be owner here. No, I'll have no dram. I want to get away.'

The car was now heard coming round, and drawing up at the door.

'Goodbye, Lindsay, and thank you for your kindness. We may never meet again, but I shall not forget.'

These were last words, and the next moment he was shut in and speeding away, the open gates with their watchful faces left behind.

5

Richard reached London only to fall ill. The doctor diagnosed influenza, but seemed to think his system had received a shock: as to this he was not communicative. He had a week in bed, and another of tardy convalescence, a prey to depression and all the ills resulting from exhaustion. A fortnight had gone by since he left Mount Verney, when he received a communication from Fryer and Fryer asking for an interview. Mr Fryer wished to see Mr Richard Quinton on a matter of business, and would be obliged if he could make it convenient to call.

'I ought to have written to the old bird, to tell him I am out of the running,' was Richard's comment, spoken to himself. 'But, as I have been remiss, I had better go and hear what he has to say. I shall have to take a taxi.'

He had no strength left for the walking distance, and even the office stairs were something of a trial. He was shown in at once to Mr Fryer, and began with an apology.

'I have only just ascertained your address,' said the man of law. 'Are you aware, Mr Quinton, that your cousin and late host is dead?'

'Indeed no, sir, I was not aware.' And that Richard was shocked by the intelligence was plain to see.

'He died suddenly of heart-failure the night after you left.

And, so far as Dr Lindsay and I can ascertain after a careful search through all his papers, he has left no will.'

This communication did not seem to inform Richard; he was still too dazed by what he had just heard.

Mr Fryer tapped the blotting-pad before him, which was a way he had when irritated.

'You don't realise what that means? The whole property goes to you, both real estate and personal. Mount Verney, and all that it contains.'

Richard gave a cry, which sounded more like horror than elation.

'You are telling me – that I am the owner of Mount Verney?'

'If no will is discovered later, certainly you are the owner.'

'And does this bind me to live there? Because I cannot – I will not. I told Mr Quinton so before leaving, and, as he made it a condition, I refused the inheritance.'

'So I understand from Dr Lindsay. No, you are bound to nothing. You can live where you please. And, as soon as the legal processes of succession are gone through, you can sell the property, should you prefer investment abroad.'

Richard still sat half-stunned, slowly taking it in. He could rid himself of Mount Verney and all that it contained, and Quinton Court, the home of his desire, would be his own.

'You would have wished, of course, to attend your cousin's funeral, but you had quitted the address left with me, and we were unable to let you know in time. He was cremated, according to his own often-expressed desire. There is one thing, Mr Quinton, I would like to say to you – to suggest, though you may think I am exceeding my province. Your cousin's intestacy benefits you, but there are others who suffer by it. Old Peters, a servant who had been with him from boyhood: he would have been provided for without doubt. Probably there would have been gratuities to the other domestics, according to their length of service; and his resident doctor, Lindsay, would have come in for a legacy. Of course it is quite at your option what to do.'

'I will thank you, sir, to put down what you would have advised Mr Quinton in all these cases, had you prepared his will, and I will make it good.'

It was not always easy to divine Mr Fryer's sentiments, but he seemed to receive the instruction with pleasure. Lawyer and client shook hands, and then Richard was in the street again, hurrying away. O, what a letter – what a letter he would have to write to Nan!

※

Legal processes take time, and summer was waning into autumn before Richard was fully established as owner of the Quinton property. Up to now he had sedulously avoided Mount Verney, though he had been in the near neighbourhood, and had several times visited Quinton Court. He knew only by the agent's report that his orders were carried out, the heads removed from the gate-pillars and the statue from the grove, which was a grove no longer, as the young oaks had been felled and carted away. The Roman relics had been presented to a local museum, and the house was now shut up, and emptied of most of its furniture. Lindsay, at Richard's desire, had chosen such of the plenishings as he cared for and could make useful, receiving these in addition to the money gift advised by Mr Fryer.

All this was accomplished, the last load removed, and now the big white villa was shut up and vacant, and Clement Quinton's heir was about to enter for the first time as its possessor. But, strange to say, he had elected to make the visit late at night and in secret, so planning his approach across country that his coming and going might be unnoticed and unknown. A thief's visit, one would have said, rather than that of the lawful owner, who could have commanded all.

The latter part of the journey was made on foot, and throughout he carried with him, under his own eye and hand, a large and heavy Gladstone bag. He had studied incendiary methods when serving in France, and materials for swift destruction were contained within.

It was a wild evening; a gale, forestalling the equinox, hurtled overhead, tearing the clouds into shreds as they flew before it, and making clear spaces for some shining of stars. Rain was not yet, though doubtless it would fall presently. The wind would help Richard's purpose, rain would not, though he thought it could hardly defeat it. That intermittent shining of the stars gave little light. The night was very nearly 'as dark as hell's mouth', and Richard had much the feeling that he was venturing into the mouth of hell.

It had needed the mustering of a desperate courage, this expedition on which he was bent, but he could entrust his purpose to no other hand. Purification by fire: there could be, it seemed to him, no other cleansing. He intended no oblation to the infernal gods, that was far from his thought: what he dimly designed was a final breaking of their power.

With this purpose in mind he turned into the dark avenue, the shut gates yielding to his hand, between the pillars from which the satyrs' heads were gone. Did faces pry on him from between the close-ranked trees? He would not think of it: and for this night at least he would shut the eyes of his soul, the eyes with which he had perceived before, or he might happen upon something which would make him altogether a coward. In the darkness he left the road more than once, and blundered into the plantation, needing to have recourse to the electric torch in his pocket before he could find the way. But at last he came upon the open sweep of drive, and there was the villa before him, stark and white, eyeless and shuttered, the corpse of a house from which the soul had gone out.

This new owner had been careful to carry with him the keys which admitted. He unlocked a side door and entered, and now the torch was a necessity in the pitch darkness which prevailed within. His first act was to go through the lower rooms, unshuttering and opening everywhere, so as to let in a free draught of air. Here a certain amount of the heavier furniture still remained: Lindsay had been moderate in his selection, though he might, with Richard's approval, have grasped at all. Then he mounted to the attics, opening as he went, and here the incendiary work started. The flames were beginning to creep over the floors and about the back staircase, when he turned his attention to the better apartments on the first floor, entering and igniting one after another. He left Mr Quinton's private rooms until the last; the rooms where those momentous interviews had taken place, and where the devils had issued from the glass.

The private den had been wholly stripped, both of furniture and books; no doubt Lindsay, who was free to take what he pleased, had valued these mementoes of a patient who was also a friend. Richard was glad to find the apartment empty; there was less to recall the past. But as he moved the illuminating torch from left to right in his survey, it seemed to him for an instant that a tall figure stood before him – long enough to realise its presence, though gone in the space of a couple of agitated heart-beats. He never doubted that it was Quinton, present to reproach him, to arrest the course of destruction if that were possible. But in spite of what he had seen – if indeed he did see – he gritted his teeth and went on.

The inner cabinet was next to enter. Here nothing had been removed or changed; the writing-table in the window still had its equipment of inkpot and blotting-pad, and on the latter, Richard noticed, a sheet of. blank paper was spread out. The velvet cover thrown over the high stand, no doubt concealed the uncanny crystal into which he had been forced to look. No one would look into it again after the destruction of this night! And then somehow, he knew not how, his attention was drawn to the white paper on the table.

Most of us have seen the development of a photographic plate, and how magically the image starts into view on a surface which before was blank. That was what appeared to happen under his eyes upon the paper, and the image was the imprint of a large hand, a man's hand, red as if dipped in blood.

The same awful sensation of sick faintness experienced before with the crystal, overcame him once again. It was a marvel to him afterwards that he did not fall unconscious, to perish in the burning house. He saved himself by a desperate effort of will, flinging what was left of his incendiary material behind him on the floor. As he gained the staircase, a rush of air met him from below, and this was perhaps his salvation. But the house was now filling with smoke, and from the upper regions came already the crackle of spreading flame.

The crackle of flame, and something more. Something which sounded like the clatter of hoofs over bare floors, and a cackle of hellish laughter; unless his senses were by this time wholly dazed and confused, hearing bewitched as well as sight. He found the door by which he entered, locked it behind him and fled into the night, now no longer bewilderingly dark, but faintly illuminated by the rising moon.

He did not take the direction of the avenue and the road, but climbed fences and made his way up the hill behind; and when on the wind-swept summit he turned to look back. He had done his work effectually; the white villa was alight in all its windows, fiercely ablaze within, and, as he still lingered and watched, a portion of the roof fell in, and flame and smoke shot up into the sky.

※

From the local paper of the following Saturday.

We regret to state that the mansion of Mount Verney, recently the residence of the late Clement Quinton, Esquire, and now the property of Mr Richard Quinton, was destroyed by fire on Tuesday night. The origin of the fire is wrapped in mystery, as the house was unoccupied and shut up, and the electric light disconnected, so there could have been no fusion of wires. Much valuable property is destroyed, and part of the building is completely gutted. The blaze was first noticed between twelve and one o'clock, by a man driving home late from market. He gave notice to the police, but by the time the fire-engines arrived, the conflagration had taken such bold that it could not be checked, though abundant water was at hand in the Mount Verney lake. The loss to Mr Richard Quinton will be very considerable, as we understand no part of it is covered by insurance.

From the same paper in the following December.

We understand that a gift has been made to our hospital fund, of the shell of the Mount Verney house with the grounds that surround it, to be converted into a sanatorium for the treatment of tuberculosis, and Mr Richard Quinton also adds to the subscription list the sum of £1,000. This munificent donation of money and a site will enable the work to be put in hand at once; and it is believed that what is left of the original mansion can be incorporated in the scheme.

The Mount Verney house, which, as will be remembered, was destroyed by a disastrous fire about three months ago, was not insured, and Mr Richard Quinton had no wish to rebuild for his own occupation. He will, we understand, make his future residence at Quinton Court, the ancestral home of his family, so soon as he returns from Canada with his bride.

5 View From A Hill (1925)

M R JAMES

How pleasant it can be, alone in a first-class railway carriage, on the first day of a holiday that is to be fairly long, to dawdle through a bit of English country that is unfamiliar, stopping at every station. You have a map open on your knee, and you pick out the villages that lie to right and left by their church towers. You marvel at the complete stillness that attends your stoppage at the stations, broken only by a footstep crunching the gravel. Yet perhaps that is best experienced after sundown, and the traveller I have in mind was making his leisurely progress on a sunny afternoon in the latter half of June.

He was in the depths of the country. I need not particularize further than to say that if you divided the map of England into four quarters, he would have been found in the south-western of them.

He was a man of academic pursuits, and his term was just over. He was on his way to meet a new friend, older than himself. The two of them had met first on an official inquiry in town, had found that they had many tastes and habits in common, liked each other, and the result was an invitation from Squire Richards to Mr Fanshawe which was now taking effect.

The journey ended about five o'clock. Fanshawe was told by a cheerful country porter that the car from the Hall had been up to the station and left a message that something had to be fetched from half a mile farther on, and would the gentleman please to wait a few minutes till it came back? 'But I see,' continued the porter, 'as you've got your bysticle, and very like you'd find it pleasanter to ride up to the 'All yourself. Straight up the road 'ere, and then first turn to the left – it ain't above two mile – and I'll see as your things is put in the car for you. You'll excuse me mentioning it, only I thought it were a nice evening for a ride. Yes, sir, very seasonable weather for the haymakers: let me see, I have your bike ticket. Thank you, sir; much obliged: you can't miss your road, etc, etc.'

The two miles to the Hall were just what was needed, after the day in the train, to dispel somnolence and impart a wish for tea. The Hall, when sighted, also promised just what was needed in the way of a quiet resting-place after days of sitting on committees and college-meetings. It was neither excitingly old nor depressingly new. Plastered walls, sash-windows, old trees, smooth lawns, were the features which Fanshawe noticed as he came up the drive. Squire Richards, a burly man of sixty odd, was awaiting him in the porch with evident pleasure.

'Tea first,' he said, 'or would you like a longer drink? No? All right, tea's ready in the garden. Come along, they'll put your machine away. I always have tea under the lime-tree by the stream on a day like this.'

Nor could you ask for a better place. Midsummer afternoon, shade and scent of a vast lime-tree, cool, swirling water within five yards. It was long before either of them suggested a move. But about six, Mr Richards sat up, knocked out his pipe, and said: 'Look here, it's cool enough now to think of a stroll, if you're inclined? All right: then what I suggest is that we walk up the park and get on to the hill-side, where we can look over the country. We'll have a map, and I'll show you where things are; and you can go off on your machine, or we can take the car, according as you want exercise or not. If you're ready, we can start now and be back well before eight, taking it very easy.'

'I'm ready. I should like my stick, though, and have you got any field-glasses? I lent mine to a man a week ago, and he's gone off Lord knows where and taken them with him.'

Mr Richards pondered. 'Yes,' he said, 'I have, but they're not things I use myself, and I don't know whether the ones I have will suit you. They're old-fashioned, and about twice as heavy as they make 'em now. You're welcome to have them, but *I* won't carry them. By the way, what do you want to drink after dinner?'

Protestations that anything would do were overruled, and a satisfactory settlement was reached on the way to the front hall, where Mr Fanshawe found his stick, and Mr Richards, after thoughtful pinching of his lower lip, resorted to a drawer in the hall-table, extracted a key, crossed to a cupboard in the panelling, opened it, took a box from the shelf, and put it on the table. 'The glasses are in there,' he said, 'and there's some dodge of opening it, but I've forgotten what it is. You try.' Mr Fanshawe accordingly tried. There was no keyhole, and the box was solid, heavy and smooth: it seemed obvious that some part of it would have to be pressed before anything could happen. 'The corners,' said he to himself, 'are the likely places; and infernally sharp corners they are too,' he added, as he put his thumb in his mouth after exerting force on a lower corner.

'What's the matter?' said the Squire.

'Why, your disgusting Borgia box has scratched me, drat it,' said Fanshawe. The Squire chuckled unfeelingly. 'Well, you've got it open, anyway,' he said.

'So I have! Well, I don't begrudge a drop of blood in a good cause, and here are the glasses. They *are* pretty heavy, as you said, but I think I'm equal to carrying them.'

'Ready?' said the Squire. 'Come on then; we go out by the garden.'

So they did, and passed out into the park, which sloped decidedly upwards to the hill which, as Fanshawe had seen from the train, dominated the country. It was a spur of a larger range that lay behind. On the way, the Squire, who was great on earthworks, pointed out various spots where he detected or imagined traces of war-ditches and the like. 'And here,' he said, stopping on a more or less level plot with a ring of large trees, 'is Baxter's Roman villa.'

'Baxter?' said Mr Fanshawe.

'I forgot; you don't know about him. He was the old chap I got those glasses from. I believe he made them. He was an old watch-maker down in the village, a great antiquary. My father gave him leave to grub about where he liked; and when he made a find he used to lend him a man or two to help him with the digging. He got a surprising lot of things together, and when he died – I dare say it's ten or fifteen years ago – I bought the whole lot and gave them to the town museum. We'll run in one of these days, and look over them. The glasses came to me with the rest, but of course I kept them. If you look at them, you'll see they're more or less amateur work – the body of them; naturally the lenses weren't his making.'

'Yes, I see they are just the sort of thing that a clever workman in a different line of business might turn out. But I don't see why he made them so heavy. And did Baxter actually find a Roman villa here?'

'Yes, there's a pavement turfed over, where we're standing: it was too rough and plain to be worth taking up, but of course there are drawings of it: and the small things and pottery that turned up were quite good of their kind. An ingenious chap, old Baxter: he seemed to have a quite out-of-the-way instinct for these things. He was invaluable to our archaeologists. He used to shut up his shop for days at a time, and wander off over the district, marking down places, where he scented anything, on the ordnance map; and he kept a book with fuller notes of the places. Since his death, a good many of them have been sampled, and there's always been something to justify him.'

'What a good man!' said Mr Fanshawe.

'Good?' said the Squire, pulling up brusquely.

'I meant useful to have about the place,' said Mr Fanshawe. 'But was he a villain?'

'I don't know about that either,' said the Squire; 'but all I can say is, if he was good, he wasn't lucky. And he wasn't liked: I didn't like him,' he added, after a moment.

'Oh?' said Fanshawe interrogatively.

'No, I didn't; but that's enough about Baxter: besides, this is the stiffest bit, and I don't want to talk and walk as well.'

Indeed it was hot, climbing a slippery grass slope that evening. 'I told you I should take you the short way,' panted the Squire, 'and I wish I hadn't. However, a bath won't do us any harm when we get back. Here we are, and there's the seat.'

A small clump of old Scotch firs crowned the top of the hill; and, at the edge of it, commanding the cream of the view, was a wide and solid seat, on which the two disposed themselves, and wiped their brows, and regained breath.

'Now, then,' said the Squire, as soon as he was in a condition to talk connectedly, 'this is where your glasses come in. But you'd better take a general look round first. My word! I've never seen the view look better.'

Writing as I am now with a winter wind flapping against dark windows and a rushing, tumbling sea within a hundred yards, I find it hard to summon up the feelings and words which will put my reader in possession of the June evening and the lovely English landscape of which the Squire was speaking.

Across a broad level plain they looked upon ranges of great hills, whose uplands – some green, some furred with woods – caught the light of a sun, westering but not yet low. And all the plain was fertile, though the river which traversed it was nowhere seen. There were copses, green wheat, hedges and pasture-land: the little compact white moving cloud marked the evening train. Then the eye picked out red farms and grey houses, and nearer home scattered cottages, and then the Hall, nestled under the hill. The smoke of chimneys was very blue and straight. There was a smell of hay in the air: there were wild roses on bushes hard by. It was the acme of summer.

After some minutes of silent contemplation, the Squire began to point out the leading features, the hills and valleys, and told where the towns and villages lay. 'Now,' he said, 'with the glasses you'll be able to pick out Fulnaker Abbey. Take a line across that big green field, then over the wood beyond it, then over the farm on the knoll.'

'Yes, yes,' said Fanshawe. 'I've got it. What a fine tower!'

'You must have got the wrong direction,' said the Squire; 'there's not much of a tower about there that I remember, unless it's Oldbourne Church that you've got hold of. And if you call that a fine tower, you're easily pleased.'

'Well, I do call it a fine tower,' said Fanshawe, the glasses still at his eyes, 'whether it's Oldbourne or any other. And it must belong to a largish church; it looks to me like a central tower – four big pinnacles at the corners, and four smaller ones between. I must certainly go over there. How far is it?'

'Oldbourne's about nine miles, or less,' said the Squire. 'It's a long time since I've been there, but I don't remember thinking much of it. Now I'll show you another thing.'

Fanshawe had lowered the glasses, and was still gazing in the Oldbourne direction. 'No,' he said, 'I can't make out anything with the naked eye. What was it you were going to show me?'

'A good deal more to the left – it oughtn't to be difficult to find. Do you see a rather sudden knob of a hill with a thick wood on top of it? It's in a dead line with that single tree on the top of the big ridge.'

'I do,' said Fanshawe, 'and I believe I could tell you without much difficulty what it's called.'

'Could you now?' said the Squire. 'Say on.'

'Why, Gallows Hill,' was the answer.

'How did you guess that?'

'Well, if you don't want it guessed, you shouldn't put up a dummy gibbet and a man hanging on it.'

'What's that?' said the Squire abruptly. 'There's nothing on that hill but wood.'

'On the contrary,' said Fanshawe, 'there's a largish expanse of grass on the top and your dummy gibbet in the middle; and I thought there was something on it when I looked first. But I see there's nothing – or is there? I can't be sure.'

'Nonsense, nonsense, Fanshawe, there's no such thing as a dummy gibbet, or any other sort, on that hill. And it's thick wood – a fairly young plantation. I was in it myself not a year ago. Hand me the glasses, though I don't suppose I can see anything.' After a pause: 'No, I thought not: they won't show a thing.'

Meanwhile Fanshawe was scanning the hill – it might be only two or three miles away. 'Well, it's very odd,' he said, 'it does look exactly like a wood without the glass.' He took it again. 'That *is* one of the oddest effects. The gibbet is perfectly plain, and the grass field, and there even seem to be people on it, and carts, or *a* cart, with men in it. And yet when I take the glass away, there's nothing. It must be something in the way this afternoon light falls: I shall come up earlier in the day when the sun's full on it.'

'Did you say you saw people and a cart on that hill?' said the Squire incredulously. 'What should they be doing there at this time of day, even if the trees have been felled? Do talk sense – look again.'

'Well, I certainly thought I saw them. Yes, I should say there were a few, just clearing off. And now – by Jove, it does look like something hanging on the gibbet. But these glasses are so beastly heavy I can't hold them steady for long. Anyhow, you can take it from me there's no wood. And if you'll show me the road on the map, I'll go there tomorrow.'

The Squire remained brooding for some little time. At last he rose and said, 'Well, I suppose that will be the best way to settle it. And now we'd better be getting back. Bath and dinner is my idea.' And on the way back he was not very communicative.

They returned through the garden, and went into the front hall to leave sticks, etc, in their due place. And here they found the aged butler Patten evidently in a state of some anxiety. 'Beg pardon, Master Henry,' he began at once, 'but someone's been up to mischief here, I'm much afraid.' He pointed to the open box which had contained the glasses.

'Nothing worse than that, Patten?' said the Squire. 'Mayn't I take out my own glasses and lend them to a friend? Bought with my own money, you recollect? At old Baxter's sale, eh?'

Patten bowed, unconvinced. 'Oh, very well, Master Henry, as long as you know who it was. Only I thought proper to name it, for I didn't think that box'd been off its shelf since you first put it there; and, if you'll excuse me, after what happened –'. The voice was lowered, and the rest was not audible to Fanshawe. The Squire replied with a few words and a gruff laugh, and called on Fanshawe to come and be shown his room. And I do not think that anything else happened that night which bears on my story.

Except, perhaps, the sensation which invaded Fanshawe in the small hours that something had been let out which ought not to have been let out. It came into his dreams. He was walking in a garden which he seemed half to know, and stopped in front of a rockery made of old wrought stones, pieces of window tracery from a church, and even bits of figures. One of these moved his curiosity: it seemed to be a sculptured capital with scenes carved on it. He felt he must pull it out, and worked away, and, with an ease that surprised him, moved the stones that obscured it aside, and pulled out the block. As he did so, a tin label fell down by his feet with a little clatter. He picked it up and read on it: 'On no account move this stone. Yours sincerely, J Patten.' As often happens in dreams, he felt that this injunction was of extreme importance; and with an anxiety that amounted to anguish he looked to see if the stone had really been shifted. Indeed it had; in fact, he could not see it anywhere. The removal had disclosed the mouth of a burrow, and he bent down to look into it. Something stirred in the blackness, and then, to his intense horror, a hand emerged – a clean right hand in a neat cuff and coatsleeve, just in the attitude of a hand that means to shake yours. He wondered whether it would not be rude to let it alone. But, as he looked at it, it began to grow hairy and dirty and thin, and also to change its pose and stretch out as if to take hold of his leg. At that he dropped all thought of politeness, decided to run, screamed and woke himself up.

This was the dream he remembered; but it seemed to him (as, again, it often does) that there had been others of the same import before, but not so insistent. He lay awake for some little time, fixing the details of the last dream in his mind, and wondering in particular what the figures had been which he had seen or half seen on the carved capital. Something quite incongruous, he felt sure; but that was the most he could recall.

Whether because of the dream, or because it was the first day of his holiday, he did not get up very early; nor did he at once plunge into the exploration of the country. He spent a morning, half lazy, half instructive, in looking over the volumes of the County Archaeological Society's transactions, in which were many contributions from Mr Baxter on finds of flint implements, Roman sites, ruins of monastic establishments – in fact, most departments of archaeology. They were written in an odd, pompous, only half-educated style. If the man had had more early schooling, thought Fanshawe, he would have been a very distinguished antiquary; or he might have been (he thus qualified his opinion a little later), but for a certain love of opposition and controversy, and, yes, a patronizing tone as of one possessing superior knowledge, which left an unpleasant taste. He might have been a very respectable artist. There was an imaginary restoration and elevation of a priory church which was very well conceived. A fine pinnacled central tower was a conspicuous feature of this; it reminded Fanshawe of that which he had seen from the hill, and which the Squire had told him must be Oldbourne. But it was not Oldbourne; it was Fulnaker Priory. 'Oh, well,' he said to himself, 'I suppose Oldbourne Church may have been built by Fulnaker monks, and Baxter has copied Oldbourne tower. Anything about it in the letterpress? Ah, I see it was published after his death – found among his papers.'

After lunch the Squire asked Fanshawe what he meant to do.

'Well,' said Fanshawe, 'I think I shall go out on my bike about four as far as Oldbourne and back by Gallows Hill. That ought to be a round of about fifteen miles, oughtn't it?'

'About that,' said the Squire, 'and you'll pass Lambsfield and Wanstone, both of which are worth looking at. There's a little glass at Lambsfield and the stone at Wanstone.'

'Good,' said Fanshawe, 'I'll get tea somewhere, and may I take the glasses? I'll strap them on my bike, on the carrier.'

'Of course, if you like,' said the Squire. 'I really ought to have some better ones. If I go into the town to-day, I'll see if I can pick up some.'

'Why should you trouble to do that if you can't use them yourself?' said Fanshawe.

'Oh, I don't know; one ought to have a decent pair; and – well, old Patten doesn't think those are fit to use.'

'Is he a judge?'

'He's got some tale: I don't know: something about old Baxter. I've promised to let him tell me about it. It seems very much on his mind since last night.'

'Why that? Did he have a nightmare like me?'

'He had something: he was looking an old man this morning, and he said he hadn't closed an eye.'

'Well, let him save up his tale till I come back.'

'Very well, I will if I can. Look here, are you going to be late? If you get a puncture eight miles off and have to walk home, what then? I don't trust these bicycles: I shall tell them to give us cold things to eat.'

'I shan't mind that, whether I'm late or early. But I've got things to mend punctures with. And now I'm off.'

✕

It was just as well that the Squire had made that arrangement about a cold supper, Fanshawe thought, and not for the first time, as he wheeled his bicycle up the drive about nine o'clock. So also the Squire thought and said, several times, as he met him in the hall, rather pleased at the confirmation of his want of faith in bicycles than sympathetic with his hot, weary, thirsty, and indeed haggard, friend. In fact, the kindest thing he found to say was: 'You'll want a long drink to-night? Cider-cup do? All right. Hear that, Patten? Cider-cup, iced, lots of it.' Then to Fanshawe, 'Don't be all night over your bath.'

By half-past nine they were at dinner, and Fanshawe was reporting progress, if progress it might be called.

'I got to Lambsfield very smoothly, and saw the glass. It is very interesting stuff, but there's a lot of lettering I couldn't read.'

'Not with glasses?' said the Squire.

'Those glasses of yours are no manner of use inside a church – or inside anywhere, I suppose, for that matter. But the only places I took 'em into were churches.'

'H'm! Well, go on,' said the Squire.

'However, I took some sort of a photograph of the window, and I dare say an enlargement would show what I want. Then Wanstone; I should think that stone was a very out-of-the-way thing, only I don't know about that class of antiquities. Has anybody opened the mound it stands on?'

'Baxter wanted to, but the farmer wouldn't let him.'

'Oh, well, I should think it would be worth doing. Anyhow, the next thing was Fulnaker and Oldbourne. You know, it's very odd about that tower I saw from the hill. Oldbourne Church is nothing like it, and of course there's nothing over thirty feet high at Fulnaker, though you can see it had a central tower. I didn't tell you, did I? that Baxter's fancy drawing of Fulnaker shows a tower exactly like the one I saw.'

'So you thought, I dare say,' put in the Squire.

'No, it wasn't a case of thinking. The picture actually *reminded* me of what I'd seen, and I made sure it was Oldbourne, well before I looked at the title.'

'Well, Baxter had a very fair idea of architecture. I dare say what's left made it easy for him to draw the right sort of tower.'

'That may be it, of course, but I'm doubtful if even a professional could have got it so exactly right. There's absolutely nothing left at Fulnaker but the bases of the piers which supported it. However, that isn't the oddest thing.'

'What about Gallows Hill?' said the Squire. 'Here, Patten,

listen to this. I told you what Mr Fanshawe said he saw from the hill.'

'Yes, Master Henry, you did; and I can't say I was so much surprised, considering.'

'All right, all right. You keep that till afterwards. We want to hear what Mr Fanshawe saw to-day. Go on, Fanshawe. You turned to come back by Ackford and Thorfield, I suppose?'

'Yes, and I looked into both the churches. Then I got to the turning which goes to the top of Gallows Hill; I saw that if I wheeled my machine over the field at the top of the hill I could join the home road on this side. It was about half-past six when I got to the top of the hill, and there was a gate on my right, where it ought to be, leading into the belt of plantation.'

'You hear that, Patten? A belt, he says.'

'So I thought it was – a belt. But it wasn't. You were quite right, and I was hopelessly wrong. I *cannot* understand it. The whole top is planted quite thick. Well, I went on into this wood, wheeling and dragging my bike, expecting every minute to come to a clearing, and then my misfortunes began. Thorns, I suppose; first I realized that the front tyre was slack, then the back. I couldn't stop to do more than try to find the punctures and mark them; but even that was hopeless. So I ploughed on, and the farther I went, the less I liked the place.'

'Not much poaching in that cover, eh, Patten?' said the Squire.

'No, indeed, Master Henry: there's very few cares to go–'

'No, I know: never mind that now. Go on, Fanshawe.'

'I don't blame anybody for not caring to go there. I know I had all the fancies one least likes: steps crackling over twigs behind me, indistinct people stepping behind trees in front of me, yes, and even a hand laid on my shoulder. I pulled up very sharp at that and looked round, but there really was no branch or bush that could have done it. Then, when I was just about at the middle of the plot, I was convinced that there was someone looking down on me from above – and not with any pleasant intent. I stopped again, or at least slackened my pace, to look up. And as I did, down I came, and barked my shins abominably on, what do you think? a block of stone with a big square hole in the top of it. And within a few paces there were two others just like it. The three were set in a triangle. Now, do you make out what they were put there for?'

'I think I can,' said the Squire, who was now very grave and absorbed in the story. 'Sit down, Patten.'

It was time, for the old man was supporting himself by one hand, and leaning heavily on it. He dropped into a chair, and said in a very tremulous voice, 'You didn't go between them stones, did you, sir?'

'I did *not*,' said Fanshawe, emphatically. 'I dare say I was an ass, but as soon as it dawned on me where I was, I just shouldered my machine and did my best to run. It seemed to me as if I was in an unholy evil sort of graveyard, and I was most profoundly thankful that it was one of the longest days and still sunlight. Well, I had a horrid run, even if it was only a few hundred yards. Everything caught on everything: handles and spokes and carrier and pedals – caught in them viciously, or I fancied so. I fell over at least five times. At last I saw the hedge, and I couldn't trouble to hunt for the gate.'

'There *is* no gate on my side,' the Squire interpolated.

'Just as well I didn't waste time, then. I dropped the machine over somehow and went into the road pretty near head-first; some branch or something got my ankle at the last moment. Anyhow, there I was out of the wood, and seldom more thankful or more generally sore. Then came the job of mending my punctures. I had a good outfit and I'm not at all bad at the business; but this was an absolutely hopeless case.

It was seven when I got out of the wood, and I spent fifty minutes over one tyre. As fast as I found a hole and put on a patch, and blew it up, it went flat again. So I made up my mind to walk. That hill isn't three miles away, is it?'

'Not more across country, but nearer six by road.'

'I thought it must be. I thought I couldn't have taken well over the hour over less than five miles, even leading a bike. Well, there's my story: where's yours and Patten's?'

'Mine? I've no story,' said the Squire. 'But you weren't very far out when you thought you were in a graveyard. There must be a good few of them up there, Patten, don't you think? They left 'em there when they fell to bits, I fancy.'

Patten nodded, too much interested to speak. 'Don't,' said Fanshawe.

'Now then, Patten,' said the Squire, 'you've heard what sort of a time Mr Fanshawe's been having. What do you make of it? Anything to do with Mr Baxter? Fill yourself a glass of port, and tell us.'

'Ah, that done me good, Master Henry,' said Patten, after absorbing what was before him. 'If you really wish to know what were in my thoughts, my answer would be clear in the affirmative. Yes,' he went on, warming to his work, 'I should say as Mr Fanshawe's experience of to-day were very largely doo to the person you named. And I think, Master Henry, as I have some title to speak, in view of me 'aving been many years on speaking terms with him, and swore in to be jury on the Coroner's inquest near this time ten years ago, you being then, if you carry your mind back, Master Henry, travelling abroad, and no one"ere to represent the family.'

'Inquest?' said Fanshawe. 'An inquest on Mr Baxter, was there?'

'Yes, sir, on – on that very person. The facts as led up to that occurrence was these. The deceased was, as you may have gathered, a very peculiar individual in 'is 'abits – in my idear, at least, but all must speak as they find. He lived very much to himself, without neither chick nor child, as the saying is. And how he passed away his time was what very few could orfer a guess at.'

'He lived unknown, and few could know when Baxter ceased to be,' said the Squire to his pipe.

'I beg pardon, Master Henry, I was just coming to that. But when I say how he passed away his time – to be sure we know 'ow intent he was in rummaging and ransacking out all the 'istry of the neighbourhood and the number of things he'd managed to collect together – well, it was spoke of for miles round as Baxter's Museum, and many a time when he might be in the mood, and I might have an hour to spare, have he showed me his pieces of pots and what not, going back by his account to the times of the ancient Romans. However, you know more about that than what I do, Master Henry: only what I was a-going to say was this, as know what he might and interesting as he might be in his talk, there was something about the man – well, for one thing, no one ever remember to see him in church nor yet chapel at service-time. And that made talk. Our rector he never come in the house but once. "Never ask me what the man said"; that was all anybody could ever get out of *him*. Then how did he spend his nights, particularly about this season of the year? Time and again the labouring men'd meet him coming back as they went out to their work, and he'd pass 'em by without a word, looking, they says, like someone straight out of the asylum. They see the whites of his eyes all round. He'd have a fish-basket with him, that they noticed, and he always come the same road. And the talk got to be that he'd made himself some business, and that not the best kind – well, not so far from where you was at seven o'clock this evening, sir.

'Well, now, after such a night as that, Mr Baxter he'd shut

up the shop, and the old lady that did for him had orders not to come in; and knowing what she did about his language, she took care to obey them orders. But one day it so happened, about three o'clock in the afternoon, the house being shut up as I said, there come a most fearful to-do inside, and smoke out of the windows, and Baxter crying out seemingly in an agony. So the man as lived next door he run round to the back premises and burst the door in, and several others come too. Well, he tell me he never in all his life smelt such a fearful – well, odour, as what there was in that kitchen-place. It seem as if Baxter had been boiling something in a pot and overset it on his leg. There he laid on the floor, trying to keep back the cries, but it was more than he could manage, and when he seen the people come in – oh, he was in a nice condition: if his tongue warn't blistered worse than his leg it warn't his fault. Well, they picked him up, and got him into a chair, and run for the medical man, and one of 'em was going to pick up the pot, and Baxter, he screams out to let it alone. So he did, but he couldn't see as there was anything in the pot but a few old brown bones. Then they says "Dr Lawrence'll be here in a minute, Mr Baxter; he'll soon put you to rights." And then he was off again. He must be got up to his room, he couldn't have the doctor come in there and see all that mess – they must throw a cloth over it – anything – the tablecloth out of the parlour; well, so they did. But that must have been poisonous stuff in that pot, for it was pretty near on two months afore Baxter were about agin. Beg pardon, Master Henry, was you going to say something?'

'Yes, I was,' said the Squire. 'I wonder you haven't told me all this before. However, I was going to say I remember old Lawrence telling me he'd attended Baxter. He was a queer card, he said. Lawrence was up in the bedroom one day, and picked up a little mask covered with black velvet, and put it on in fun and went to look at himself in the glass. He hadn't time for a proper look, for old Baxter shouted out to him from the bed: "Put it down, you fool! Do you want to look through a dead man's eyes?" and it startled him so that he did put it down, and then he asked Baxter what he meant. And Baxter insisted on him handing it over, and said the man he bought it from was dead, or some such nonsense. But Lawrence felt it as he handed it over, and he declared he was sure it was made out of the front of a skull. He bought a distilling apparatus at Baxter's sale, he told me, but he could never use it: it seemed to taint everything, however much he cleaned it. But go on, Patten.'

'Yes, Master Henry, I'm nearly done now, and time, too, for I don't know what they'll think about me in the servants' 'all. Well, this business of the scalding was some few years before Mr Baxter was took, and he got about again, and went on just as he'd used. And one of the last jobs he done was finishing up them actual glasses what you took out last night. You see he'd made the body of them some long time, and got the pieces of glass for them, but there was somethink wanted to finish 'em, whatever it was, I don't know, but I picked up the frame one day, and I says: "Mr Baxter, why don't you make a job of this?" And he says, "Ah, when I've done that, you'll hear news, you will: there's going to be no such pair of glasses as mine when they're filled and sealed," and there he stopped, and I says: "Why, Mr Baxter, you talk as if they was wine bottles: filled and sealed – why, where's the necessity for that?" "Did I say filled and sealed?" he says. "O, well, I was suiting my conversation to my company." Well, then come round this time of year, and one fine evening, I was passing his shop on my way home, and he was standing on the step, very pleased with hisself, and he says: "All right and tight now: my best bit of work's finished, and I'll be out with 'em tomorrow." "What, finished them glasses?" I says, "might I have a look at them?" "No, no," he says, "I've put 'em to bed for to-night, and when I do show 'em you, you'll have to pay for peepin', so I tell you." And that, gentlemen, were the last words I heard that man say.

'That were the 17th of June, and just a week after, there was a funny thing happened, and it was doo to that as we brought in "unsound mind" at the inquest, for barring that, no one as knew Baxter in business could anyways have laid that against him. But George Williams, as lived in the next house, and do now, he was woke up that same night with a stumbling and tumbling about in Mr Baxter's premises, and he got out o' bed, and went to the front window on the street to see if there was any rough customers about. And it being a very light night, he could make sure as there was not. Then he stood and listened, and he hear Mr Baxter coming down his front stair one step after another very slow, and he got the idear as it was like someone bein' pushed or pulled down and holdin' on to everythin' he could. Next thing he hear the street door come open, and out come Mr Baxter into the street in his day-clothes, 'at and all, with his arms straight down by his sides, and talking to hisself, and shakin' his head from one side to the other, and walking in that peculiar way that he appeared to be going as it were against his own will. George Williams put up the window, and hear him say: "O mercy, gentlemen!" and then he shut up sudden as if, he said, someone clapped his hand over his mouth, and Mr Baxter threw his head back, and his hat fell off. And Williams see his face looking something pitiful, so as he couldn't keep from calling out to him: "Why, Mr Baxter, ain't you well?" and he was goin' to offer to fetch Dr Lawrence to him, only he heard the answer: "'Tis best you mind your own business. Put in your head." But whether it were Mr Baxter said it so hoarse-like and faint, he never could be sure. Still there weren't no-one but him in the street, and yet Williams was that upset by the way he spoke that he shrank back from the window and went and sat on the bed. And he heard Mr Baxter's step go on and up the road, and after a minute or more he couldn't help but look out once more and he see him going along the same curious way as before. And one thing he recollected was that Mr Baxter never stopped to pick up his 'at when it fell off, and yet there it was on his head. Well, Master Henry, that was the last anybody see of Mr Baxter, leastways for a week or more. There was a lot of people said he was called off on business, or made off because he'd got into some scrape, but he was well known for miles round, and none of the railway-people nor the public-house people hadn't seen him; and then ponds was looked into and nothink found; and at last one evening Fakes the keeper come down from over the hill to the village, and he says he seen the Gallows Hill planting black with birds, and that were a funny thing, because he never see no sign of a creature there in his time. So they looked at each other a bit, and first one says: "I'm game to go up," and another says: "So am I, if you are," and half a dozen of 'em set out in the evening time, and took Dr Lawrence with them, and you know, Master Henry, there he was between them three stones with his neck broke.'

Useless to imagine the talk which this story set going. It is not remembered. But before Patten left them, he said to Fanshawe: 'Excuse me, sir, but did I understand as you took out them glasses with you to-day? I thought you did; and might I ask, did you make use of them at all?'

'Yes. Only to look at something in a church.'

'Oh, indeed, you took 'em into the church, did you, sir?'

'Yes, I did; it was Lambsfield church. By the way, I left them strapped on to my bicycle, I'm afraid, in the stable-yard.'

'No matter for that, sir. I can bring them in the first thing tomorrow, and perhaps you'll be so good as to look at 'em then.'

Accordingly, before breakfast, after a tranquil and well-earned sleep, Fanshawe took the glasses into the garden and directed them to a distant hill. He lowered them instantly, and looked at top and bottom, worked the screws, tried them again and yet again, shrugged his shoulders and replaced them on the hall-table.

'Patten,' he said, 'they're absolutely useless. I can't see a thing: it's as if someone had stuck a black wafer over the lens.'

'Spoilt my glasses, have you?' said the Squire. 'Thank you: the only ones I've got.'

'You try them yourself,' said Fanshawe, 'I've done nothing to them.'

So after breakfast the Squire took them out to the terrace and stood on the steps. After a few ineffectual attempts, 'Lord, how heavy they are!' he said impatiently, and in the same instant dropped them on to the stones, and the lens splintered and the barrel cracked: a little pool of liquid formed on the stone slab. It was inky black, and the odour that rose from it is not to be described.

'Filled and sealed, eh?' said the Squire. 'If I could bring myself to touch it, I dare say we should find the seal. So that's what came of his boiling and distilling, is it? Old Ghoul!'

'What in the world do you mean?'

'Don't you see, my good man? Remember what he said to the doctor about looking through dead men's eyes? Well, this was another way of it. But they didn't like having their bones boiled, I take it, and the end of it was they carried him off whither he would not. Well, I'll get a spade, and we'll bury this thing decently.'

As they smoothed the turf over it, the Squire, handing the spade to Patten, who had been a reverential spectator, remarked to Fanshawe: 'It's almost a pity you took that thing into the church: you might have seen more than you did.

Baxter had them for a week, I make out, but I don't see that he did much in the time.'

'I'm not sure,' said Fanshawe, 'there is that picture of Fulnaker Priory Church.'

6 Curse of the Stillborn (1926)

MARGERY LAWRENCE

'Dammit – why can't you let 'em bury their dead in their own way?'

The words were blurted out. Mrs Peter Bond raised her sandy eyebrows and stared at the speaker with outraged virtue written large upon her square determined face, burnt brick-red with the Egyptian sun. Little Michael Frith wilted, but stuck to his point.

'I'm sorry – didn't mean to swear, Mrs Bond – but don't you see what I mean, really?' His brown wrinkled brow was lined with distress.

Mrs Bond pursed her lips disapprovingly. Upright and heavily built, in uncompromisingly stiff white piqué, her thick waist well-belted, her weather-beaten face surmounted by a pith helmet, she looked impregnably solid and British, reflected Frith exasperatedly – three years among these people and no nearer comprehending them. He tried again.

'You see – Mefren's a child of the desert … and her old mother's a pure-bred nomad … wild as a hawk. Why can't you let 'em bury their dead in peace?'

'I am surprised at your attitude, Mr Frith! I'm sorry, but I can't undertake to advise my husband any differently. These people are ignorant, childish, superstitious … I and my husband stand here to try and teach them better. And you actually suggest that I allow Mefren to bury her baby as she likes – presumably in the Desert, with I don't know what awful sort of heathen rites – when my husband is here a minister of the Lord, ready and anxious to give the poor little thing decent Christian burial! I must say I don't think this side of it can have struck you, Mr Frith!'

Mrs Bond's voice was genuinely shocked. Restlessly little Michael Frith stirred and kicked a booted foot against the whitewashed wall. He frowned – how could he explain? The native point of view ... and this good-hearted, narrow, stubborn woman!

Vaguely his mind fled to Mefren, small, slender brown creature, and her mother, Takkari, silent and haggard, with black burning eyes beneath her voluminous *haik*. Wanderers both, they had appeared at the door of his tent one dawn with a request for food ... he was encamped on the lip of the Valley of Blue Stones, a deep cleft between two ridges a few miles away from the tiny town of Ikh Nessan, where Peter Bond's little whitewashed church brooded over the tangle of mud huts like a white hen mothering a scattered handful of brown and alien chicks. Always soft-hearted, Frith had fed them both, and seeing the girl's condition and obvious exhaustion, had sent them into Ikh Nessan with a note to Mrs Bond – of whose kind heart, despite her irritating ways, none of the tiny colony had the least doubt. Food and shelter were at once forthcoming, and none too soon, for it came to pass, only a few days after the wanderers' arrival at Ikh Nessan, that the girl's time came upon her, but too soon ... and a child was born, but dead – stillborn.

Full of well-meaning sympathy and a genuine desire to help, Mrs Bond had hurried to inform Takkari, grimly silent, crouched in the shadows of the mud hut that sheltered the weeping girl, that despite the fact that the child, poor little soul, had died too early for baptism, her husband was ready at once to conduct the burial service. She was met by blank silence and a vigorous shake of the head. Dashed, and considerably annoyed, the Englishwoman demanded her reasons. Glowering silence again, but repeated attacks elicited the brusque information, in halting English, that

'Kistian bury no good. Come night, her bury self – come night, her go aways.'

Naturally Mrs Bond was outraged, and withdrew to consult her husband. I fear, had it not been for Nature, whose heavy hand on the young mother forbade anything in the way of flight, Takkari and her daughter would have been away, lost in the heart of the Desert they came from, before that night. But the evening brought little Peter Bond, full of anxious sympathy for this frail member of the flock he genuinely loved, though shocked beyond measure at his wife's report of Takkari's refusal, and the sullen, stubborn silence with which she faced him. It was while awaiting the result of this, Mrs Bond felt, most momentous interview, standing at the rickety gate of the little walled garden, the evening sun warm on the tamarisks that sprawled, green and lusty, across the whitewashed wall, that Michael Frith, dusty and hot, trudged by and paused with a cheery word. Full of her story, she had poured it forth, and her surprise and indignation were great to meet his gaze at the end – a look in which politeness warred with frank disapproval. His sympathies were entirely with Mefren and her dour, free-striding old nomad mother; why should they who were, at best, mere birds of passage, be obliged to conform to the hidebound ideas of this stupid Englishwoman? Left to himself 'Peterkin', as the little chaplain was affectionately known, would have been a sympathetic, understanding father to these wayward children of his – it was the insistent domination of this well-meaning, sincerely religious, but supremely narrow-minded wife of his that drove him into insisting on the 'Church's rights'. The phrase was on Mrs Bond's lips as Frith aroused himself from his reverie; she was still talking, her square, hard-featured face stern with strong disapproval as she eyed him.

'Towards a member of his flock – I told my husband he must not admit argument on the subject. As a Father, he must be Firm ...'

'But surely, it's not as if Mefren was a Christian,' objected Frith drily; 'if it was a member of your husband's congregation ...'

'Oh, but she is!' Mrs Bond was eagerly assertive. 'They are both Christians ... I took care to inquire about that when they came first, and Takkari assured me that both she and Mefren had been baptised!'

Michael Frith smiled drily. He could see Takkari's sombre eyes at that first interview, summing up the unconscious Mrs Bond, and assenting gruffly to any suggestion put forward – anything for a shelter and good food for her ewe-lamb in her trouble. But what was there to say? He shrugged, none too politely.

'Well ... I don't agree, I'm afraid, Mrs Bond. You see, I know these people pretty well. And frankly, I warn you again I should let them have their own way.'

As he spoke there was a quick step from the house, and the Revd Peter appeared on the threshold. Wiping his moist forehead with a large red handkerchief, he smiled uncertainly on Michael Frith, and turned with a mild air of triumph to his wife. She asked eagerly:

'Well – have you succeeded?'

'With the blessing of the Lord,' said Peterkin solemnly. 'Poor child – poor child! I feel for her ignorance, and for her mother, though I fear Takkari is still stubborn. But I wrought mightily with Mefren for the soul of her child, and at last I prevailed ...!'

A shadow seemed to fall upon the group. Old Takkari stood behind them, her lean, muscular feet muffled in the dusty earth. From the dark hooding of her brown *haik*, pulled close about her head, her uncanny eyes shone out, moving from one face to the other in silence. Mrs Bond started and drew a sharp breath – the woman was standing at her elbow before she had seen her, and the grim wrinkled face was pregnant with meaning. There was a moment's tense silence, then, turning to Frith, Takkari said something in a low tone, ending with a sardonic laugh … and was gone, flitting through the open gate and down the dusty road towards the little town. The group moved, and Mrs Bond found her tongue.

'Well, really!' she began, then curiosity fought indignation and conquered. 'Whatever did she say to you, Mr Frith?'

Frith, feeling his patience, like his politeness, nearing its end, moved away in the track of the tireless brown feet that had left delicate tracks, like a greyhound's, in the white dust.

'Nothing in particular,' he said over his shoulder, 'only a warning. An old Arabic proverb to the effect that your blood must be upon your own head.'

As he strode away he saw Mrs Bond beckon to Said Ullah, idling with a few cronies under the nodding palms, to come and dig the grave.

※

Like a lean dark wolf returning to its lair at evening, Takkari crept back to her daughter's side that night. Burials are not things, in the tropical heat of Egypt, to be postponed, and already a newly-turned mound beneath a clump of aloes marked the cradle – first and last – of the poor little scrap of humanity that never saw the sun. Alone the chaplain and his wife had committed the tiny body to the warm earth, watched Said Ullah, lean and nonchalant, fill in the grave as they prayed … Mefren was still in a semi-delirious state, and the sound of her distant moaning was disturbing. Mrs Bond walked down after supper with offers of help, but was confronted by a silent, scowling Takkari in the doorway, whose determined headshake and glowering expression frankly daunted her. She retired, huffed, but somehow not feeling sufficiently sure of herself to adopt the attitude of dignity she felt the situation needed … defeated by the grim silence, the dark hut with its sinister single light spreading a dull red carpet behind the still dark figure of Takkari in her hooded draperies. The stealthy rustle of the bushes that brushed her skirts, the crooning of the faint wind that crept about the garden, combined with the velvet darkness of the night to defeat Mrs Bond completely, and she beat a retreat to the shelter of the little 'parson-house' as graceless Said Ullah called it, in a state of nerves very unusual with her. In fact, she took herself severely to task for her weakmindedness in not reproving Takkari for her lack of manners, but a curious feeling of reluctance to face that silent hut again kept her from a second attempt, and with a frown at herself and a mental note to rectify this leniency by increased severity on the morrow, Mrs Bond settled herself down to write.

She was a most efficient clerk, in truth, and all the financial affairs, indeed the entire organisation of the secular side of her husband's life, was in her large and capable hands; every evening she set aside an hour at least for checking every item of the day, entering up accounts, engagements made for herself or her husband, requests for help, the thousand and one minor arrangements that make up a parson's life, who, like a doctor, can scarcely dare to call an hour his own. Laboriously on the opposite side of the table little Peter Bond, his high forehead grotesquely wrinkled under the pushed-up glasses, sat writing out his next Sunday's sermon; he was a painstaking preacher, and spent days upon one sermon – conscientious, entirely ineffective orations. It was a pleasant little room, despite the cheap and horrid 'Eastern' bazaar stuff with which it was crammed. An oil lamp with a preposterous red shade, not unlike a rakishly poised hat, stood at the chaplain's elbow between him and his wife – the contrast between his slowly scratching pen and frequent pauses and her swiftly decisive scribbling was curiously symbolical of both characters. The room was silent, and outside the lazy, fat-bodied, night moths lunged and bumped against the pane. As a rule the intrusion of the insect tribe after lamp-time was the one thing that maddened Mrs Bond, but tonight, oddly enough, the room was entirely empty; the churring of the myriad flies that usually found their way in to circle wildly round the lampshade was absent. It may have been the unwonted silence – one misses even a nuisance quite amazingly at first – but once or twice Mrs Bond stopped her rapid writing, and raising her head, listened intently. The third time she frowned, and spoke.

'Peter – doesn't it strike you how quiet it is? Is there a storm gathering? I feel there must be.'

The Revd Peter raised his large mild blue eyes and regarded her solemnly. In the dead stillness of the room her voice had sounded curiously loud and harsh.

'A storm – I really couldn't say, my dear. There may be one of those desert storms brewing … He stared over at the window, screwing up his eyes. 'You may be correct, my dear. Indeed, I think there is something electrical in the air tonight. For instance, the lamp is burning very badly – very low indeed. Yes.'

'Electricity – rubbish! Mrs Bond's voice was snappy; now she remembered that the unusually poor light had struck her, subconsciously, and for some obscure reason this worried her faintly. After the manner of many women, the inexplicable always had the effect of sharpening her temper; she hated any deviation from the ordinary as a cat hates getting wet. 'Electric conditions can't affect an oil lamp, Peter. Don't be silly – oh!'

The exclamation was, as it were, wrung out of her, for suddenly the lamp, already perceptibly lower, sank to a mere pool of faint light on the table; even as they both exclaimed, though, it flared up again, and irritably Mrs Bond pulled off the shade to examine it.

'Light the other lamp, Peter. There must be something in the oil, or the wick's a bad one, or something ...' Mrs Bond was an expert at managing a lamp, as she was at most household tasks, and the room sank into silence again as the Revd Peter resumed his labours beneath a fresh lamp, and his better half wrestled with the internal secrets of the red-shaded one at a little table.

After ten minutes or so spent in patient analysis of the erring lamp, however, she pushed it on one side with an annoyed 'Tcha! ... There's nothing wrong with it, as far as I can see – it must have been the oil. Well, I can't waste any more time over it.'

The Revd Peter, deep in his sermon, grunted absently, and silence fell again upon the room. Outside the night brooded over the little group of buildings, huts, chapel, the few low-roofed bungalows that, greatly daring, clustered together at the very threshold of the dour, stark Desert. The wind rose among the whispering tamarisks, and the brushing of their green-tufted branches made a dry siffling sound against the low window-sill of the lighted room; the wide sky, a sheet of black-purple velvet, patterned sequin-like with stars, yawned above the Desert, vast, illimitable, a dome of immensity which was at once comforting and menacing. Comforting, at least, it had till now always been to Mrs Bond, a sincerely pious woman in her stern way. Many a night in her first six months in Egypt she had gazed up at that wide dark peace, and telling herself that that same sky had shone above the Birth at Bethlehem – a star like those immense, unwinking stars had led the Wise Men over hill and dale to their goal at last – the same age-old silence shrouded Joseph and Mary on their flight from Herod's blood-drenched swords. She had gazed up at the stars and felt contentment, peace, a solace in the thought that she, too, lay beneath the Shelter that had made the stars ... but for the first time, something faint, tiny, unexplained, seemed to have jarred the usual peaceful spell of the night.

Mrs Bond felt, bit by bit, her attention wander from her work; irritated, she shrugged the feeling off at first, but it returned, slyly persistent, jogging her shoulder, whispering in her ear – the utter absence of the usual buzz and murmur of the circling insects worried her, at first subconsciously, then consciously. She found herself concentrating on this problem, to the exclusion of anything else; her writing became spasmodic, erratic, and at last ceased altogether. Pushing back her chair with an irritated sigh, she rose from the table.

'Peter – I really think I must have a touch of the sun! Can't concentrate in the least tonight somehow – it must be the heat.'

The Revd Peter looked up solicitously.

'Try an aspirin, my dear,' he suggested mildly. His wife shook her head impatiently.

'No – that's no good. I feel oppressed, nervy, somehow – perfectly idiotic, I know, but there it is. It's this – awful stillness, not even a fly in the room. Don't you feel it, too, Peter – or has this life got on my nerves till I'm imagining things?'

'Well – now you come to mention it, I've been feeling a little odd for some time. And now you point it out, it is curious, the absence of the – er – usual insect life around the lamp. It must be a storm brewing – or, as you say, we are both a little overdone.'

The words were valiant, but there was trepidation in the little man's mild blue eyes – trepidation vague, formless but present. Mrs Bond struck her hand on the wall in a spasm of irritation, born of the quick inrush of fear that had now seized her, like a stealthy enemy rendered suddenly bolder, at the discovery that the same creeping dread had been working its spell upon her husband's peace of mind as well.

'Peter!' She spoke firmly. 'This is either sheer foolishness on our part, of which we ought to be thoroughly ashamed – or else someone is trying to play tricks upon us ... for doing our duty as Christians to our flock, despite their ignorant prejudices.'

It was odd how, instinctively, it seemed, her mind reverted to the matter of Takkari and Mefren – the former's menacing, sullen eyes.

The little clergyman looked frankly frightened. 'You mean you think Takkari! ...' His sentence was unfinished.

'Oh, I don't mean anything *really* – what's-its-name – uncanny!' Mrs Bond snapped. 'I should hope I'm too good a Christian for that – but I wouldn't be surprised if Takkari and some of her precious friends tried to work some of their jugglers' tricks on us, to frighten us ... pure nastiness, of course! Nothing else is possible ...'

Her tone was a shade too decided; against her will as she talked, partly at random, she could not but realise that the weight and monotony of the silence seemed rising like a sea about them – and ... was it so, or was it a trick of her agitated imagination? The fresh lamp now seemed to cast a ring of smaller size, of decreased brilliance; shadows, surely, surely, loomed more deeply in the corners behind the bamboo chairs! There was a curious break in Peter Bond's voice as he answered a little quake of fear.

'Are you sure, Matilda? I thought so ... but tonight, I kept thinking of the witch who tempted Samuel – the Witch of Endor ... of Our Lord's strange words of wickedness in high places. ... And I wondered ...'

With a decisive movement, Mrs Bond strode over to the window and slammed it to, pulling the curtains together to shut out the night – and reeled away with a strangled shriek of terror! Rushing to her assistance, her frightened husband peered out into the darkness, but all was still, save the faint rustling among the tamarisks as the little wind crept through them.

There was no light in the distant hut that housed Takkari and her sullen anger. At the table Mrs Bond shivered and gasped, gradually regaining her self-control.

'What, my dear ... what happened?' The dead silence, the crowding shadows, seemed to listen for her reply. With a huge effort the woman sat up and gulped down her terrors, replying with a steadiness that spoke well for her pluck.

'Peter – something – something awful seized my wrist as I pulled those curtains! Now don't you tell me I'm mad – I was never saner! I grant I was feeling a little nervy – things seem odd tonight somehow – but just at that moment I was perfectly balanced. What – what you said about the ... well, you know what you said – suddenly made me realise we were allowing ourselves to become – well, foolishly, unchristianly frightened at nothing at all – it must be nothing at all! – and I went to pull the curtains, to shut out the night and the wind and make ourselves cosy and sensible. I was going to suggest we played Patience ... and all of a sudden a hand took me by the wrist, strongly, and tried to prevent the curtains being pulled! I told you Takkari was up to something ... though how ...'

Her eyes, frightened, angry, bewildered, met her husband's – and read there a greater terror than hers.

'Wait!' His voice was a mere whisper. 'I can tell you now ... but I did not dare to tell you, Matilda, lest it be a mere hallucination on my part. I know' – the humiliated tears were very near – 'alas, I am a weak man, Matilda! ... I thought perhaps the stillness of the night and – and my own foolish fears, for I must freely admit that I have been far from easy the whole of the evening – were working upon me till I saw, or thought I saw …'

'What?' Mrs Bond's face was strained; beads of perspiration speckled the little chaplain's lean jaw as he answered, in a voice that shook uncontrollably in the now definitely gathering gloom.

'Something – something swathed and indefinite, but Something that wasn't a shadow – I swear – stand beside you and bend over to watch you write!'

Mrs Bond shrank back with an involuntary cry of terror. The bald statement was horrible, and the woman shuddered as she listened.

The Revd Peter's knees were shaking, his voice gathering speed, a hoarse whisper as he rushed on, his frightened eyes seeking from side to side … and still the lamp sank lower and the silence gathered, fold on fold, about the trembling pair.

'I stared and stared … and looked away and forced myself to write. I prayed and sweated and dared not look again, dared not speak for fear it was hallucination and you might think my brain going with the heat and work – till you spoke. Then I dared look – and it was gone! Thank God … I spoke, I believe, rationally enough … and then you rose to draw the curtain, and Matilda, as I am a priest of God and hope for salvation, suddenly It rose at your side again, and Its face pressed close to yours … and the horror of it was Its face was no human face at all, but a gilded mask!'

The hurrying voice rose high and culminated in a half shriek – for on the last word the lamp, now a dying flicker on the table, went out, and with one stride darkness entered the room.

Utterly unnerved, Peter Bond collapsed whimpering on the table, but although shaking in every limb, his wife rose dauntlessly, and biting her lips to still their quivering, faced the darkness that had entered into possession of the room.

Silence, dead, heavy, menacing, ruled supreme, broken only by the sobs of the terrified chaplain, the heavy breathing of his wife. Like a cornered creature at bay, she backed sturdily against the table, panting hard, turning her head from side to side, her hands clammy with moisture, clenching and unclenching. There was, indeed, something pathetically valiant about this woman driven thus to fight so hopelessly one-sided a battle, for, in the dire, stealthy strength of the Force that she now dimly realised was arrayed against her, all her shivering, gallant bravery went for no more than a reed's feeble stand against the gale. Upright in the swirling shadows that clustered about her, she stood, clutching hard at her sanity, her self-control, while her little narrow soul shrank within her and grew shrivelled and puny with terror, like a last year's walnut in its shell. She knew now – she knew the Thing behind all this in some way some streak of lightning clarity had told her – somewhere behind this awful manifestation moved Something that belonged to Egypt, that had demanded Its right of Its land, and had through her been denied it ... yet, though sweating with terror, shaking in every limb, Mrs Bond, true to her stern type, held grimly to her convictions, and her shaking lips muttered prayer on prayer, while her soul crawled in terror, but not regret ... But the end was at hand, and mercifully. With a final huge effort to throw off the spell, with some vague idea that even to try and light the lamp, anything humdrum, ordinary, might break the influence that held her so bound, Mrs Bond stretched out a fumbling hand along the table for the matches ... and touched another hand! Dry and cold and leathery, with sharply pointed nails, it lay alongside hers, and as she touched it, withdrew sharply, but it was too late. Even as Mrs Bond, her last quivering defences down, opened her mouth to shriek, It grew beside her swiftly in the darkness, indefinite, macabre, and of a terror unspeakable; a Thing swathed and clumsy and vague, shapeless, yet dreadfully, appallingly powerful, a blind Horror seeking vengeance …

In a frenzy of fear the woman flung herself backwards across the table where crouched poor little Peter Bond, gibbering, hysterical, in his panic … but the Shape rose above her against the moving dark, the crowding shadows, and she saw It clearly, bulbous eyes in a horrible still face of gleaming gold, sinister and pitiless as It bent over her and … as her senses mercifully left her, laid Its ghastly cheek to hers!

✵

Frith knocked out his pipe. As the echoes of his voice died away into the tense silence a little ripple stirred the intent group of listeners, held in the grip of sheer horror. Dennison, the soldier, was the first to find his voice:

'Good Lord – what a beastly yarn! But go on, Frith – that can't be the end? You've got us all on tenterhooks!'

Frith smiled drily.

'That's just where the clever storyteller should leave his audience! I'd rather leave things where they are – on the pitch of the climax, but, of course, there is an aftermath. Fact is, I happened to be strolling near the chapel that night and heard Mrs Bond scream – rushed in and found her lying in a faint, with poor little Bond perfectly hysterical at her side, burbling wildly, and quite unstrung – for the moment a complete lunatic. Oh, yes, the lamp flared up again just as I got inside the room – no, I saw nothing; but I tell you what I *did* notice – the awful smell in the room!'

'What sort of a smell?' asked Hellier sharply.

'Bitumen,' said Frith simply. 'Bitumen and natron and dried spices and the intolerably ancient smell of the grave – the smell of the burial rites of old Egypt – stern, undying. The place stank like a newly-opened tomb!'

'But what, actually, was it? The Thing with the gold face, I mean?' My curiosity was greater than my shyness as I put the question.

Frith raised his eyebrows as he poured himself out another liqueur brandy.

'Ah – well, that no one can say for certain. Egypt keeps her secrets now as well as ever she did, but I think I can give a good guess, at least. If I knew the history of Takkari, a strange old daughter of the Nile sands, with the blood, perhaps, of Pharaohs dead ten thousand years ago in her veins ... you see, it's true that the system of embalmment died out long ago, yet, like other strange ceremonies, religions, beliefs, no one can swear, even now, that it is utterly dead and forgotten ... and who knows what age-old memories, what instincts, what fears, may have haunted those two women from the mysterious Desert as they suffered and agonised over the Stillborn!'

We fell silent, spellbound, as he went on, his voice thrilling, his eyes distant on the blue-gold ancient country he so greatly loved. 'You see – in the old days, unless the body of a stillborn child, immediately on its birth, was embalmed with the full ritual, the swathings, the amulets, the golden mask, all the strange symbolic trappings and ceremonies of a full grown being – the Ka, the soul that it had meant to incarnate, would rise in rage and anger at the neglect of the honours due to it, and turn against the house where it was born and all therein, become the evil demon, the Maleficence haunting the unfortunate being who had dared to do it this wrong ...'

'Then you think this was the direct result of Mrs Bond's insisting on Christian burial – that Takkari and her daughter, urged by who knows what instinctive dread and knowledge, meant to secretly steal away with their dead to the Desert, to bury it there with spices and cerements and ceremony to propitiate the Ka thwarted by death of its incarnation?'

133

Hellier's eyes were alight with interest – Frith nodded.

'Yes. That's what I do think, frankly. In utter ignorance, blundering and narrow, Mrs Bond forced her weak husband to pit his puny might against a great and ancient Force, and thwarted of its right, the outraged Ka rose against these presumptuous ones ... and won ... very dreadfully won. In the morning the grave was found empty; the women had dug up the body of their dead in the night and fled with it to the silence of the Desert, which opened and swallowed them. There, perhaps, they laid it to rest in their own way – in Egypt's way. At least the Horror, having worked its will upon those poor well-meaning fools, passed away. I spent many nights after that in the house, and it was perfectly normal. Poor Mrs Bond – she has paid bitterly enough for her folly, poor soul. She has never been able to tell me what she felt at that supreme moment of horror, when the Thing rose over her and pressed its cheek to hers, except that it was utterly impalpable, no actual touch at all, but a ghastly coldness that scored and burnt like the searing finger of an icicle ... then she lost consciousness, thank Heaven. But that terrible moment has left a mark on her that she will never lose. When I picked her up I saw her face was twisted, all wried sideways ... where the Gilded Mask had touched.'

7 The Cure (1929)

ELEANOR SCOTT

It was, I know my fault but though she never may – and I pray that she never will – realise it, it was even more Freda's. For it was Freda who implored me to undertake the whole thing saying in her brisk and decisive way 'He must *vegetate*, Spud. It's his nerves. You understand. Let him just be quiet – do nothing and think nothing.' And, again, 'Make him into a *real vegetable* won't you?' Which shows, of course, that she knew nothing of Erik, though she was his twin. You could no more make a vegetable of Erik Storm than you could make a doorscraper of a violin. Though I didn't know that then. It's one of the things I learnt, down at Crows' Hall. And I learnt, too, that when it's the thoughts of a man that are distorted and flaming like a jungle it's the wickedest and silliest thing you can do to give his mind complete rest. Then, like a spider, his Idea (for everyone has an Idea that is the driving-power of his whole mind) begins to work and weave, out of its own substance, a filmy web that grows and tangles the mind until –

Well, you see how it is. I know these things now. I was, at the beginning of this story – if it is a story – the stolidest and stupidest of creatures. Which is exactly why Freda chose me as Erik's companion.

I'd grown up next door to the Storms, and we three – Erik and Freda and I – had played together. Erik invented the games out of his head – wonderful games, I daresay, for he was a wonderful boy; but Freda, who was quick and practical, and I, who was slow and literal, used to shriek with laughter sometimes over his wild fancies; and we could never see, as he could, all manner of beauties and terrors by 'just thinking'. So it generally ended in Erik's going off, sore and furious, to the bare sea-marshes, while Freda and I played the normal, ordinary games in the pretty secluded garden. When our games gave out – (two is a small number, and we were uninventive) – we used to go out and find Erik, sitting in the sea-lavender with his hands clasped round his knees, crooning to himself; or standing, silent, listening to the lonely wind creeping round the dunes. Most unhealthy. He'd generally forgotten all about the quarrel then. He never did remember his human relationships very well.

We didn't go to the same school. Erik went to some queer Scandinavian place – did I say that Mr Storm was Scandinavian? Swedish or Norwegian or Danish, I forget which – and I went to a 'lesser public school' near home. I was only a weekly boarder, and so I saw a lot of Freda still. She was a good pal – far more of a boy than a girl, though a good housewife even then. And I'm afraid we didn't miss Erik much. Then he went to Oxford; and I, who was far too stupid for a University, and had no desire whatever for one, took to farming in Sussex. Freda went on her brisk, interested way alone until she got married to a decent quiet chap called Martin. And then for some years I lost sight of the Storms – heard vaguely of Freda's babies – that Erik had gone abroad to Russia – that he was spending six months in Iceland – that he was doing research into Northern folklore. So *like* Erik, I thought.

Then, one day when I was in town on business, Freda and I ran into each other in Baker Street.

'Spud!' she said, rather breathlessly. 'It's like a miracle. I believe I was praying to see you.'

She slurred her r's, as she always did when she was excited.

'Were you?' I said stupidly. I hadn't seen her for over four years, but we always met like that – as though one of us had just been out of the room for a moment and had come back. 'What's up?' I went on, for she looked quite disturbed.

'I can't tell you here,' she said, looking round. 'Can't we go somewhere and talk?'

'Madame Tussaud's –' I began. I was quite surprised when she began to laugh a little wildly.

'Spud! How like you!' she cried. 'We meet after four years – you come like a miracle – and you propose to go to a waxwork show!'

'Not to see the waxworks,' I explained patiently. I'd never seen Freda like that before. 'To talk. It's quiet. It's generally empty at this time of year.'

'I didn't even know there was really such a place … Well, let's go – anywhere to talk in peace – I *must* talk to you, Spud.'

So we went. It was nearly empty – I knew it would be, in June – and we ordered tea in the place there. And Freda told me.

'It's Erik,' she said, taking off her gloves very carefully. 'He's – so funny, Spud.'

I nodded. That was nothing unusual.

'He's … Well, you know how he went off into the North to find out sagas and charms and things? He found out a l ot … and … I can't quite follow it all. He was alone, you know, alone there in the dark and the ice … He seemed – fascinated … He went about, farther and farther north. He opened tombs and things … and he found odd things, and heard – dreadful things … Spud, I think he got sort of – possessed. He used to go out alone at night to those awful old dead places … and he'd learned spells and charms and rites … And – and, Spud – I'm – afraid.'

She broke off sharply. She was quite pale.

'He got ill. Of course he did, going out at night into that ghastly cold. I went to him. He was – I've never seen him like that before. He was frightened – oh, I can't tell you – *terrified*!

He was delirious – he *shrieked* – and then he'd whisper, and whisper … Just scraps, but enough …'

Her voice was shaking so that she had to stop. After a little she went on more quietly.

'Well, I brought him home, back to the sun and warmth. His nerves are all to pieces. He's more or less controlled, now, but – Well, honestly, Spud, I don't like having him in the house with the children. Peter's timid as it is, and he and Erik are always together. And then you came into my mind … I thought you might help … I don't know what to do.'

I'd never seen Freda so distressed. 'Is he still ill – apart from nerves I mean?' I asked.

'Oh no – his body's all right. He needs to *vegetate* you know. He's been so worked up – so excited over all this silly magic business. And you're such a calm old thing Spud –'

It was then that she made the remark about my making a vegetable of Erik.

Well I needn't detail the whole thing. I went and saw – Freda ostensibly, but really the situation. Erik looked all right, I thought – pale and thin of course, but then he'd been ill; and his eyes looked odd. People's eyes often do, though, when their faces are thin. He was quiet enough, except that once, at dinner, he started up trembling all over and rushed into the garden. When he came back he muttered some silly rot about having heard a bat. Now one doesn't, you know, in Hampstead – or anywhere, as a rule, they squeak too high; I thought it a thin explanation … Oh yes, and he did get quite excited once when he noticed a queer old ring I was wearing. I always wear it since I turned it up one day when I was ploughing up on Wether Down – an ugly, heavy thing of some dull metal with queer shapes – runes, don't you call them? – cut on it. He got quite worked up – wanted the thing, and behaved like a spoilt child when I refused to part with it. I got quite annoyed – I am obstinate, I know. And Erik suddenly got up and went off somewhere alone, just as he used to when we were kids. Lord knows where he went to, though, in Hampstead …

Of course Freda had her way. I could see that Erik was nervy – Lord! what an inadequate word! But it really was all that I saw then – and Freda was naturally worried. And I am far too lazy to be anything but obliging. So, as I was going back to Sussex anyhow, I invited Erik. Freda and I thought that the farm would be just the place for him – so quiet, so uneventful, so calm … God! What fools sensible people are!

Now, I want to make two things quite clear. I never had, and didn't then, begin to understand Erik or anything about him. But I was tremendously sorry for him – he was so white and miserable and silent and (I know now) *haunted*. I wanted to do my best for him; only I didn't know what to do. I could only think of the silliest, most obvious attentions that one would pay to an invalid aunt.

I met him the night he came. I drove to the little station where there are three trains a day, because it seemed the thing to do. I remember it was a threatening looking night, and I hoped the rain wouldn't come just yet and beat down the hay. Erik was the only passenger, and he was absurdly glad to see me. I was quite moved.

'I was so afraid you wouldn't be here,' he kept saying.

'Well, it wouldn't have been so far to walk if I hadn't come,' I said once. 'You could have left your stuff at the station.'

He looked at me oddly and didn't answer.

'Besides, you'd probably have had company on the road,' I went on.

He started then, and shivered violently. I remembered his illness, and told him to pull up the rug …

He seemed very listless at first – wouldn't even unpack

properly, so my housekeeper, Mrs Burns, told me. She is very tidy, and she seemed a bit annoyed. I can't risk that. So one evening I said to Erik:

'Got straight upstairs yet, Erik?'

'N-not yet,' he said very slowly. 'You see, I-I've brought a lot of stuff … unnecessary … curios, you know. I haven't sorted my things since I came south …'

He seemed quite confused about it.

'Well, would you like me to come up and give you a hand? Rather miserable, isn't it, having your collars and socks mixed up with coins and junk like that?'

He flushed scarlet. 'Oh, I-I don't – I'm afraid' I was extremely puzzled by his manner. Then he burst out: 'Well, if you really wouldn't mind coming *with* me.'

It sounded like a kid afraid of the dark! But I just thought that he was too tired after his illness to want to do anything on his own. I've never been ill, and I felt quite bright for thinking of it.

We went up to his room – and really I didn't blame Mrs Burns. I'm not what you'd call neat myself, but this –! I'd never seen such a muddle. Bags and boxes and rucksacks all open and bulging with sweaters and shoes and books and all manner of things.

'You see, I wanted to find something – something … not valuable, at all, but … I can't remember where I put things … I was ill, you know, and – *and I must find it*,' he broke out.

He was awfully worked up.

'Well, let's put everything away,' I said, 'and we're bound to find it, if it's here. What is the thing, anyway?'

But he only muttered to himself, something in a language I didn't understand. I don't think it was the stuff he and Freda used to talk, though. It sounded more uncouth than that.

We'd nearly finished when he found the box. Quite an ordinary wooden box. He threw himself on it, like a kid with a toy. Then he began to open it, with a kind of rather horrible eagerness; and then – he suddenly began to tremble visibly, got deadly white, and hurled the thing to the other end of the room. It must have been fairly heavy, for it made quite a thud, and I thought I heard a chinking sound, like metal.

'Here! Don't go chucking treasure trove about like that!' I said, making a desperate effort to be jocular because I was too bewildered to do anything else.

I went across to pick the thing up, but Erik jumped at me and clutched my arm.

'Don't *touch* it, don't *touch* it,' he kept gabbling in a queer hoarse whisper. 'Come away – do come away ...'

I was afraid he was going to be ill again. He looked like death.

Now, as I say, I hadn't the faintest idea what the chap was after or what to do; but I was simply aching with pity. So I thought I'd better just do what he wanted – humour him, you know. We went downstairs together. He clung on to my arm all the way, and, though his hands shook and trembled, there were bruises there when I went to bed.

Well, I'm not what's called imaginative, Lord knows! But it was a queer business, wasn't it? and Erik – I simply can't begin to tell you what he looked like with his white face and staring black holes of eyes, and his terror – for it was nothing else. I'd never in my life – then – been afraid; not of the dark when I was a kid nor of animals nor accidents nor people nor, I'm afraid, God or the Devil. I suppose it was because I had no imagination. But that night I felt – well, uncomfortable, no more – for the first time in my life.

The sight of my cheery room with its wood fire and the bright warm light and the curtains and sporting prints put me right before I knew I was wrong. It was a ripping room, that. Pity I shall never see it again ...

Even Erik seemed better in there. We sat down, one on

each side of the fire (it was a chilly night, I remember, for June) and I, to give him time to recover himself, messed about with my pipe, which didn't need any attention whatever. Again I rather patted myself on the back for my tact in this. But there was no betting on Erik.

'For heaven's sake stop scraping that pipe, Spud,' he cried quite suddenly. 'It doesn't want it, and – and I can't bear it ...'

I'm afraid I gaped. He was beyond me. I'd no idea anyone could mind a little noise like that.

He smiled at me suddenly, like a kid.

'Oh, Spud, I'm sorry! I am an ungrateful brute,' he said. He was the most disarming chap.

'Bosh, old thing,' I said. 'Only, you see I'm such a tough sort of bear. You'll have to tell me every time I get on your nerves, because I simply don't know enough to keep off.'

He smiled again. Now I've never seen any eyes in the least like Erik's. They could be so bright and blue that they quite startled you and then in a second they'd be dead black – not what you generally call black but real black, all over. Extraordinary they were. And you could generally tell his mood by the colour of his eyes. Now they were as blue as the sea is on an August afternoon when you look over from Wether Down.

'Spud, you're a – I mean, I'm most tremendously glad you're here,' he said. 'I want – I say, may I tell you something – something about what happened –'

I quite forgot Freda and the cure.

'I wish you would,' I said.

'I don't know if you'll ever understand,' said Erik slowly. 'It'll sound the most putrid rot, I expect. Perhaps it is! Anyhow, I can't tell whether it is or not until I say it out to somebody else. If you go on turning a thing over in your own head you can get to believe *anything*.'

Now I know that he was right. You can. But then I said,
'Rot! Either a thing's true or it isn't. No amount of thinking
will make truth into a lie or a lie into truth.'

He smiled again, rather sadly. 'Well – I don't know,' he said.
'Anyhow, I want to tell you.'

So he began telling me how he'd gone to Norway and
Iceland and these other places to do research into a dead
life. Folklore and charms and dead religions and legends and
things. He found out quite a lot, apparently: anyhow he got
absolutely fascinated.

'I can't tell you how it gripped me,' he said. 'It was –
extraordinary stuff. And the more I looked the more I found.
I simply can't tell you … I went north, and I met a man – old –
oh, incredibly old. And he showed me how to see and to hear
… One night, after he knew me a bit, we went to a barrow …'

His breath seemed to stop completely. He was quite white,
like paper, and his eyes seemed to have gone into his head.
They were black and dead.

I couldn't understand in the very least. What was there to
alarm or disturb the chap? He didn't say what he'd seen and
heard, of course, but still –!

'My dear Erik,' I said, 'what a kid you are! You get an old
Swede or Dane or something to tell you ghost stories, and
you go out at night with him to some old tomb thing – and
you're upset for months! What did you do at the barrow?' He
shuddered violently. He tried to say something, but his voice
died before I could hear it.

'What does one do at a barrow?' I went on jocularly: 'You
bury old kings and warriors, don't you, with jewels and cups
and things, in chambers inside a burial mound? Did you look
for any loot?'

He nodded; and suddenly I saw light. 'What – the box
upstairs? You pinched some treasure? Oh, Erik, you *priceless*

old fool!' I was weak with laughing. 'I'm going to have a look.'

I ran upstairs whistling and went into Erik's room. There lay the box where he'd pitched it. I went towards it, when something rushed past me, snatched it up, and hurled it right through the window.

It was Erik. He turned on me, eyes blazing, chest heaving – looked as if I'd tried to murder him!

'My dear chap!' I said when I could speak. 'I wasn't going to hurt the thing. What the devil's the matter? – Don't stare at me like that!' I snapped. 'You've lost the bally thing now, not me. And you've broken a window into the bargain.'

His face changed. He got a bit more colour and his eyes looked saner. He looked like a man waking out of a dream, bewildered and a little ashamed.

'I – I'm awfully sorry,' he muttered. 'I don't know – I can't explain. Let's go downstairs. I'm awfully sorry,' he repeated.

When we were back before the fire I tried to get him to tell me what had happened at the barrow and what was in the box and why he'd got so mad: but he would say not one word. I'd shut him up for good. Only, just as we were going up to bed, he turned to me at the door in his old frank way.

'Spud,' he said, 'look here. I'm no end sorry about this. It shan't happen again. I'm going to chuck all this stuff – these dead things. I'm going to be sane – *if I can*. You'll help me, won't you, not to go back to them?'

'Why the devil should you ever go near Iceland again if you don't want to?' I said. He puzzled me hopelessly.

'I don't necessarily mean Iceland … Oh, I can't explain! I hate it, and I long for it – I loathe it, and I must have it! It's like a drunkard … Spud, keep me away from it!'

It was like a frightened kid asking you to keep ghosts off. All I could say was, 'It'll be quite all right, old chap. This isn't Iceland, you know. No icefields and barrows here. Only good farmed land and friendly country … Now let's get to bed.'

'It isn't only Iceland,' he said slowly. 'It's everywhere – if you look ... But I won't look. I'll chuck it. I *will*.'

And for some days after that he was quite normal and cheerful – seemed quite interested in the farm and the beasts and labourers and so on. Asked a lot about the history of the place, I remember, and why the valley behind Wether Down, where the mounds are, was called Kings Bottom ... He spent the day fooling round, picking up stories from the countryfolk and getting to know the lie of the land. I only saw him at meals, and then he was so contented and happy that I cheered loudly and wrote to tell Freda that our cure was working and that Erik had quite forgotten his old dead ghosts and gods.

It was, perhaps, a week after that that I had to ride over to Marden le Winken, which is a village about a mile from the farm. It's the sort of little place that I like because it has a small life of its own, and – oh, well, it's homely. Artists come there and gas about the green and the old well and the church, until in sheer self-defence I retort with plain speaking about sanitation, which generally makes them sheer off. Well, that day – a very clear, hot, July day with a cloudless sky that looked as if it never could change or darken – I pulled up on the green; and there, sitting on the well coping I saw Erik and another person, I couldn't quite make out whom. They were staring down the well as if they'd lost something. Now I'm always a bit anxious when nervy people start gazing earnestly at water or down cliffs or anything like that; so I called out to Erik.

'Oi! Erik!' I shouted. 'Come here half a tick, will you?'

He got up and came over, walking as if he were in a trance. And then I got a start. Erik, of course, was queer and one made allowances, but his companion was Murky Glam the village idiot!

Now I'm not an absolute brute and I've a kind of respect for 'God's children' as Sussex people still call imbeciles. But I don't like them. I don't like anything deformed or abnormal. Still, I'd often spoken to Murky Glam – (no one knew why he was called that or what his real name was) – and he'd sometimes been over to Crows' Hall with a message or something; and often and often, when I've been ploughing up on the downs above Kings Bottom, I've come across Murky sitting there on one of the humps that stand above the valley where the ancient yew trees grow. But it's one thing to speak civilly to a chap when you meet him, and quite another to sit with him for hours looking down a well. And I didn't think that a village idiot was a very good companion for Erik anyway.

Well, it was a blazing hot day, and I'd been annoyed at having to leave the farm, and I'd been delayed by a man on the way in, and then Erik had startled and almost frightened me; so I snapped at him.

'What the devil were you doing at that well?' I asked.

Erik looked straight through me as if I wasn't there. I don't believe he knew who I was. He said nothing at all.

'Erik!' I said angrily.

He seemed to wake up.

'Oh! Did anyone – did you speak to me?' He asked in the queer half-foreign accent he always had when he was dreaming.

'Yes,' I snapped, 'I did. I should think you could have heard me half a mile away. What the deuce are you doing with that chap?' And I jerked my head towards Murky Glam.

Erik looked at me and I felt like a blustering bully.

'I was talking,' he said very quietly.

'You weren't,' I said bluntly.

He flushed scarlet and turned away.

'Erik!' I said, 'hold on. I'm sorry. I didn't mean to be rude. But you know –'

He didn't seem to be listening. He was walking very slowly back to the well. Murky Glam took no notice whatever of either of us. It really was a bit uncanny. Broad midday – glorious summer weather – the homely little village green – and that chap dressed in rags, with odd bright patches and a broken cock's feather stuck in his hat, sitting staring at the well. The water, like a bright eye twinkling in the sun, seemed to stare back. And there was Erik – my vegetating charge – walking straight into this fantastic picture.

I can't tell you why, but I felt quite alarmed. It was like seeing a child walk over the edge of a cliff.

I vaulted down and caught Erik up.

'Erik!' I said, laying hold of his arm. 'Erik – you *said* you'd chuck it.'

I didn't myself know what he was to chuck.

He stood quite still; slowly he turned and faced me. Then he looked back at the well. Murky Glam was sitting up now, and looking at us with an idiot's silly smile.

'You promised,' I said again.

'Yes. I know I did,' muttered Erik, his eyes on Murky Glam. 'I will – I *will*.'

And he turned and went slowly off down the road to Crows' Hall. He'd made quite a sensation in the village – of course he had! – and I knew there'd be endless chatter, which I hate. I was awfully annoyed. I made the best of it by turning into the inn, and casually mentioning that Erik was interested in imbeciles – I'm afraid I purposely gave the impression that he was a doctor on a holiday – and then I went on to the woman who calls herself Murky Glam's mother and told her that I wouldn't have the chap coming down to Crows' Hall. It would have been about as useful to tell the fire not to let the kettle boil …

I was, even for a working farmer, quite exceptionally busy just then. The harvest was coming on in that sudden rush that sometimes happens when a hot August follows a wet July. There were storms knocking about, too, and I wanted to harvest as soon as possible. Then Bates, my excellent cowman, slipped on a greasy stone floor and broke his leg, and, as I didn't trust his boy, I had to do most of the cow work myself. I'm not trying to make excuses. I know now that I ought to have lost the crops and even let the cows suffer rather than have allowed what happened. And I ought to have had my eyes opened, too, after that hot blue morning in Marden le Winken. But on a farm you lose sight of everything but the land and the beasts. I thought myself lucky if I got off with a seventeen-hour day, and I rolled into bed only to sleep like a log. Even at meals I was preoccupied with plans and details of farm work, and only noticed that Erik was very quiet, and often late for meals. Sometimes I hardly saw him all day, for he cut out his food altogether as far as we could see, and only said he'd been 'out' when I questioned him.

It was Gibson, my head carter, who finally put me on to the track. We were making the arrangements for the great harvest supper that is always held at Crows' Hall, whoever the owner, on August 15th – Lammas Night. It's the event of the year there. There's a big meal first, with lots of beer and cider, and afterwards there's a 'bale-fire' on the biggest mound in Kings Bottom. We had just finished our plans when Gibson made his remark.

'Mr Storm seems rare taken up wi' they mounds over to Kings Bottom,' he said. 'Always down among 'em he is, along o' that wastrel Murky Glam.'

I jumped, I don't deny it.

'Murky Glam?' I said. 'I warned him off my land days ago.'

'Big mound ain't Crows' Hall prop'ty, not by rights it ain't,' said Gibson. 'You stops at second mound sir, if all was as it should be.'

'Then how can I have the bale fire on the big mound, you

fool?' I cried. I was annoyed for we'd spent valuable minutes in discussing that very fire and Gibson had seemed to take the site for granted.

'That'll be all right, sir,' answered Gibson placidly. Good chap, he knew what a time I'd been having, and he made allowances for me, though he did have that maddening air that country people so often have of kindly pity for the poor idiot who doesn't know their customs. 'Lammas Fire's always been on that mound, long's any on us can mind. That's the place for 'im. But if you'll allow me, sir,' (a favourite phrase of Gibson's, that) 'you'll take care on 'en this year. See, it's the seventh year.'

'*What's* the seventh year?' I asked, bewildered and a bit exasperated.

'It's like this, sir. Bale-fire, he always goes up on big mound, like I was a-tellin. Only, once in seven years, summat happens, like. Old folks they say it's the toll taken by *him*?' He jerked his thumb up at the mound. He was desperately solemn. 'Seven year ago it were Ben Puckey – nice serious chap as you'd wish to see, Ben were, and booklearned along wi' it. Left supper early, he did, an' never went 'ome. Nex' day he weren't at work. "I'll tell 'ee where to find 'en," says old gaifer Gregory. "Look in ashes up on big mound," he says. An' true, there he were … Poor Ben, a nice young chap as you'd meet. Seven year afore that it were young Mr Jerrold from Combes – young chap up at Oxford College. Not so much loss he weren't. Afore that it were old Gaffer Tomlyn and afore that –'

'Gibson! Don't be an ass!' I shouted. 'Do you want me to believe that someone's bound to die on the mound every seventh year?'

"Tain't what I asts you to believe,' said Gibson with dignity. 'It's truth, take it what way you like.'

I thought a minute. One has to be rather careful, even with

the most sensible men, over their pet beliefs; and I'd certainly heard something about young Jerrold – yes, and about Ben Puckey too …

'Gibson, look here,' I said. 'I don't deny that there have been deaths there. I'm not a fool, and facts are facts. But don't you think it's just because people expected them? They think there'll be one – and so of course there is. Look at these men you've mentioned. Gaffer Tomlyn was "toteling", wasn't he? Over ninety, I've heard. He'd got it on his mind that there must be a death there that year. Young Mr Jerrold – well, you all know he was in with a wild set – drink and Hellfire Club and devil worship and the rest. And poor Ben had books and legends and charms on the brain. They were all ripe for it. So when the seventh year came, they – they just –'

'Quite so, sir,' said Gibson in his politest and most chilling manner, which he always put on when he didn't in the very least agree with me and meant to stick to his own way. 'All I say is, sir – best be careful come Lammas. It's been like that long's I can mind.'

That was so like the Crows' Hall men. 'Been so as long as we can mind' – and therefore always must be so! The job I had to get them to take to new methods and machinery you simply wouldn't believe … I just shrugged my shoulders.

'Oh! all right,' I said; and made a private resolution to talk to Erik.

I didn't forget to; but it wasn't so easy to get the chance. I hardly ever saw him, and when I did he – how can I put it? – he didn't seem to know I was there. It was as if we lived in different worlds. Sitting at the same table, or beside the same hearth, we were like beings of two different creations, unable to understand or speak or even see each other. Like disembodied spirits in different spheres – or a man and a spirit. I expect that's nearer the truth …

August 15th was a blazing day. I remember thinking there must be thunder about behind the fierce purplish sky, and my joy as I thought that, after this one field, all the crops would be in. The men worked like Trojans, for I'd said that three of them could go to prepare the fire if the others made up for their absence. We slaved and sweated in that field, and, as I write, I can smell the dry scent of the ripe wheat and the baked earth, and see the tiny flowers, speedwell and pimpernel, that we trod underfoot ... The sea, five miles away over Wether Down, shimmered in a haze. The new rick looked silvery white against the deep intensity of the sky.

I hadn't time to eat or speak or think that day. Apart from the ordinary work, there was the big barn to prepare for the harvest supper, the carving to do, the beer and cider to tap, the fire to prepare. I worked like a man possessed. I forgot everything but the jobs that seemed to press in on me in an endless and urgent succession. I only remember one extraneous thought – and that was that I wished Erik would help a little. Looking back now, that thought seems to me the grimmest comment possible on that night.

The supper was, I believe, a great success. I know I carved and poured and poured and carved for what seemed like hours, and the men ate and drank enormously, and finally cheered and cheered. Then we went out to Kings Bottom.

The moon was up by then – a great pearl, floating in a kind of insolent calm over the rolling fields. It was miraculously clear. Every blade of stubble, every stone, every leaf, seemed etched in the flood of light. The sky was huge and empty and only a moonlit sky is empty. Oddly enough, for me, a line of poetry slid into my mind

The moon doth with delight look round her when the heavens are bare.

The country was like an incarnation of that line. And then, quite suddenly, with a rush and a roar of flame, the bale-fire sprang into life.

It was magnificent. In that remote valley under the quiet darkening sky, the huge fire leaped and towered upon the tomb of a long-dead king; and the men stood round it, grave, patient, like the soil itself. I seemed to have a sudden glimpse of some truth I'd always known and never understood – some truth about men and the earth and the kinship of things …

Then someone began a song, and there was a certain amount of skylarking, and people went through old, half-forgotten rites and charms; and the quiet moon sailed higher in the darkling sky, as if contemptuous of our antics.

I was suddenly very tired. The fire was sinking and the fun was over. I thought of bed, and decided that I needn't wait. I rather wished Erik had been there – he'd have been interested in the charms and things – and then I thought, impatiently, God forgive me! what a hopeless chap he was to have to do with, and that if he preferred to fool round with an idiot he could – I couldn't dry-nurse him, in addition to all my other tasks. I decided to clear out. After all, I'd done my job. They'd had their feed and their fire, and the crops were in, and Gibson's gloomy croakings about the seventh year were disproved, and all was well. So I said goodnight, and went back to Crows' Hall.

Yes, all was well, I thought again, going down through the reaped fields, and the rickyard with the big firm solid stacks, and the quiet farmyard where the horses moved a little, heavily, in their stalls, and the young calves rustled in their litter. Thunder might come, and rain and hail; but for me at least all was well.

I fell asleep at once. It was the heavy, dreamless sleep that you get after hours of heavy outdoor work and a good bit of anxiety that ends in peace. It must have been some hours later when I woke and saw the light on my wall.

My first thought was of lightning; then I knew it was fire, and thought of the rickyard. Then, at the window, I saw it, streaming up from the King's Mound – a column of fire, steady as a pillar, vivid under the night sky, the quiet empty fields spreading round it.

At first I saw no one; then, quite unmistakably, even at that distance, I saw the weird figure of Murky Glam.

He moved slowly round the solitary fire, making odd fantastic gestures which were yet solemn, and to me, horribly impressive. And then, quite suddenly, I saw something in the midst of the flame.

I think I knew even then what it was. I tore out of the house like a man possessed. I don't think anyone has ever run as I ran that night, barefoot and terrified, to the big mound that overlooks the sea lying like the rim of a silver shield beyond it. I ran blindly, in a red mist that seemed to me to be the light of the bale-fire: my ears roared, and I thought it was the flames, and ran on. I could taste the salt of my own sweat as it ran into my mouth; the breath tore roughly at my heart and throat. And even as I ran I knew I was too late ...

The fire had sunk when I got there. A few little flames flickered timidly in the ashes, and licked at the hands of the man on the mound.

Murky Glam had vanished. Erik lay quite alone, his face turned up to the moon, his mouth smiling. His hands, lying on his breast, were folded about a little pile of ashes, where lay lumps of shapeless metal. Only his hands were singed badly. Above them a knife haft protruded from his bare breast. On the tomb the sacrifice had been offered; and the eternal moon looked down on the quiet and fruitful earth.

8 Ho! The Merry Masons (1933)

JOHN BUCHAN

The Thursday Club – the successor of the old Runagates Club of which I have compiled a few chronicles – is not quite the same home of wild tales as its progenitor. Its newer members are too pre-occupied with the cares of life, and are apt to engage in grave discussions of current problems. But now and then the conversation strays into fantastic paths, and sometimes a story emerges.

One April night, when the street corners were scented with wallflowers, and oysters were no longer on the dinner menu, the company was small, for half a dozen members had gone after salmon to the Dee, the Wye, and the Blackwater. Burmester, who was in the chair, brought the news of the death of one who had often been a guest, Sir Alwyn Thomasson, the retired diplomat, who had recently settled in Gloucestershire. 'Rotten bad luck,' he said. 'He was only in his early seventies, and as healthy as a blood-horse. I'd have given him another ten or fifteen years. You had heard about it, Ned?' and he turned to Leithen. 'Wasn't he a near neighbour?'

Leithen nodded. 'I went over to Scaip yesterday. It's a melancholy business, and that poor girl of his has a lonely future.'

Some man asked what he had died of.

'Heart failure, they say,' Burmester replied, 'though he didn't look like a man with a heart. But you never know with a fellow that has lived in hot countries and led a pretty gruelling life. Had you any suspicions, Ned?'

'No. And I don't believe he had himself.' Leithen's fine-drawn sallow face was curiously grave, as if this death meant more to him than that of an ordinary country neighbour, and Burmester discreetly passed from the subject.

That evening, I remember, was like one of the old Runagates sederunts. It was a soft spring night, the windows were left open and the curtains undrawn, and the only light came from the unshaded candles which burned without a flicker. The talk wandered discursively from the dangers of yellow fever spreading to East Africa, through the latest pronouncements of Mussolini, to certain speculations in the physics of hyper-space which a Cambridge professor had just made public. Peckwether, who was scientist as well as historian, had something to say about the last, and he stirred up Anthony Hurrell, the ornithologist.

'Have you ever considered,' Hurrell asked, 'that physics may provide a scientific explanation of certain ghost stories? There are some, you know, which are perfectly authenticated as facts, but are wholly inexplicable. Ordinary causality simply doesn't apply. But our new physics may provide the missing link.'

Leithen, who had spoken little at dinner, now found his voice. 'That was what Hollond used to say. Did any of you ever know Hollond? He perished years ago on the Chamonix Aiguilles. A genius in his way, and, though he is superseded now, he was the forerunner of Einstein and Planck and all that lot. He used to say that he could not see why some event should not have left an indelible mark on the ether, and that under certain conditions that mark might become audible or visible or present in some way to the human consciousness. There are places, you know, where you can wake an echo only by striking a particular note; to any other note in the scale the place is dumb.'

Burmester observed that the ether was a dashed queer thing. Someone had been telling him that every sound made since the beginning of time was still tucked away in the ether, and that some day scientific instruments might be devised which would be capable of eliciting them. He had been told that it might even be possible to dig out the actual Sermon on the Mount and Caesar's 'Et tu, Brute', if Caesar ever said it, and Philip Sidney's dying words, and the notion had solemnised him.

But Hurrell was not to be diverted by Burmester's fantasies. He said that he agreed with Hollond, whom he had known a little. 'Suppose you have some great crisis of human emotion – panic, lust, hate, self-sacrifice – a murder, a great renunciation – anything which strains the nerves to the extreme limit. We talk about an atmosphere being tense, and the tenseness may be not merely subjective. Why shouldn't human passion create some subtle physical dislocation which abides in the air of a particular place, and which may be recalled if somehow the *trait d'union* appears again? That would explain certain ghost stories – or, at least, it would point the way to their explanation.'

I do not know if Hurrell was serious – possibly not – but to our surprise Leithen was serious enough. This shrewd, matter-of-fact lawyer, who rejoiced to prick most speculative bubbles, suddenly revealed an unexpected credulity.

'It needn't be only in the air,' he said. 'Why should it not be in the whole physical environment – stones, trees, a glen, a hillside? We do not know what queer intricate effects the human soul may have on inanimate things. A physical environment may be charged with psychical stuff as a battery is charged with electricity, and, when the right conductor appears there may be the deuce to pay.'

He stopped.

'Go on,' said Hurrell. 'Explain yourself.'

'I can't,' said Leithen. 'It's only a whimsy, and won't bear explanation.'

Then Burmester showed his acumen. 'There's a story here,' he said. 'Let's have it, Ned.' Leithen looked embarrassed.

'There is a story. It's about Scaip – where Thomasson died. But I'm not sure that I should tell it.' He hesitated. 'Yet, I don't know. We were all friends of his – and I've rather got it on my mind … I think I should like to tell it you. I can trust your discretion, for, as you'll see, it's not a thing that should be talked about.'

※

It all happened years ago, he said, just after I acquired Borrowby. Borrowby was rather a ruin, and I had to do a good deal to make it habitable, besides putting in bathrooms and lighting and that sort of thing. I employed a young architect who understood what I wanted, but I was so desperately keen that I couldn't keep away from the place, and was always running down to see how the builders were getting on. So that year, when the courts rose before Easter, I decided to spend my vacation in the Cotswolds. I meant to put up at a local pub, but suddenly out of the blue came an invitation from Barnes Lacey to stay with him at Scaip. Scaip is only five miles from Borrowby, so I gladly accepted.

You remember old Lacey? Bankers often dabble in scholarship, but he was the only stockbroker I have ever known who cultivated the Muses. Pretty arid Muses they were, for his hobby was the backstairs of the Middle Ages – all the dustiest backstairs, too, for he didn't care a rush for poetry and art, but only for conundrums in law and custom. He has been dead for some time, and I gather that his reputation is growing – constantly quoted by the pundits, for apparently he had some original theories which Maitland pooh-poohed, but which people nowadays are inclined to accept. He was the genuine antiquary and never so happy as when he was up to the neck in grubby charters. How he was so successful in the City I can't explain, but he was. He made a pot of money, and was just about to retire and look for a country house, when he inherited the family place from a distant cousin.

Scaip was the right kind of house for him. It is in one of those steep little valleys that cut into the west side of the Cotswold escarpment. Coming from the east, you cross the upland plateau with its stone walls and beech clumps and wild thorny meadows, and come suddenly to an edge and look over the Severn to the Welsh hills forty miles off. The glen drops straight from your feet, with a stream in it that lower down is dammed into a string of ponds. Near the top on a shelf is the village of Greenbourton, one of the prettiest in England – thirteenth-century church, green, cross, well spreading into watercress beds, and twenty grey stone-roofed cottages that look as ancient as hillside boulders – the most delicious place on earth, especially in April when it is smothered in a foam of cherry-blossom. Half a mile down on the next shelf stands the manor house of Scaip, to which all the glen and about ten square miles of the uplands belong.

Have you ever seen Scaip? Well, go and look at it, for you won't forget the first sight of it. It has all the gloom and mystery of the back world of England. Seen from the hill above it appears to be a little town, with all manner of tiny quadrangles and falling terraces, but if you look up at it from below it is more like some Tyrolese Schloss, a dark, craggy, impenetrable fortress. Or it is like a Border keep built to protect the gates of the Marches. There is Norman work in it, but the tower dates from just before the Wars of the Roses, and tacked on to it is the main block built about the time of Henry VII. It is the austerest kind of early Tudor, a grim façade broken up by a few shallow rectangular bow windows. The remarkable thing about it is that it has not been altered, except for a classical Jacobean porch at the main entrance, and a kitchen built out in the eighteenth century. Below it, dropping to the stream and the ponds, are funny little stone curtains, and terraces flanked with things like dovecots, and twisting stone stairways. All the purlieus are a maze of fantastic stonework, but the house itself rises above them as solid and self-contained as a mountain.

Inside it was the last word in discomfort, for it had been scarcely lived in for a century, the Laceys having another place in Norfolk which was not entailed and so had not descended to Barnes. The staircases ran at impossible angles, and to find your way about was a perpetual game of hide-and-seek. A good deal of the furniture was three centuries old and I have never seen such a museum of day-beds and settles and chairs in which ease was impossible. Barnes, who liked his comforts, had done his best, and he had excellent servants, but we had to bathe in hip-baths, and all the water had to be fetched from the courtyard well, and the food was apt to be cold, since it had to be brought about a quarter of a mile from the kitchen. His antiquarian conscience would not allow him to alter much, so he himself roosted in a medieval bed-chamber which smelt of mould, and put up with tepid meals. But he had introduced some reasonable armchairs and had the chimneys altered so that they did not smoke, and he knocked two rooms on the terrace together so as to make one decent guest chamber. I, being a disconsidered bachelor, had a medieval cubby hole next to his own.

The weather when I arrived was the quiet, hazy, early April kind before the riot of spring begins. I arrived late and saw nothing of Scaip till the next morning, and then it seemed to me the last word in perfection, so that I fell sadly out of conceit with my own Borrowby. I looked from my window over the falling courts and gardens to the shining waters of a little lake, and beyond to a green shoulder of hill where sheep were feeding. I couldn't lie in bed, so I went for a walk before breakfast and looked into the terrace guest-room. It had not been spoiled by the reconstruction, and the small dark panels, the stone fireplace, the exquisite plaster mouldings of the ceiling, and the tapestry of the bed hangings and the curtains, were as they might have been three or four centuries ago. The view outside, too, had nothing modern in it, and I had a pleasant feeling of having cheated time as I paced the terrace. There was a far-off sound of bleating sheep, and a great cawing of rooks from the hillside beeches, and somewhere very distant the slow sweet chiming of bells. I thought what a kind and habitable land our England was, and how Scaip had an extra share of its graciousness. No harshness, I told myself, could ever have broken the peace of this happy vale.

On the second afternoon of my visit Barnes took me for a walk along the slopes of the hills in brisk shiny weather. A south wind was blowing that made the buds swell visibly. He wanted to show me the church at Fanways, which I had never seen, and which contained several Lacey tombs. We came to it about four o'clock, which I have always considered the cheerfullest hour in the day. I won't try to describe Fanways, for I daresay most of you have been there, for it is the show place of that bit of country. The village straggles on both sides of a narrow road and the cottages are perched high up on the banks with, below them, rock-gardens which were blazing with *aubrietia* and *arabis*. The church is at the foot, rising out of the water meadows like a baron's keep, and dwarfing the village, dwarfing even the hills. You cannot imagine anything more snug and comfortable than that string of ancient homesteads, each sending up its drift of smoke from its stone chimneys. But not so the famous church. Even in the clear April sunshine it threatened and commanded, pulled the mind out of its ease and warned it of the mystery of life and the terrors of death. Seen under a wild December sunset, it must be a solemnising spectacle.

I had this impression strong on me as we passed through the churchyard yews to the main porch. Barnes didn't seem to share it. He became the pitiless antiquarian, calling my attention to all kinds of architectural tit-bits, and talking a language I imperfectly understood. In the interior gloom, heavy with incense, for the vicar was an extreme Anglo-Catholic, he scarcely showed decent reverence, for he was eager to point out a dozen things in the carved woodwork and stonework which he pronounced to be grotesque and obscene. Other people had discoursed to me of the traces of diabolism in the holy places of our ancestors, and I did not pay much attention to Barnes.

But as we were leaving, and stood under the great eastern buttress, he suddenly revealed a sensitiveness with which I had not credited him. 'A noble house of God,' he said. 'Yes, but I swear that the Devil had a good deal to do with the building of it.'

He held the point of his stick at my breast in a way he had when he wanted to be emphatic.

'There's no greater nonsense,' he said, 'than the stuff the modern medieval sentimentalist talks about simple piety flowering into stone and lime and craftsmen working solely to the glory of God. There was a little of that, no doubt, but there was a pretty ugly other side. A great church often had its origin in the vulgarest rivalry. One magnate wanted to score off another, and that was the best way he could do it in public. "As sure as God's in Gloucestershire," the proverb says. Well, I've unearthed some pretty queer tales which show that the Almighty can't have been very happy about some of the houses built for him.'

'Not only that,' he went on. 'Someone ought to tell the truth about the medieval craftsmen. They had their gilds as you know, close corporations which were often guilty of the bloodiest tyranny. Our innocent trade unions today don't know the first thing about their jobs. Some of them – the masons especially – had secret societies with a fairly devilish side to them. They were under the special protection of the Church, you see, in their work, and made sure of Heaven at their death, so in their lives they could dabble with impunity in Hell. They might be building a shrine for the Virgin or St Peter, but it was Priapus or Nodens or Vaunus, or some other old Pagan miscreant that often inspired their work. You can find it here and in many other places – there's a spirit in the stone, a spirit of black malice and blood and cynical mockery. They were queer lads, some of those old masons, and they have left behind them something which is not quite dead. Often their work speaks to me, and what it says scares me. So when I read rhapsodies about the Ages of Faith, and the consecration of the old builders, and their gentle ribaldry which belongs only to people who are assured in their faith, I'm inclined to laugh. I know too much about the merry masons.'

That night, I remember, Barnes buried himself in family papers which he was trying to put into some order, for the Lacey muniment room had been neglected. It was a chilly evening and we sat in two new armchairs before a blazing fire, in what I suppose had once been the withdrawing-room behind the dining-hall and was now the library. I was re-reading *Guy Mannering* for the tenth time, and he had a pile of documents beside him on the floor from which he was making notes. He had another pile on an adjacent table, which he would often get up to consult, and he had a vast family tree opened out on another table to which he added pencil jottings. His occupation made him a restless companion, especially as he kept frowning and muttering to himself as if he were being constantly puzzled.

'What's shortness of breath?' he suddenly asked me.

'The thing we all die of,' I said.

'I know. But why should anyone want to set down that as the cause of death? It's foolish tautology – like saying a man died because he ceased to live.'

'Not worse than heart failure,' I said, 'and that's a common finding of the doctors.'

'No. Heart failure is a specific thing. It means that there is something organically wrong with the heart. But shortness of breath! Unless something like asthma is meant. But I don't see …'

'What have you got there?' I asked.

'I've been trying to find out what my forebears died of, the few who happened to die in their beds. And "shortness of bryth" spelled in twenty different ways, seems to have been their favourite affliction. It must mean some definite disease, like asthma or lung trouble. But I don't see how it could have been that either, for apparently it took them suddenly. Here is Giles Lacey, who was one of the strongest men of his time, and Henry VIII's favourite boon companion. He carries all before him in the tilt-yard in London, comes back here, and forthwith dies of shortness of breath. Don't tell me that a fellow who could clear the lists in plate armour that must have weighed a ton was a consumptive. His nephew Christopher was one of Raleigh's men, and a sun-dried, whipcord mariner. Same thing happened to him after he had ridden from Plymouth in thirty hours, which must have been a fairish achievement. Sir John Lacey came here after Naseby to hide, and was dead in two days of the same ailment. There's a funny sentence in his brother's letter about him. "Poor Jack," he says, "hath scaped the sword of the godly and the stranger to be the prey of his familiar devils." Now, what on earth did he mean by that?'

'It looks like some disease in the blood,' I said.

'It does,' he replied. 'But what could it be that carried off strong men without warning in the prime of their strength?'

I told him that there were very odd ailments in older days. 'Could it have been some pestilence that lingered in this valley?' I suggested. 'Or in this house?'

He was clear that it could not have been in the valley. The place, he said, was about the healthiest in England; he had made inquiries and there was never any legend of maladies in the village. He thought much the same about the house. 'It's stuffy, of course,' he said, 'like all very old buildings, but I had it carefully vetted, and there's not a hint of dry rot, and the water is perfectly pure. I daresay that in old days the absence of drains was appalling, but bad plumbing wouldn't kill a strong man in twenty-four hours. Besides, that would have meant a fever, and fever is never mentioned. Only shortness of breath.'

I asked what the later record had been, and was told that the Laceys had left Scaip shortly after the Restoration for Bartleham, in Norfolk, which had come to them by marriage. And that's also a queer thing,' he said. 'They were great sportsmen and mad about hunting and fowling. Bartleham was quite a little place till it was added to in the time of George III, and it lies in a dull unsporting county, whereas Scaip had everything that a sportsman could wish. But once they migrated they never returned here, except on a short visit, though they saw that it didn't fall into disrepair. They never let it, either – perhaps they couldn't find a tenant. Another thing – at Bartleham there seems to have been no more shortness of breath. They took to perishing of surfeits and apoplexies and paralytic strokes and such-like Christian diseases. I'd give a good deal to know what ailed them at Scaip.'

As I went to bed in my powdering-closet I puzzled a little over Barnes' tale and concluded that his ancestors had probably suffered from some form of congenital epilepsy. But what stuck in my memory were his words that afternoon at

Fanways, and I wondered in what kind of spirit my beloved Borrowby had been built. I had a sort of nightmare about it, for I saw myself on Borrowby lawn surrounded by a host of little men with trowels and mallets, horrid red-eyed fellows, who leered at me and sang 'Ho, the merry masons'.

Next day we motored over to Coldbrook to the local point-to-point. I had been keeping horses there and hunting regularly that winter, and had entered a mare for the Hunt Cup. I am not much of a performer over the sticks, and had ridden in few races except in the Bar Point-to-Point, but since I was settling in the neighbourhood I thought I might as well do the thing thoroughly. The course was an easy one, in good condition, and I was getting on nicely, till the second time round, at the second fence from the finish, I was cannoned into by a half-witted undergraduate. The consequence was a bad take-off, and a most hearty spill. I didn't quite roll clean, and got kicked by the mare just above my left eye.

As is usual in a concussion, I remembered nothing after the moment we lined up for the start. I was unconscious for about half an hour and came to myself in the kitchen of an adjacent farmhouse, where the local doctor was preparing to sew up the cut. It was deep, right down to the bone, but the skull was unharmed, and he promised me a good recovery if I would lie up for a week. Barnes was in a great fuss and wanted to get a nurse, but the doctor told him that the case was simple and that all I needed was quiet. 'Scaip's the very place for him,' he said. 'Thick walls and not a railway whistle or a motor-horn within hearing. He'll probably have a headache for twenty-four hours and then feel as fit as a fiddle. No. There's no dope for that kind of headache. He must grin and bear it.'

Barnes took me home at a snail's pace, and decided that I must have the new guest-room on the terrace, so as to avoid the steep stairs. So about six o'clock I found myself in a great four-post bed, with a fire crackling on the hearth, and the windows filled with the green April twilight. I was given a light dinner and told to go to sleep as soon as possible, since I must neither read nor talk. Barnes's butler, a man called Thistle, attended to me and, since there was no electric light at Scaip, he put matches and a couple of candlesticks on the bedside table. There was also an electric bell with its own battery. He informed me that he slept two storeys above me, but that Mr Lacey had experimented and that the bell could easily be heard in his room. The doctor was coming first thing in the morning, and his chief injunction was that I was to keep perfectly still.

My feeling, I remember, when he left me was one of great comfort and peace. I did not regret my accident, for I would have a few quiet days for reflection, and I had too few of such spells in my life. I lay for a little with both candles burning, watching a small corner of the ceiling, which was all I could see because of the bed curtains. The plastering was new and an admirable piece of work, but everything else in the room was hoar-ancient. The walls with their dark panelling were in gloom, broken only at one point by the glow of the fire. I had the fancy that the tiny bit of plaster moulding I could see was my one link with the familiar world, and that for the rest I had been snatched back into the deep comforting shadows of the past. It was what I hoped to achieve at Borrowby, and I blew out the light with a pleasant sense of bodily and spiritual well-being.

The doctor was wrong. I had no headache, but I had the most devastating dreams. I fell asleep at once, but it was not proper sleep for I seemed to remain half-conscious of my environment. I was having a long argument with a solicitor, one of my best clients, who insisted on keeping his face hidden. That I remember, for I had heard that he had shaved his beard and wanted to see what he looked like, but he obstinately evaded me. The place seemed to be my Temple chambers, but it was also Scaip, and at one end was the choir of the Fanways church. Presently I woke feeling outraged, for the solicitor was cocking snooks at me – I saw his hands and was exasperated because I could not see more of him.

I lay awake for a little, telling myself that this was the kind of thing I might expect after a concussion. My bodily comfort had gone, and I felt restless and rather hot. The fire had sunk to one red coal.

In my second dream there could be no doubt about the place. I was in the Scaip guest-room, and, though there was no light anywhere and the windows were shuttered, I could see it clearly. The bed had gone and also the furniture; the chamber was perfectly bare, and, what is more, it did not seem to be quite finished. There was a hole where the fireplace should have been, and above it, instead of panelling, a patch of wet mortar. I disliked the place intensely, disliked it and dreaded it in the irrational way one has in dreams. But at the same time I knew I was dreaming. Though I could not see myself I was aware that I was lying somewhere in the room. I was even aware that I had had an accident and must not move – otherwise I wanted to get up and go away.

And then, suddenly, I was aware of something else in the room, which I could feel, but could not see. It was somewhere near the hole which should have been the fireplace. My eyes, in the dream, saw nothing; but my mind received the impression of something menacing and horrible. I saw no movement, but all the same I was certain that the presence was advancing towards me. Terror awoke me, and I found my bandaged forehead damp with sweat.

I lit a candle with shaking fingers, and there was the corner of new plaster-work on the ceiling and all around the silent shadows. I was having an abominable night, and I had a childish longing to ring the bell merely for the sight of Thistle's honest features. But I resisted the impulse and forced myself to lie still on my back, while I repeated all the cheerful poetry I remembered. I went over the details of the library I was fitting up at Borrowby, and by and by I fell asleep again.

This time I had the worst nightmare of all. I was still in the room, but now I could see nothing whatsoever. Darkness, like thick black velvet, muffled the air. But I could hear, and what I heard was a faint tapping, like the sound of a mason's mallet. Steadily, rhythmically, it continued, and sometimes it was accompanied by a hollow sound, as if the worker was beating on the rim of some cavity. I had the impression that the space round me was becoming constricted; that if I stretched out my hands I might touch raw stone and wet mortar. This time I had no subconscious awareness that it was a dream. It seemed to me an awful reality, and I did not dare to put out an arm to make the test, for I believed that in a minute I should want all my strength to fight off a burden that would suffocate me ...

And then, in the dark, the lineaments of a face slowly took shape. I remember nothing about it except that it was the face of a human being in the last agonies. The mouth was open, the eyes protruding, the cheeks livid, the veins on the forehead black and swollen. It did not menace me, but it made me suffer with it. I felt a clutch at my throat and a ton's weight on my chest, and I awoke gasping.

I was terrified – I freely admit it – but I think my discomfort was more of body than of mind. For my difficulty in breathing did not end with the nightmare. I was lying broad awake, and I had the same horrible constriction of breath that I had had in my dreams. I lit a candle and decided that the trouble was the curtains of the four-poster and the heavy windows. Yet the bed-curtains had been looped up high, and I remembered that Thistle at my request had opened the upper part of the windows.

I had a struggle not to ring the bell. What prevented me was the thought that all this might be the result of my accident. I had never had a concussion before, and this one might be behaving according to form. That reflection did a good deal to lessen my fright, but it did not make my breath more comfortable. I seemed to be shut up in a chest, and was gasping like a fish out of water. The air I inhaled did not fill my lungs, and my heart was fluttering wildly, just like a man suffering from claustrophobia. But I took a pull on myself and managed to keep quiet till I became a little easier. I was resolved not to fall asleep, for I was in terror of seeing that livid, tortured face again.

But the upshot was that towards morning I did fall asleep and had no further dreams. I woke to find the candles burned down to their sockets, and Thistle undoing the curtains and letting in the light of the spring morning. He expressed the hope that I had had a good night, as he set my early tea beside me.

The doctor came after breakfast and was very displeased with me. He re-did my bandages and informed me that my temperature was up. 'What have you been doing with yourself?' he asked. 'No headache, you say? But you have got quite a lot of fever. How did you sleep?'

I told him that I had had the most infernal nightmares.

'That's odd,' he said. 'You're a strong man, suffering from nothing but a clean hole in your head and a slight concussion. Last night you were the perfect patient, and this morning you are all to bits. You haven't anything to worry you by any chance?'

When I told him that my conscience was clear, he answered that he would call in in the evening and, if necessary, give me a sedative. The temperature, he expected, would go down during the day.

It did, but I had a very disturbed time for all that. It was glorious weather, and through the open window came the spring scents and the sun, and the sound of birds and sheep. Barnes sat with me for most of the morning, and read me the newspaper. Thistle brought me admirable meals, at which I only pecked. The trouble was that I was wrestling with cowardice. I was in a blind funk of another night in that room, and longed to ask Barnes to move me back to my old powdering-closet, and at the same time I was heartily ashamed of myself.

I never spent a more miserable day. I was certain that I had no fever, and after luncheon I had a couple of hours of quiet sleep. Barnes had tea with me and complimented me on my obedience to doctor's orders. The doctor came about six and was better pleased with me. He was willing to give me some sort of mild dope, but I refused, for I had a notion that I mustn't sleep soundly, for if I did I might be caught by the gaping, agonised face.

The weather all day had been still and fine, but about twilight there came a brisk April shower. It stirred up all sorts of echoes in the old house. The wind sang in the chimney, and the raindrops pattered on the terrace and drifted against the window panes. To my ear there was a tune in the place, a jigging dance tune with an odd wild catch in it. Now, as you know, I am the most unmusical creature on God's earth, but I have a good memory for airs – the rudiments of them, for I get the details all wrong. You remember Summerfield, who was the great authority on old folk music and published several collections. Well, Summerfield used to play some of his discoveries to me on a flute or a penny whistle, and one took my fancy. When I asked about it he looked wise. 'That's witch music,' he said. 'I had the devil of a job to find it, and there are places in England and Wales even today where the old folk wouldn't let you even hum it. If you started it in a public house, the tap-room would empty. Heaven knows what antique devilry was at the making of it.'

Well, it seemed to me that I was hearing Summerfield's tune somewhere in the joists and the panelling. It had a good effect on me, for it made me ashamed of my babyishness. I told myself angrily that I was behaving like a fool, and the result was that I screwed up my resolution. Once for all I would put this nonsense outside my mind. When Thistle brought me my dinner I was quite cheerful, and told him that I was feeling better. But before he tucked me up for the night I bade him leave the curtains undrawn and open the windows at the bottom, though he protested that it was early April and the night might be chilly. I also bade him leave the door ajar which opened on to the terrace. The room was in a projecting buttress of the house, and the terrace door opened at the side into an alcove which was shielded from the wind, so there was no question of draughts. I gave these orders – at least, so I told myself – not because I was any longer nervous, but because I believed that somehow the place got unbearably stuffy during the night.

I lay for some time in a fairly comfortable mood, watching the fire which flickered in the light airs that blew from the windows, and the gently shaken curtains, and the window squares which were ebony dark before moonrise. Slowly, I must have drifted into sleep, and the first hour or two must have been peaceful. I know that from the timing of what happened later, for the moon did not rise till nearly midnight.

When I began to dream I was conscious only of a deep unhappiness. There was no fright in it, but the bottom seemed to have dropped out of everything and left an aching emptiness. I knew where I was – with my mind, for I saw nothing with my eyes. I was in Scaip, and Scaip was a shrine of the uttermost sorrow. I felt, so acutely that it seemed like ice in my veins, the misery of life. I am a cheerful being and never in my days had I known anything like it. Wave upon wave of abysmal distress seemed to flow over me and paralyse me.

And then a form of words began to run in my brain. I traced them afterwards – they were from one of Lord Rosebery's perorations about the Empire. 'Cemented with men's blood and tears' – a harmless platitude you will say. But, as they came to me out of the void, they were like a dreadful incantation. They sharpened my consciousness of my environment, for they were the voice of the walls that surrounded me. I knew I was in a place which had been built out of the heart of darkness. The mortar had been wet with tears and blood, and death had plied the mallets.

Suddenly, I seemed to be looking into a gulf of unimaginable evil. I say 'unimaginable', for it bore no relation to the world I knew. It was something that had rotted in the hoary past and on which God had mercifully shut the door. It was only an impression you understand – I remember no details, only the blank, heavy cloud of horror. Things had been wrought here – in these walls and in this room – which came from the nether Pit, things aeons removed from the common trivial wickedness of mankind. The weight of them suffocated my mind and senses, and, though my soul shuddered at them, my body and will were atrophied and I could only sink – sink.

I woke to find myself stifling. Not my mind, but my body. There was no weight on my chest, no clutch at my throat, but I simply could not breathe. Honest fear galvanised my impotence. I fumbled for the electric bell, and tried to press the button, but there was no strength in my fingers. I put my knuckles on it, but my fist seemed to have become as frail as gossamer.

I was now in the uttermost panic. Somehow or other I rolled out of bed, and lay gasping on the floor. The moon was up, and I saw the windows as squares of light. If I could reach them I might breathe free air.

I crawled towards an open sash – reached it – and found no comfort. Outside was the quiet moonlit night and a green hill with sheep on it. If I could clamber over the sill I knew I could breathe, but I was too weak for that. The terrible room had me in its clutches. It made a curtain of suffocation beyond which I could not penetrate, though only an inch or two separated me from freedom.

I felt that I was dying, that in a few seconds more I should be a corpse on the floor … There was a thin streak of moonlight at the terrace door which Thistle had left ajar. I struggled towards that, as a drowning man struggles towards a life-belt. Of that awful moment I have no clear memory, but I must have reached the door, for when Thistle opened it he found me at the threshold.

Yes, the bell had rung somehow, and Thistle says he skipped down at once. There cannot have been more than a few minutes between my waking and his finding me … They took me to the cottage hospital, for I couldn't have stayed in that house another hour. As it was, I was a sick man for most of the summer, not the concussion, which never troubled me, but an odd kind of low fever which puzzled the doctors.

※

'Explanation?' Leithen said, when he had finished his tale. 'You may take any you like, for I have none. You may say that it was the result of a crack on the head combined with a peculiar nervous system, though I've never considered myself neurotic. You may take Hurrell's view, that I was chosen by Providence to be the spark that fired some old devilry that was built into the walls of Scaip.'

'What became of Lacey?' Peckwether asked.

'Dead. He gave up Scaip in the same year as my story –
said the place did not suit his health – and went to live in
Cornwall. Scaip had no tenant till poor Thomasson leased it
last autumn. If I could prevent it, it wouldn't have another.'

Leithen answered the unspoken question in Hurrell's eye.

'Yes. I mean that. I went over there yesterday, as I've told
you Thomasson occupied the terrace room, the one I had. He
died in it. The doctor called it heart failure, which no doubt
it was in the end. But something came before – shortness of
breath.'

9 Roman Remains (1948)

ALGERNON BLACKWOOD

Anthony Breddle, airman, home on sick leave from India, does not feel himself called upon to give an opinion; he considers himself a recorder only. The phrase *credo quia impossibile* had never come his way; neither had Blake's dictum that 'everything possible to be believed is an image of truth.'

He was under thirty, intelligent enough, observant, a first-rate pilot, but with no special gifts or knowledge. A matter-of-fact kind of fellow, unequipped on the imaginative side, he was on his way to convalesce at his step-brother's remote place in the Welsh mountains. The brother, a much older man, was a retired surgeon, honoured for his outstanding work with a knighthood and now absorbed in research. The airman glanced again at the letter of invitation:

'... a lonely, desolate place, I'm afraid, with few neighbours, but good fishing which, I know, you adore. Wild little valleys run straight up into the mountains almost from the garden, you'll have to entertain yourself. I've got lots of fishing rods for you. Nora Ashwell, a cousin you've never met, a nurse, also on sick leave of sorts but shortly going back to her job, is dying for companionship of her own age. She likes fishing too. But my house isn't a hospital! And there's Dr Leidenheim, who was a student with me at Heidelberg ages ago, a delightful old friend. Had a Chair in Berlin, but got out just in time. His field is Roman Culture – lots of remains about here – but that's not your cup of tea, I know. Legends galore all over the place and superstitions you could cut with a knife. Queer things said to go on in a little glen called Goat Valley. But

175

that's not down your street either. Anyhow, come along and make the best of it; at least we have no bombing here …'

So Breddle knew what he was in for more or less, but was so relieved to get out of the London blitz with a chance of recovering his normal strength, that it didn't matter. Above all, he didn't want a flirtation, nor to hear about Roman remains from the Austrian refugee scholar.

It was certainly a desolate spot, but the house and grounds were delightful, and he lost no time in asking about the fishing. There was a trout stream, it seemed, and a bit of the Wye not too far away with some good salmon pools. At the moment, as rain had swollen the Wye, the trout stream was the thing to go for; and before an early bed that night he had made the acquaintance of the two others, Nora and Emil Leidenheim. He sized them up, as he called it: the latter a charming, old-fashioned man with considerable personality, cautious of speech, and no doubt very learned; but Nora, his cousin, by no means to his taste. Easy to look at certainly, with a kind of hard, wild beauty, pleasant enough too, if rather silent, yet with something about her he could not quite place beyond that it was distasteful. She struck him as unkempt, untidy, self-centered, careless as to what impression she made on her company, her mind and thoughts elsewhere all the time. She had been out walking that afternoon, yet came to their war-time supper still in shorts. A negligible matter, doubtless, though the three men had all done something by way of tidying up a bit. Her eyes and manner conveyed something he found baffling, as though she was always on the watch, listening, peering for something that was not there. Impersonal, too, as the devil. It seemed a foolish thing to say, but there was a hint in her atmosphere that made him uncomfortable, uneasy, almost gave him a touch of the creeps. The two older men, he fancied, left her rather alone.

Outwardly, at any rate, all went normally enough, and a fishing trip was arranged for the following morning.

'And I hope you'll bring back something for the table,' his brother commented, when she had gone up to bed. 'Nora has never yet brought back a single fish. God knows what she does with herself, but I doubt if she goes to the stream at all.' At which an enigmatic expression passed across Dr Leidenheim's face, though he did not speak.

'Where is this stream?' his brother asked. 'Up that Goat Valley you said was queer, or something. And what did you mean by "queer"?'

'Oh, no, not Goat Valley,' came the answer; 'and as for "queer", I didn't mean anything particular. Just that the superstitious locals avoid it even in the daytime. There's a bit of hysteria about, you know,' he added, 'these war days, especially in god-forsaken places like this –'

'God-forsaken is good,' Dr Leidenheim put in quietly, giving the airman an impression somehow that he could have said more but for his host's presence, while Breddle thought he would like to tap the old fellow's mind when he got the chance.

And it was with that stressed epithet in his ears that he went up to his comfortable bedroom. But before he fell asleep another impression registered as he lay on that indeterminate frontier between sleeping and waking. He carried it into sleep with him, though no dream followed. And it was this: there was something wrong in this house, something that did not emerge at first. It was concerned with the occupants, but it was due neither to his brother, nor to the Austrian archaeologist. It was due to that strange, wild girl. Before sleep took him, he defined it to himself: Nora was under close observation the whole time by both the older men. It was chiefly, however, Dr Leidenheim who watched her.

The following morning broke in such brilliant sunshine that fishing was out of the question; and when the airman got down to a late breakfast he was distinctly relieved to hear that Nora was already out of the house. She, too, knew that clear skies were no good for trout; she had left a verbal excuse and gone off by herself for a long walk. So Breddle announced that he would do the same. His choice was Goat Valley, he would take sandwiches and entertain himself. He got rough directions from Dr Leidenheim, who mentioned that the ruins of an ancient temple to the old god, Silvanus, at the end of the valley might interest him. 'And you'll have the place to yourself,' said his brother, laughingly, before disappearing into his sanctum, 'unless you run across one of the young monsters, the only living things apparently that ever go there.'

'Monsters! And what may you mean by that?'

It was Dr Leidenheim who explained the odd phrase.

'Nothing,' he said, 'nothing at all. Your brother's a surgeon, remember. He still uses the words of his student days. He wants to scare you.'

The other, finding him for once communicative, pressed him, if with poor results.

'Merely,' he said in his excellent English, 'that there have been one or two unpleasant births during these war years – in my language, *Missgeburt* we call them. Due to the collective hysteria of these strange natives probably.' He added under his breath, as if to himself, something about *Urmenschen* and *unheimlich*, though Breddle didn't know the words.

'Oh,' he exclaimed, catching his meaning 'that sort of thing, eh? I thought they were always put out of the way at birth or kept in glass bottles –'

'In my country, that is so, yes. They do not live.'

The airman laughed. 'It would take more than a *Missgeburt* to scare me,' he said, and dropped the unsavoury subject before the old archaeologist got into his stride about the temple to Silvanus and Roman remains in general. Later he regretted he had not asked a few other questions.

Now, Anthony Breddle must be known as what is called a brave man; he had the brand of courage that goes with total absence of imagination. He was a simple mind of the primitive order. Pictures passed through it which he grouped and regrouped, he drew inferences from them, but it is doubtful if he had ever really thought. As he entered the little valley, his mind worked as usual, automatically. Pictures of his brother and the Austrian flitted across it, both old men, idling through the evening of their day after reasonable success, the latter with a painful background of bitter sufferings under the Nazis. The chat about collective hysteria and the rest did not hold his interest. And Nora flitted through after them, a nurse maybe, but an odd fish assuredly, not his cup of tea in any case. Bit of a wild cat, he suspected, for all her quiet exterior in the house. If she lingered in his mind more vividly than the other two it was because of that notion of the night before – that she was under observation. She was, obviously, up to something, never bringing in a fish, for instance, that strange look in her eyes, the decided feeling of repulsion she stirred in him. Then her picture faded too. His emotions at the moment were of enjoyment and carefree happiness. The bright, sunny morning, the birds singing, the tiny stream pretending it was a noisy torrent, the fact that 'Operations' lay behind him and weeks of freedom lay ahead … which reminded him that he was, after all, convalescing from recent fevers, and that he was walking a bit too fast for his strength.

He dawdled more slowly up the little glen as the mountain-ash trees and silver birch thickened and the steep sides of the valley narrowed, passed the tumbled stones of the Silvanus temple without a glance of interest, and went on whistling happily to himself – then suddenly wondered how an echo of his whistling could reach him through the dense undergrowth. It was not an echo, he realized with a start. It was a different whistle. Someone else, not very far away, someone following him possibly, someone else, yes, was whistling. The realization disturbed him. He wanted, above all, to be alone. But, for all that, he listened with a certain pleasure, as he lay in a patch of sunshine, ate his lunch, and smoked, for the tune, now growing fainter, had an enticing lilt, a haunting cadence, though it never once entered his mind that it was possible a folk tune of sorts.

It died away; at any rate, he no longer heard it; he stretched out in the patch of warm sunshine, he dozed; probably, he dropped off to sleep …

Yes, he is certain he must really have slept, because when he opened his eyes he felt there had been an interval. He lay now in shadow, for the sun had moved. But something else had moved too while he was asleep. There was an alteration in his immediate landscape, restricted though that landscape was. The absurd notion then intruded that someone had been near him while he slept, watching him. It puzzled him; an uneasy emotion disturbed him.

He sat up with a start and looked about him. No wind stirred, not a leaf moved; nor was there any sound but the prattle of the little stream some distance away. A vague disquiet deepened in him. Then he cupped his ears to listen, for at this precise moment the whistling became audible again with the same queer, haunting lilt in it. And he stiffened. This stiffening, at any rate he recognized; this sudden tautening of the nerves he had experienced before when flying. He knew precisely that it came as a prelude to danger: it was the automatic preparation made by body and mind to meet danger; it was – fear.

But why fear in this smiling, innocent woodland? And that no hint of explanation came, made it worse. A nameless fear could not be met and dealt with; it could bring in its wake a worse thing – terror. But an unreasoning terror is an awful thing, and well he knew this. He caught a shiver running over him; and instinctively then he thought he would 'whistle to keep his courage up', only to find that he could not manage it. He was unable to control his lips. No sound issued, his lips were trembling, the flow of breath blocked. A kind of wheeze, however, did emerge, a faint pretence of whistling, and he realized to his horror that the other whistler answered it. Terror then swept in; and, trying feebly again, he managed a reply. Whereupon that other whistling piper moved closer in, and the distance between them was reduced. Yet, oh, what a ravishing and lovely lilt it was! Beyond all words he felt rapt and caught away. His heart, incredibly, seemed mastered. An unbelievable storm of energy swept through him.

He was brave, this young airman, as already mentioned, for he had faced death many times, but this amazing combination of terror and energy was something new. The sense of panic lay outside all previous experience. Genuine panic terror is a rare thing; its assault now came on him like a tornado. It seemed he must lose his head and run amok. And the whistler, the strange piper, came nearer, the distance between them again reduced. Energy and terror flooding his being simultaneously, he found relief in movement. He plunged recklessly through the dense undergrowth in the direction of the sound, conscious only of one overmastering impulse – that he must meet this piper face to face, while yet half unconsciously aware that at the same time he was also taking every precaution to move noiselessly, softly, quietly, so as not to be heard. This strange contradiction came back to memory long afterwards, hinting possibly at some remnant of resisting power that saved him from an unutterable disaster.

His reward was the last thing in the world he anticipated.

That he was in an abnormal condition utterly beyond his comprehension there can be no doubt; but that what he now witnessed registered with complete and positive clarity lay beyond all question. A figure caught his eye through the screen of leaves, a moving – more – a dancing figure, as he stood stock still and stared at – Nora Ashwell. She was perhaps a dozen yards away, obviously unaware of his presence, her clothes in such disorder that she seemed half naked, hatless, with flowers in her loosened hair, her face radiant, arms and legs gesticulating in a wild dance, her body flung from side to side, but gracefully, a pipe of sorts in one hand that at moments went to her lips to blow the now familiar air. She was moving in the direction away from where he stood concealed, but he saw enough to realize that he was watching a young girl in what is known as ecstasy, an ecstasy of love.

He stood motionless, staring at the amazing spectacle: a girl beside herself with love; love, yes, assuredly, but not of the kind his life had so far known about; a lover certainly – the banal explanation of her conduct flashed through his bewilderment – but not a lover of ordinary sort. And, as he stared, afraid to move a step, he was aware that this flood of energy, this lust for intense living that drove her, was at work in him too. The frontiers of his normal self, his ordinary world, were trembling; any moment there might come collapse and he, too, would run amok with panic joy and terror. He watched as the figure disappeared behind denser foliage, faded then was gone, and that he stood there alone dominated suddenly by one overmastering purpose – that he must escape from this awful, yet enticing valley, before it was too late.

How he contrived it he hardly remembers; it was in literal panic that he raced and stumbled along, driven by a sense of terror wholly new to all his experience. There was no feeling of being followed, nor of any definite threat of a personal kind; he was conscious more of some power, as of the animal kingdom, primitive, powerful, menacing, that assaulted his status as a human being ... a panic, indeed, of pagan origin.

He reached the house towards sunset. There was an interval of struggle to return to his normal self, during which, he thanked heaven, he met no member of the household. At supper, indeed, things seemed as usual ... he asked and answered questions about his expedition without hesitation, if aware all the time, perhaps, that Dr Leidenheim observed him somewhat closely, as he observed Nora too. For Nora, equally, seemed her usual, silent self, beyond that her eyes, shining like stars, somehow lent a touch of radiance to her being.

She spoke little; she never betrayed herself. And it was only when, later, Breddle found himself alone with Dr Leidenheim for a moment before bedtime, that the urgent feeling that he must tell someone about his experiences persuaded him to give a stammering account. He could not talk to his brother, but to a stranger it was just possible. And it brought a measure of relief, though Leidenheim was laconic and even mysterious in his comments.

'Ah, yes ... yes ... interesting, of course, and – er – most unusual. The combination of that irresistible lust for life, yes, and – and the unreasoning terror. It was always considered extremely powerful and – equally dangerous, of course. Your present condition – convalescing, I mean – made you specially accessible, no doubt ...'

But the airman could not follow this kind of talk; after listening for a bit, he made to go up to bed, too exhausted to think about it.

It was about three o'clock in the morning when things began to happen and the first air raid of the war came to the hitherto immune neighbourhood. It was the night the Germans attacked Liverpool. A pilot, scared possibly by the barrage, or chased by a Spitfire and anxious to get rid of his bombs, dropped them before returning home, some of them evidently in the direction of Goat Valley. The three men, gathered in the hall, counted the bursts and estimated a stick had fallen up that way somewhere; and it was while discussing this that the absence of Nora Ashwell was first noticed. It was Dr Leidenheim, after a whispered exchange with his host, who went quickly up to her bedroom, and getting no answer to their summons, burst open the locked door to find the room empty. The bed had not been slept in; a sofa had been dragged to the open window where a rope of knotted sheets hung down to the lawn below. The two brothers hurried out of the house at once, joined after a slight delay by Dr Leidenheim who had brought a couple of spades with him but made no comment by way of explaining why he did so. He handed one to the airman without a word. Under the breaking dawn of another brilliant day, the three men followed the line of craters made by the stick of bombs towards Goat Valley, as they had surmised. Dr Leidenheim led them by the shortest way, having so often visited the Silvanus temple ruins; and some hundred yards further on the grey morning light soon showed them what was left of Nora Ashwell, blasted almost beyond recognition. They found something else as well, dead but hardly at all injured.

'It should – it *must* be buried,' whispered Dr Leidenheim, and started to dig a hole, signing to the airman to help him with the second spade.

'Burnt first, I think,' said the surgeon

And they all agreed. The airman, as he collected wood and helped dig the hole, felt slightly sick. The sun was up when they reached the house, invaded the still deserted kitchen and made coffee. There were duties to be attended to presently, but there was little talk, and the surgeon soon retired to his study sofa for a nap.

'Come to my room a moment, if you will,' Dr Leidenheim proposed to the young airman. 'There's something I'd like to read to you; it would perhaps interest you.'

Up in the room he took a book from his shelves. 'The travels and observations of an old Greek,' he explained, 'notes of things he witnessed in his wanderings. Pausanias, you know. I'll translate an incident he mentions.'

It is said that one of these beings was brought to Sylla as that General returned from Thessaly. The monster had been surprised asleep in a cave. But his voice was inarticulate. When brought into the presence of Sylla, the Roman General, he was so disgusted that he ordered it to be instantly removed. The monster answered in every degree to the description which poets and painters have given of it.

'Oh, yes,' said the airman. 'And – er – what was it supposed to be, this monster?'

'A Satyr, of course, 'replied Dr Leidenheim, as he replaced the volume without further comment except the muttered words, 'One of the retinue of Pan.'

10 Cracks of Time (1948)

DOROTHY QUICK

It was when the cocktail party I was giving for Myra was at its height that I first saw the face.

I had been listening to the one hundred and fourth 'But my dear, your engagement was such a surprise – You know you have all my best wishes – Now I want to congratulate the lucky man,' and wondering how Myra ever found the right words to reply. Marvelling, too, at the ease with which she did so, and passed the people on to Henley, who managed them equally well. They were a good pair, my younger sister Myra and Henley Bradford. They'd have a happy marriage.

It was to hide the rush of tears to my eyes that I looked down, and saw the face. The sun room's floor was done with tiles Jason and I had brought from Spain while on our honeymoon – when we had been happy. They were a sea green-blue, some with geometric designs, some perfectly plain, their only ornamentation the patina of the glazing and the dark lines, or cracks, which time had given them. In this particular tile that caught my eyes the cracks had patterned a face. It was only a vague outline, the profile of a man with full, thick lips – sensuous lips, slanted eyes, and a forehead from which the hair rose up into a point that looked like a horn. There was nothing more that was definite. The rest was blurred and vague, like some modern, impressionistic picture, of the shadowy school which suggests its subject, rather than portrays it.

I was about to call out and tell the crowd what I'd discovered. I thought I'd make a game of it, because, in a way, it was like 'statues', or finding shapes in clouds. The words 'See what I've found!' were actually on my lips when the eye of the face looked a warning from under its slanting lid, and then the lid came down, covering the eye.

It was a trick of lighting, of course. The face was in profile and the eye was open. The shadow of someone's foot in passing must have made the effect of the lid closing. The eye looking at me in warning was imagination plus several cocktails. But what I had been going to say was still-born. I didn't mention the profile but kept looking at it as the afternoon progressed, and it seemed to me that the face became clearer and more sharply etched. I began thinking it resembled the ancient sculptures of Pan.

By the time the guests had drunk themselves into a state of hilarity I had forgotten the face. I didn't notice it again until Jason came over to me and, in a rare mood of affection, put his arm around my shoulder. 'Sheila,' he whispered in a voice liquor had thickened, 'you're the best-looking girl here. Why don't we kiss and make up?'

I knew he wouldn't have said that, sober, I also knew that our quarrelling had gone beyond the point where we could follow his suggestion. Jason's charms were legion but so was his drinking and the other women that went with it. I had out-forgiven myself – there just wasn't any more of that virtue left in me. Still, perhaps I should try once more. Maybe it wouldn't be right to reject this offer.

It was then I looked down and the face was moving from side to side, obviously saying 'no' to my charitable inclinations. 'No, no, no!' I caught myself up sharp. This was ridiculous; I was letting my imagination run away with me. The afternoon shadows were tricky things and I certainly couldn't let shifting light betray my better impulses.

So, when Jason repeated his question, kissing the place behind my ear that he called his, I said 'Yes, Jason.'

It seemed to me then that the one eye of the face completely closed and that I saw a tear trickle down the high-boned cheek. It was ridiculous but that's the impression I received.

'Hi, folks,' Jason was calling, as he swirled me around in a wild dance. 'Let's have another round. I'm celebrating the fact I've got the loveliest wife in the world, the kindest, the sweetest –'

I didn't hear the rest of the adjectives. My handkerchief had dropped during the turns we'd made. As Jason talked I bent down for it. The tiny square of white had fallen over the face. When I picked it up, it was wet. Liquor? Something spilled from a cocktail? That's what I thought, but when I lifted it to my nose there was no alcoholic odour. I touched it to my lips, the tip end of my tongue, and there, was the bitter salt taste of tears.

And I had seen a tear roll down the face! Incredible, but in my mouth was the tang of a man's tears. I looked down. The face *was* much clearer; the back of the head was completely filled in, with the hair clustered on it dark and curly. The eye was open now and it had acquired depth and perspective. It looked down at me with admiration and a kind of pathetic appeal. The full lips trembled. It was as though they were calling out for me to lean over and touch them.

So strong was the illusion that in another moment I might have done so, but Jason came back just then with two cocktails. 'Here you are, darling.' He handed one to me.

I took it, and he encircled me with his arm. 'Sweet, let's drink to us!' He was very tight, but his charm was in the ascendancy. I drank with him and forgot about the face.

The reconciliation proved very absorbing. Not since our honeymoon and the first year of our married life had Jason been so completely devoted. It was as though the five miserable years through which we had quarrelled had not existed. We were suddenly back, continuing the first twelve months of our felicity. I had fully intended to examine the tile with the face most carefully, the next day, when there would be no feet to cast shadows, no liquor to give ideas. But as it happened it was over a week before I went in the sun porch.

To begin with, there was the new devoted Jason, a round of parties for Myra, and days of rainy weather, which always put the desirability of the sun porch at low ebb.

The cocktail party had been on a Saturday. It was exactly ten days later – Tuesday, to be definite – that the sun shone so brightly I said I'd have my lunch in the sun room. I had completely forgotten the face by then.

But once seated on the red bamboo chair with my lunch tray on a matching table before me, the face obtruded itself into my vision. It was slightly to my right and not as much *en profile* as I'd thought. It was more three-quarter; there was a glimpse of the other cheek, more than a suggestion of the other eye. The original one looked at me reproachfully.

I caught my breath. The effect was really amazing. Since I'd seen it the face had gained dimensions too. There was depth and thickness to it now, and it was larger – the hair had spread over to the next tile. I leaned over and examined the lines – the cracks of time. They were deep, almost fissure-like, quite outstanding against the blue-green glaze. It was almost as though some artist had made a sketch freehand of Pan, before the tiles went to the kiln, and it had lain under the glaze for years until time and wear had brought it back to the surface. I had no hesitancy about knowing it was meant to be Pan; the little forehead horns were very clear now, and the full, sensuous lips could have belonged to none other. Pan in the deep wood, admiring a dryad, with all the connotations of a satyr.

I wasn't particularly interested in my lunch but I went on eating it automatically, watching the face as I did so, surprised to see the reproach melt away to admiration, then longing, and finally desire undisguised.

189

At that point I caught myself up sharply. 'Sheila, you're being ridiculous,' I said aloud.

Johnson, the maid, appeared in the doorway. 'Did you call?' she asked.

'No.' I was amused. She'd heard me talking to myself. 'But now you're here, you can take the tray. I'll just keep my tea.'

When she came over I pointed down to the tile. 'Look, Johnson. Don't you think it's funny the way those lines on that tile make a face?'

She peered down and then drew back. 'It is, indeed, Madame, a strange face – not quite human, although it's not very clear, is it?'

The outlines weren't vague to me now but they had been when I had first seen them. Suddenly there was a voice in my ear. 'You have tasted the salt of my tears; that is why you see more clearly.'

The tea cup I had been holding crashed to the floor, the china ringing hard against the tiles as it shattered into bits. I found control of myself quickly. 'Oh, Johnson, I am sorry. It just slipped out of my hands.'

'And your good china, too,' she sighed. 'I'll clean up, Madame, and give that tile a bit of an extra rub, too. Maybe we'll be able to wipe that ugly face out.'

But I knew she'd never be able to erase it from my mind.

Or the floor, either!

In fact, her efforts only made it more distinct to me, although she seemed to think she had obliterated some of it.

When she had finished and gone, I sat there trying to figure it out. There *was* an outline of a face on the tile. Johnson saw it, so it wasn't entirely imagination. She wasn't educated enough to know about Pan; if she had been, she too would have seen the resemblance. So I wasn't completely off track. There was a face. It was inhuman, but there actuality stopped. The rest had to be imagination. The cracks of time could make a face but they couldn't make it weep or speak. That had been my own mind, and, yet what it had said made sense in a way: 'you have tasted the salt of my tears; that is why you see more clearly.'

There was a fairy tale I remembered from my youth and Andrew Lang's coloured fairy books. It was called 'Elves' Ointment' as I recollect, and it was the story of a midwife brought to attend the birth of an elf. Given ointment to put on the new baby's eyes she had inadvertently gotten some on her own, and had seen everything differently thereafter – that is, until the elves caught on and took her new sight away from her, with quite tragic results, as I remembered.

But the analogy held. I looked at the face again. The full lips were parted. I could almost feel the hot quickened breath on my nearby ankle.

This was getting beyond sense. I was making myself see things that couldn't be, hear a voice, feel emotions that should be kept under cover. It was incredible; yet it was so real! It was uncanny. It made me a little afraid.

I decided I would go up to the attic and see if there were any left over tiles and if there were, I'd have this one, with its cracks of time, removed as quickly as possible.

'Of course,' I told myself sternly, 'it's only because you've been emotionally stirred up these past days. What with Myra's engagement and Jason, no wonder you're full of imaginings.'

Then I heard the voice again, an ageless voice, thin and reedy, yet with a curious appeal. 'Don't fight me. Just listen to my music.'

The music was soft at first, fleeting into my brain with gently vibrating notes. From its first sound I didn't think any more. I couldn't. I could only listen to something indefinably lovely music that soothed and made me know that nothing apart from it really mattered. It held the essence of life.

Suddenly it changed and became little tongues of flame licking around me, touching me here and there like caressing winds. Then there were waves of sound that vibrated through my entire being. And it seemed as though all the magic there had ever been was in them, weaving itself around me until I was a part of it, and I knew that nothing so lovely had ever happened to me before. I was suddenly a part of nature. Soon all its secrets would be known to me, and –

Jason's voice: 'Hi, Shelley, where are you?' came from the living room, driving the music away. I didn't answer. I didn't want Jason to find me. I wanted the music back again. I wanted to lose myself in it.

'Shelley.' Jason was calling. 'Shelley.' His pet name for me, part nickname for Sheila and partly made up from my admiration for the poet.

I looked down at the face. There was a finger touching the lips, as though to enjoin silence. Another crack of time, but it looked like a finger and its meaning was plain: the music was to be our secret, there was no mistaking that. And I wasn't imagining it. There *was* a finger on the thick lips.

For a minute I thought of them touching mine, and I knew that was what I wanted most in the world – that, and the music.

'Soon. It will be soon.' The thin, reedy voice was like the notes of a pipe, coming from far-off enchanted places. A pipe. Pan's pipe.

Then Jason was in the room, exclaiming: 'What the –! Why didn't you answer me? Didn't you hear me call?'

'No. I – I guess I was half asleep.'

He leaned over and kissed me. There was warmth in his kiss but it left me cold. The wonderful music had deadened my senses to everything but its own magnificence, and Pan's, the god who had called it to being.

I looked down at the tile. The finger was no longer against the full lips. Instead, they were forming a word, 'Wait.' It was as plain to see as though I had studied lipreading.

Jason's eyes followed mine. 'Hello! Look at that cracked tile. We'll have to change that. You know, those cracks make a face, a horrible, repulsive face that gives me the shivers. I'll go to the attic tomorrow and fish out another tile and get rid of that face on the bar room floor.'

Against my will I laughed. Against the hurt look in Pan's eyes. But suddenly the expression changed to one of cunning, combined with determination.

Words came to my lips. Without any volition of my own I found myself saying, 'There's a piece of broken china still there. I broke a cup.'

Jason bent down, picked up the piece of the tea cup the maid had overlooked, which I hadn't even known was there. He swore softly and shook a few drops of blood from his finger. Aghast, I watched the full lips catch them, suck them in.

'Jason,' I cried. 'You're hurt!'

He laughed. 'Don't look so horrified; it's only a small cut.' Again he shook off a few drops of blood, which the mouth on the floor caught.

I shivered. There was something so horrible about the mouth and the blood that I forgot the music.

'Come on.' Jason caught me up. 'I'll let you put a band-aid on it and then we're stepping out. The Crawleys are waiting for us at Agello's.'

Agello's was our local '21'. Going there was always an event. I was quite excited. There in the bright lights, with the gay music, I could forget the face and the silly things it provoked me into imagining.

I thought that, and I was happy, looking forward to fun at Agello's with Jason and the Crawleys, a couple we both liked tremendously. I was quite elated. Jason had his arm around me and it felt fine – warm and vibrant.

But as we left the porch I saw the face again. The lips had colour, and they formed a word, 'Soon.' And as we left, an echo of the thin, fluting pipes sounded in my ear.

At Agello's I managed to forget. I had to forget, otherwise I would begin to think I was going mad. The face on the floor was genuine enough; Jason and the maid had both seen it. They had sensed evil. The maid had said it was inhuman, Jason that it was repulsive. So the face was all actuality. The rest had to be an overworked imagination, and I didn't like the implications of that. I made up my mind there on the crowded floor dancing with Jason that I'd help him find another tile and get rid of the one with the cracks of time as quickly as possible. After that, I proceeded to enjoy the evening.

It was late when we left Agello's. Once we were home, Jason didn't give me time to think. It was like our honeymoon all over again, and I was glad of that.

The next day was Sunday. Sunday was the day we usually had breakfast on the sun porch in our pajamas. In the light of day I wasn't worried about the face, but it was comfortable in our room. 'Let's be sissies,' I said, 'and have breakfast in bed.'

'Lazy.' Jason laughed. 'But it's too nice a day to be on the north side of the house. No, Shelley, we're going to bask in the sunlight. And just to pamper you, I'm going to carry you thither.' He leaned over the bed and gathered me into his arms.

'This is fun,' I grinned, 'but in the interests of modesty you'd better let me have a negligée.'

He held me down so I could retrieve my blue crepe housecoat from the foot of the bed. I clutched it to me, and we were ready.

On our way, Jason paused a minute before the mirror set into my closet door. 'See what a pretty picture you make,' he whispered in my ear. 'You're like a slim dryad of the woods, and I –' he squared his massive shoulders and I felt the muscles of his chest hard against me '– am Pan.'

There wasn't any music – no thin fluting or wondrous tones; only a resentment and a feeling of instinctive recoil – as though anyone could be Pan but the face. I made myself look in the mirror. Just as we were we might have posed for a calendar picture of a dryad being abducted by a satyr – not Pan. Jason's face was lascivious enough but there was no suggestion of the god in him. He was of the earth.

I, in my white satin nightie had a classic look, for the satin moulded my form and was a startling contrast to my red-gold hair.

Jason, in blue foulard pajamas, looked like an advertisment straight out of *Esquire*. Direct physiological appeal. But I knew instinctively that within him there were no nuances, none of the subtle approach, that is so dear to a woman's heart. His was not the knowledge that Pan possessed.

It was at that moment I heard the music – the faint, thin piping that shivered against my nerves and made them vibrate to its tune, music that grew louder even as I listened.

Jason started towards the door.

The music was calling to me. Calling to me to come, to give myself up to it completely.

Suddenly I was afraid. Jason was very dear, human and near. I clung to him. 'Don't go downstairs,' I begged. 'Let's stay here.' I tried to put allure into my voice. Anything to keep him here where it was safe, where I could shut the door and drown out the music that attracted me, as something evil that is yet beautiful can always do.

Jason's mind was one track. 'Breakfast first, darling.' He walked on, and the music swelled in tone. It was making me forget everything but my desire for it – and Pan, for the two were inescapably one.

Still I tried to hold to reality. 'Do you hear music?' I asked Jason, as he descended the stairway.

'Music? Lord, no! But I do hear a vibration like the jangling note of a wire that's off-key. After breakfast we'll look for it.'

'There may not be time.' The words said themselves.

'We've got all day, darling.' He was at the bottom of the steps, advancing to the living room. The music was becoming more and more pronounced. Like Wagner's fire music, little tongues of flame licking about me, growing larger and stronger.

I knew they were waiting to envelope me. I made a last effort. 'Jason, we musn't go to the sun room. There's something there – something –' 'Evil' was what I'd meant to say but the word was still-born on my lips. The music had taken possession of me. I was encased in it as surely as Brunehilde ever was on her fire-ringed mountain. Little flames of music were licking about me.

Then we were in the sun room and Jason put me down.

My wrapping the negligée around me was mechanical, and wasted, for Pan's eyes looked through the material, yes, through the skin, into my very soul. He was complete now, a full-grown figure, and even as I watched he rose from the blue-green tiles, wholly dimensional. His boring eyes held mine and the music was like a flowing river of fire, touching me, everywhere.

'So, you have answered my pipings?' It was as though he were singing.

'Yes,' I replied, 'And now that I am here?'

'Shelley, what are you talking about?' Jason's voice was impatient.

The music diminished. 'Didn't you hear?' I began.

'Wait.' Pan's voice was thunder-clear.

Suddenly arrested, I stood still. But my gaze betrayed me.

'What is it?' Jason asked. Then, when I made no reply, he became insistent. '*What is it?* What do you hear?'

That caught me up short with surprise. It didn't seem possible that he didn't hear that glorious, engrossing, enveloping music. I found words. 'But you must hear the music. It's so wonderful. And you must see –'

I looked at Pan. He was regarding me strangely and shaking his head.

I stopped short. Jason followed my gaze. 'It's that darn tile. You've been acting peculiarly ever since you saw those cracks. I'm going to dig it out.'

'No,' I cried. 'No, Jason, let it alone. There's danger!' I don't know how, I knew there was danger for Jason, perhaps it was the expression in Pan's eyes. But how, or why I knew Jason went in peril? And at that moment the urgency was upon me to save him.

'Don't be foolish, Shelley. How could there be danger in a tile – a cracked tile, at that?'

'But he's larger than you.' I was struggling against Pan and the music now, trying to save Jason from something intangible, some danger I sensed but couldn't rightly name. I was afraid, and yet, what did Jason – anything – matter, against the vibrant music that was swelling around me?

'Sheila!' Jason exclaimed. 'I think you must have a hangover – seeing things. A hangover, or be mad. That tile has bewitched you. I'm getting rid of it now – this second.'

He went to an old sea chest where he kept tools and things. He opened it and took out a hunting knife.

I could see Pan's triumphant smile.

'No, Jason, no!' I shrieked, and then the music was so loud, so beautiful, that I couldn't think of anything else. I was completely lost to the music, hypnotized as any snake by a master piper, enveloped by melody which was part of Pan.

As in a dream I saw Jason advance toward the tile, knife in hand. I saw Pan moving towards him.

The music accelerated. For one desperate moment I came to my senses. 'Jason, come away!' I screamed, and rushed to him.

Pan was before me. With one hand he thrust me back; with the other he turned Jason's arm with the knife inward, so that the knife was toward Jason's body. I saw the blue tile gleaming, crackless and pure, just like the others. Pan had left it. He had materialized. Just as I realized this, Pan pushed Jason. My husband fell, and as he did so, impaled himself on his own knife as surely as any ancient Roman running himself through with his sword.

There was a funny gurgling noise. Then Jason rolled over on his back. I knew the danger had struck. Jason was dead.

But Pan was alive!

Alive and wholly man, and the music too was a living, throbbing thing, marvellous beyond human knowing, enveloping me until I was part of it.

The wonder of the music was completely mine now. It swept me forward, into Pan's arms.

I don't mind being in prison – or the fact that I am on trial for my life, charged with the murder of my husband. I don't even care that they are saying I am mad, perhaps because I know that if I told them the truth they would be certain of it.

I don't mind being confined in this horrible cell, or any of the rest of it. I don't mind, because the cracks of time opened for me, and now the wonderful music is always in my ears, and the remembrance of Pan's kisses on my lips.

And the certainty that at the end I shall feel them again!

11 Whitewash (1952)

ROSE MACAULAY

The sea as it swung gently against the rocks was jade green, like the evening sky. I was reclining on thymy turf, reading *The Story of San Michele*. Six feet down in the sea my aunt was scrambling among broken marble wreckage that had been once an imperial bath. When she surfaced I looked up from Dr Axel Münthe and said, 'It's nice to know what an excellent man Tiberius actually was, after all one was brought up to think of him'.

My aunt coughed up water and turned on her back to float.

'I know nothing of the sort,' she said. 'I would rather believe his contemporaries than these modern whitewashers. And I have the islanders with me, to a man, woman and child.'

'Naturally,' I agreed. 'Timberio is their local industry. If he lost his wickedness, he would have nothing but a few ruined villas and baths and a rock up there by the Fato from which no one was ever thrown. What use would visitors have for a beneficent old gentleman who retired here to flee the corrupt world and commune with his soul? Suetonius and Tacitus and all the legend-makers since are the local Bible. But they are wrong. Timberio has been cleared, and I am delighted that all these villas and baths were used by so saintly an emperor.'

'One after another,' said my aunt, 'they take them from us. Nero. Tiberius. The Borgias. King John. Richard III. Are we to be deprived of all the monsters of the past? Are they all to be of the present? And how long will it be before our contemporary monsters have the whitewash buckets poured over them and emerge saints, or victims of circumstance, more sinned against than sinning? Most of us are more sinning than sinned against; why should monsters be exceptions?'

I made no effort to convert my aunt on this subject. She required monsters, and, so far as I was concerned, could have them.

'I shall go exploring some of the caves,' I said. 'Will you come?'

'Not I,' said my aunt. 'When one thinks what went on in them,' she added primly, as she climbed out of the sea. 'I am going back to the villa. Dinner at nine.'

'I'll be back,' I said.

My aunt draped herself in her scarlet bernous and set off up the steep rock stairway that would conduct her in the end to the villa. I dropped into the warm twilight sea again, and swam round the next jut of rock. Above me the island sloped down to the sea, smelling of pine and thyme and cistus and the stored heat of the August day. Below me lay Roman villas and baths that had slipped long since into the waves and got drowned. I had explored these remains often enough; what I now wanted was a cave. There was one a little further on. I swam into it; it was a deep cave, thrusting far back into the rock. Round it, just above sea level, ran a broad ledge, slippery and green with seaweed. I hoisted myself on to it and walked along it. It was almost dark inside the cave. But, after walking a few yards, I felt a draught on my right, and saw a good-sized round opening in the rock. I remembered tales told by the locals of passages that climbed up from caves to one or another of Timberio's villas. Perhaps this one did so. I entered it, meaning to explore it for a little way. It sloped gently up, and was about the height of my shoulders. But I did not get far; a cold wind suddenly came against me like a hand on my chest, pushing me back. It struck me that I would rather explore that passage by day, and that I was inexplicably shivering,

and had better get out of the cave and go home. In a few
moments I was back on the slippery ledge; the little waves
were lapping against the rock with a sound like whispering
voices – or was it sharp, frightened gasps? A frightened
crowd, it sounded like; a collection of people scared out of
their wits. I slipped down into the water, which had become
colder, and swam towards the cave's mouth. Outside was the
green evening sky, the green evening sea. At the entrance
I felt, oddly, as if a strong tide were running against me; I
swam, but made no progress; in fact, I was being pushed
back. But there was no tide, and the sea was calm. I struck
out harder, and was pushed back further. I began to panic.
What current was driving with such force into the cave
that I could not swim against it? I remembered nightmare
battles with Cornish tides that, swim as I would, carried
me out to sea, the landmarks slipping from me in a losing
race. I had been rescued by boats. There was no boat now,
and I could not get out. I was growing tired; I was not a
strong swimmer. Suppose I had to spend the night on that
slippery, slimy ledge, among that whispering, frightened
chatter? And would the sea rise? The Mediterranean is
not quite tideless. I went on struggling; for a moment it
seemed to me that I made headway. Then, looking up, I saw
a dark shape, floating quietly just outside the cave's mouth;
it was just under the surface but for a sharp, sail-shaped
fin; it seemed to wait, rolling to and fro, in no hurry, but
just waiting. That decided me; I retreated into the cave and
climbed on to the ledge. I was shaking so much that I could
scarcely make it. If the shark should enter the cave, I would
climb into the passage.

I sat on the cold ledge, huddled up, my arms round my
knees. It seemed to me that the chattering and whispering
of the sea slapping against the rocky wall was louder, quicker,
more verbal. The atmosphere in the cave was tense; it was

sheer terror. It caught me like a wave, drowning me in cold panic. I have never known fear so intense, such submerging anguish.

Then, above the whispered clamour, rose a soft, jeering voice from the passage behind me. It said, '*Veni, cete, veni*'. The next moment the cave mouth darkened; the great white shark drove in with a noise of rushing water. I saw its white belly and its row of terrible teeth. I did not wait; I plunged head first into the passage in the rock.

Then something more than a wind drove against me; it was as if some other strength met mine, pushing me back. I gripped a jut of rock with both hands; my feet were tensed against the side wall of the passage. I looked into the darkness of the corridor that wound ahead; suddenly on it there hung palely, as in phosphorescent light, a head and face I knew: I had seen it on coins, in busts, in reliefs. A handsome, sneering face, its lips curled now in a sensual smile. From them came a rich, pleased chuckling. And from the cave behind me came a snapping of jaws and a thin screaming, and splash after splash, as if things were being dragged down from the ledge into the water. At each splash came the low chuckling.

I was being pushed, but half-heartedly, as if the pusher's attention were concentrated elsewhere; or as if there were no real bodily contact. I held on to my position with hands and feet; I was not really much afraid of losing it, for I was alive, and the pusher had been dead for close on two thousand years, and what physical force can the dead and the living exert over one another? My terror was of the scene behind me; the thin screams, the snapping jaws, the splashing ... And of the leering phosphorescent face hanging in the dark rock corridor in front of me; and of that enjoying chuckle. I shut my eyes, but could not stop my ears.

I do not know how long the ghastly scene lasted. But before very long I realised that there was silence in the cave, but for a heavy, gorged, wallowing sound. Then the drawling voice said 'Abi, cete, abi hinc'; and the heavy shape seemed to flounder through the water, out of the cave into the sea beyond.

I opened my eyes. The face was gone. I seemed quite alone; the soft slap-slap of water against rock was no longer like whispering voices. I slithered down on to the ledge, staring in horror at the deep green water below me, now silvered by the first long shafts of rising moon. I don't know what I feared to see in it – mangled limbs, ripples running red ... but there was only green sea water touched with silver. All the same I did not get into it; I followed the ledge round to the cave's mouth, and peered warily out. No dark shape was in sight; no fin. I knew I was alone.

I slipped into the moon-struck sea and swam round the jut of rock to the place where we had bathed among the ruins of the Roman bath. My bathing wrap lay there. Putting it over my shivering body, I was back in the twentieth century. The tension slackened; I lay limply on the rocks and was sick.

What time it was I had no idea. Getting up, I saw *The Story of San Michele* lying open where I had put it down; I picked it up and climbed the path up the hill.

I came in through the open French window; my aunt lay smoking in a long chair.

'So there you are at last,' she said. 'I've kept your dinner for you. Do you know,' she added reflectively, 'I was beginning to fear that Timberio had got you after all.'

'I began to think so too,' I told her. 'And you will be glad to know that Suetonius and Tacitus and the locals are all perfectly right about him, and that Dr Münthe and Norman and the other whitewashers are perfectly wrong; they haven't the faintest idea what they are talking about.'

'No,' my aunt tranquilly agreed. 'Whitewashers never have. Evil does exist, and monsters have always been monsters. Nero,

Tiberius, the Borgias, Richard III, John, our contemporary tyrants ... I believe in them all.'

'Or,' I asked myself presently, when warmed and clothed and fed, 'can I have had some kind of a fit? I shall tell Norman about it tomorrow, and ask what he thinks.'

I met Norman in his favourite piazza café next morning. Though the most patriotic of islanders, he told me that I had been the victim of an erroneous mass mythology. For Timberio had been a most excellent man, kind of heart and temperate of habit.

'Only,' he added, re-filling his three glasses, 'you've hardly begun yet. Timberio, according to the Capraeans, could do much better than that. You must try some of the other caves.'

12 The Golden Ring (1954)

ALAN J B WACE

The tide of war carried me in 1917 to Salónica where I saw my friend George Evesham who was shortly afterwards mortally wounded in the fruitless Allied offensive in April of that year. Of his death I have written elsewhere, but what I have to tell now was also connected with his death to some extent. From Salónica I was sent on to Athens for special duty and it so happened that when Evesham was killed his colonel, whom I had met at Salónica, wrote to me once or twice about the disposal of Evesham's personal belongings. Later at the end of the summer when I thought that all Evesham's affairs had been settled, I was surprised to receive another letter from his colonel and with it a small packet.

The letter ran as follows:

I am sending you in a separate packet something else that belonged to poor George Evesham. It is a Greek gold ring on which he set much store and always wore round his neck like an identity disc. He was not wearing it when he was killed because one night when he was asleep two subalterns cut the string and removed it for a rag. Poor Evesham was much put out, but as this happened only one or two days before the offensive he never recovered it. Of the subalterns one was killed in the same attack and the other died of wounds. The latter gave the ring and string to a chaplain in the Casualty Clearing Station. He seemed to fancy that judging by the way poor Evesham regarded the ring as a mascot he was responsible for his death, because he was not wearing it when he was killed. The chaplain went to Malta in a hospital ship and has only just returned here and that is why we did not know about the ring before. Anyway here is the ring and it is said to be Byzantine and ever so many hundred years old BC. Still you will know all about it and what it is best to be done with it. Perhaps the Athens Museum might like it or you could give it to the British Museum. The silly bit of string to which the ring was fastened poor Evesham always wore with it and would never change. Please acknowledge on receipt ...

When I opened the little packet which accompanied this rather characteristic military letter I found, in a Bryant and May match box, a worn gold ring tied to a rough piece of woollen yarn, obviously hand spun and knotted thrice as though it had been cut. The ring was small and rather broad, but plain except for two bands of tiny gold pearls. It had a large almond-shaped bezel, also of gold, on which so far as I could see a quadruped of some kind seemed to be represented in intaglio. The type of ring I recognized at once as characteristically Mycenaean and certainly ever so many centuries old, probably thirteen at least BC, but certainly not Byzantine except to such unbelievers as told Schliemann that the royal treasures of Mycenae, which he had found, were Byzantine and therefore un-Homeric. I wondered what to do with the ring for it was so worn that it had little artistic value. Still as Evesham had always been very fond of working in the Mycenaean room of the National Museum at Athens I thought I might follow up his colonel's suggestion and see whether the museum would like it as a memorial of him.

Accordingly a few days later when I had a couple of hours free in the morning I went to the National Museum with the ring. I showed it to the then Director who was specially interested in the Mycenaean collection. After looking at it closely with a glass he said it was certainly genuine and added that the quadruped must be a bull because that was the animal most popular with the Mycenaeans for engraving on seals and gems. He promised he would have a plaster cast made so that we should be better able to judge, and then took a lump of fine beeswax from his desk and pressed the bezel of the ring into it. As he did so his fingers became entangled in the string. This annoyed him and he flew into a temper, which he did very easily, and saying that he did not want that dirty bit of string, he cut it with a pen knife from his desk. After studying the impression carefully he said he could not decide, but still was in favour of recognizing the animal as a bull. He undertook that if I would come back in two or three days he would have the plaster impression ready and that we would then go into the question more fully.

The following week when my turn for a few hours off duty came round once more I called again at the Museum. To my surprise I found it in a somewhat disturbed condition. The very day after I had seen him the Director had had a severe stroke and was now lying ill in bed at his house, speechless and helpless. The doctors said it was unlikely that he would regain the use of his faculties, but that he might survive for several months. In the meantime the assistant director had taken charge and was doing his best to cope with the situation which was made worse by the fact that one of the senior attendants had disappeared. I enquired after the ring and he called the museum technician who produced a plaster impression of the ring. We discussed the subject, but could arrive at no conclusion. I felt it was not a bull but some other animal, while both the assistant director and the technician were ready to accept the bull identification. So I asked to see the ring again. To the assistant director's horror the ring could not be found. He rummaged through the safe and the special cupboards in the director's room where it should have been, but there was no sign of it. Then an idea struck him and he asked me what day it was I had brought it. When I told him he said that on the very next day the missing attendant, Thersites Glossopoulos, had failed to put in an appearance. It was consequently suggested that the attendant had stolen the ring and perhaps other things and vanished. The police were at once informed and a strict watch was ordered to be kept on all men trying to depart from Piraeus, Patras, or any other port whence vessels sailed to other countries. The passport, police, and port authorities were supplied with his name and particulars, so that if he tried to leave even by signing on as a seaman he would be recognized and detained.

Days, however, passed and no word came of the missing man. At last it was discovered that he had a brother, a baker, at Chalcis and I gladly accepted an invitation to go with the gendarmerie officer to make enquiries. When we arrived at Chalcis, the baker was summoned to the gendarmerie station and interrogated. He said his brother had come to see him a week or two before and stayed a few days, but then had left suddenly, presumably to go back to his post in Athens. We then went on to the bakery to question his wife. She called on fire and lightning to burn her, but she knew nothing more. She was sent into an inner room and their small daughter, Koula, who was about ten or twelve, was called before the local sergeant in charge of the interrogation. He pulled a tattered notebook and a broken pencil from the lining of his cap, licked the pencil, and looked ferociously at the girl.

'Now, tell us the truth!' he thundered in his sternest official voice, 'How many gold rings did your uncle take away with him? Your father says he took only one, but we know better. He took six. Now tell us the truth or you will go to prison and never come out.'

The girl though obviously terrified was staunch and said simply that her uncle had had no gold rings and that she believed he had gone back to Athens. I felt convinced by the girl's manner that she was telling the absolute truth and so begged the officer that the unlucky baker and his family should be left in peace.

The railway officials said that the missing man had not gone back to Athens by train. A boatman, however, told us that about the time Thersites disappeared from Chalcis a Greek ship laden with magnesite from Limne had set sail for England. Further the captain of the vessel, also a native of Chalcis, was a god-brother of Thersites. We jumped to the obvious conclusion. Thersites had persuaded his godbrother to take him on as one of his crew and so had slipped inconspicuously out of the country. On our return to Athens orders were at once telegraphed to Gibraltar that the vessel should be detained and searched for the man. The man, when found, was to be sent back to Greece as soon as possible for examination. Again we waited but no news came from Gibraltar and no news came from England of the ship's arrival. The vessel, the *Aspasia Arabatzoglou*, was never heard of again. Most probably she was sunk with all hands by the Germans somewhere in the central Mediterranean where enemy submarines were then very active.

In the winter of 1917–18 I managed to get home on leave and while in England I helped Evesham's mother to prepare the little memoir of him which was prefixed to the collected edition of his poems. I thus had the opportunity of going through his notebooks and other papers and while doing so I found his notes about the ring – how he had obtained it and some other details.

It had come into his hands in 1913. That spring he happened to be in Mycenae staying at the little inn, 'The Fair Helen of Menelaus', which archaeologists always delight to patronize. One morning when he was walking up the road towards the citadel he found the road crowded with a party of shepherds who with their flocks, wives and families, dogs and cats, chickens, and other belongings were moving up into the hills for the summer. Just before Evesham reached the point where the road passes in front of the Lion Gate he overtook a group of three old women who were spinning wool as they walked along. He paid no attention to them, but one of them called him and when he turned around she showed him the ring. He took it, looked at it, and saw how worn it was and handed it back saying he did not wish to buy it. The old woman then said she did not wish to sell it, but wished to give it to him. He refused to take it because, though it had little archaeological importance, owing to its condition, it was still gold and therefore of some value. The old woman, however, insisted and so he took it and showed it would not go on his finger, as is usually the case with this type of Mycenaean ring. One of the other old women unwound a piece of the yarn from her distaff and slipped the ring on it, but she could not break the thread. So the third old woman took the scissors which were hanging by a string from her belt and cut the yarn. The first woman, the one who had produced the ring, then knotted the yarn and put it over Evesham's head.

'*Mi to khasis!* (Don't lose it!)' she said, as she did so.

'*Mi to dhosis!* (Don't sell it!)' added the second.

'*Mi to kopsis!* (Don't cut it!)' concluded the third with an air of finality.

Although he thought it all sounded rather silly, Evesham to humour them said he would always wear it and thanked them very much. He then turned off to go up to the Lion Gate, but as he did so he remembered he had never asked them where it was found. He turned back to go after them, but though he walked some distance up the path in the direction they were going, he could not find them. They seemed, he wrote, to have vanished.

Evesham does not seem to have shown the ring to anyone at the National Museum or to anyone else in Athens, but on his return to England he took the ring to the British Museum. There one of the assistant-keepers of the Greek and Roman Department treated the ring coldly, said it seemed genuine though a poor example, showed he did not think much of it, but could not decide whether the quadruped was a bull or some other four-footed beast. He handed it to one of the technicians, asking him to prepare plaster impressions to help them to decide the nature of the animal. After two days Evesham called again and the assistant-keeper rang for his technician to bring the ring and the impressions. An attendant came in to say that the technician had not yet arrived that morning. Instructions were given to telephone to his house to find out if he was ill and to bring in the ring and impressions. A little cardboard tray was produced and in it lay the ring, two plaster impressions of the design on its bezel and the woollen thread which had been cut and separated from the ring. While Evesham and the assistant-keeper were fruitlessly debating the vexed question of the identity of the quadruped, word was brought that the technician had left home at his usual hour for the Museum. Hard on the heels of that message came one from the Middlesex Hospital to say that he had been knocked down by a car, seriously injured, and had died soon after reaching the casualty ward.

Having failed to gain any enlightenment from the British Museum, Evesham took the ring with him to Oxford when he went there at the beginning of October. Oxford then boasted the possession of the chief experts in the Minoan and Mycenaean archaeology of Greece. The three most renowned of these sat for some little time arguing the case of the ring and its design from all aspects in the typical Oxonian manner. The ring they all declared was not Mycenaean but Minoan, for all the civilization of Mycenae and everything found there came from Crete. The ring therefore was Minoan, that is to say Cretan, and since the bull, as witness the Minotaur, was the legendary animal of Crete the quadruped on the ring must be a bull. They further told Evesham that the ring was an inferior specimen and obviously of late date and in such bad condition as to be almost worthless except for its metallic value. One of the experts began to cut the woollen thread, but Evesham checked him just in time. He had, however, to knot the yarn to prevent a break.

Evesham, who still believed in the ring and was determined if possible to solve the problem of the representation on it, was not discouraged by its chilly reception both in the British Museum and in Oxford. He wrote that he had a feeling somehow that the ring was connected with the history of Mycenae and never ceased to regret that he had not asked the old women where and how it was found. He wondered whether he would take it to Cambridge and see whether the rival university could help him, because the principal Oxford expert had been suddenly attacked by a serious infection of his eyes. He was advised, however, so Evesham noted, that no one in Cambridge was of any competence in Minoan or Mycenaean matters.

As we know, Evesham continued to wear the ring and constantly took it with him wherever he went, regarding it as a kind of mascot. Thus it happened that he had it with him when he was sent to join the Salónica army and, but for the untimely trick of the two subalterns, would have been wearing it in the Allied offensive in 1917 when he was mortally wounded.

After I read Evesham's notes about the ring and its history my interest and curiosity were still more excited and I resolved that, when I had an opportunity of revisiting Athens, I would again consult the authorities of the National Museum to see what further information could be gleaned. I even dreamed of visiting Mycenae and inquiring there whether it was possible to get into touch with the local shepherds and find the old women. For a moment I even fancied myself discovering some rich and hitherto unknown royal tomb hidden in the glens of Argolis, which would make my name as famous as that of Schliemann. Fortunately my opportunity came sooner than I could have hoped. So many British experts left the Aegean to attend the Peace Conference in Paris that their places had to be filled and so I was, much to my delight, once again sent out to Greece early in 1919.

As soon as I could after my arrival in Athens I called at the National Museum and found that my old friend, Dr Klavdianos, had just been made director. The previous one had recently died, after being bedridden ever since the episode of Evesham's ring. Klavdianos had obtained the keys of the late director from his widow, who had been unwilling to part with them while her husband still lived and held his post. Klavdianos was thus exploring all the cupboards in the Director's office as well as the locked drawers in his desk where his private papers had been kept. I naturally asked him if he had come upon any trace of the ring.

'What ring?' he asked, and so I explained and said that the technician ought still to have one at least of the plaster impressions. Then he pulled open one of the private drawers in the director's desk which he had just unlocked to inspect and sort the contents. From this he picked out a gold ring.

'Is this it?' he asked. It was the very ring and in the same drawer we found the cut piece of woollen yarn on which it had been fastened and a wax impression of the design on the bezel. I was delighted to see the ring again and he was equally delighted that it was now proved that Thersites Glossopoulos had never stolen it. When the news spread among the other museum attendants they also were highly pleased because the honesty of their body was at last vindicated.

I then asked Klavdianos if he would like to have the ring as a gift to the Museum. He gladly accepted it and handed it at once to be numbered and entered in the inventory while we talked over other things. A small label was typed out stating that this Mycenaean ring was presented in memory of Evesham who had fallen fighting for Greece against the Bulgarians in Macedonia, and Klavdianos asked me to go with him into the Mycenaean room and select a suitable place for its exhibition. This we did and left the ring in a case containing some of the other treasures from Agamemnon's city.

We also discussed the problem of the animal represented in the intaglio on the bezel and Klavdianos said that if I would come back in a few days he would go through the collection of Mycenaean rings and engraved gems and, sealstones and see if he could come to some satisfactory solution. So about a week later I visited the museum again.

'They have taken it!' laconically remarked the chief attendant who met me and he added some derogatory remarks about 'them'. I failed to understand him at first, but soon elicited the fact that Evesham's ring, which Klavdianos and I had put into a locked and otherwise secure glass exhibition case not a week ago, had disappeared about three days before. In reply to my inquiries he told me that that particular day was rainy and consequently the light in the museum was not good and there were loud claps of thunder and vivid lightning. Visitors were naturally few in the Mycenaean room, only three in fact, old women wearing 'Vlach' or shepherd clothing who had obviously come in to get out of the rain. The attendant on duty did not watch them very closely because they were clearly so harmless and as they moved about from case to case they exclaimed to one another in uncouth dialect about particular treasures that attracted them. His attention was distracted for a moment when the man who had repaired the roof looked in to ask whether it was watertight. When he looked round again the old women had gone and he concluded they had moved on to see the sculpture galleries. No one, however, had noticed the old women in any other gallery and no one had seen them go out, but as just at that time the sun had come out brilliantly for a brief spell, it was assumed they had taken advantage of it to go their way.

The fact that the ring was missing was not noticed until the next morning when Klavdianos came in to verify a point in connection with the comments about it he had promised me. The museum case was still locked, but the ring was gone and how it could have been abstracted no one could tell. A possible solution was that the old women were expert thieves in disguise who had taken advantage of the bad, dull weather and the thunder to employ skeleton keys on a museum case. That they had taken only the ring which was not an outstanding object was accounted for by the suggestion that they were disturbed and had just snatched at the first thing. This was the official explanation published later after a formal inquiry in which everyone was exonerated.

When I called on Klavdianos to ask if the official investigation had thrown any light on the mystery or whether he had solved the problem of the representation he turned round in his chair and took from the bookcase behind him one volume of Frazer's monumental commentary on Pausanias and turned to the page where it told the story of Atreus, Aerope, Thyestes, and the golden lamb.

Atreus vowed to sacrifice the finest animal in his flocks to Artemis. A golden lamb appeared among them, but he strangled it and kept it in a box. His wife, Aerope, granddaughter of Minos, who had been seduced by his brother Thyestes, abstracted it and gave it to her lover. The Mycenaeans were told by an oracle to elect a king from the house of Pelops and sent for Atreus and Thyestes. The latter persuaded the people that the possessor of the golden lamb ought to be king. Atreus in ignorance of his betrayal agreed.

Thyestes produced the golden lamb and became king. This was one of the main causes of the bitter feud between the two brothers which afterwards wrought such tragedy in the house of Atreus.

'You see this is a lamb and not a bull,' explained Klavdianos. 'Look at the length of the legs, the tail, and the rendering of the fleece!' As he spoke he pointed out these details on the impression, and I saw now that my original feeling that it was not a bull was perfectly correct. The Oxford and other experts to whom Evesham had shown the ring had been so convinced it must be a bull that they had not taken any other possibility seriously into consideration. Once the eye knew the solution the figure of the lamb became visible of itself.

Was this then really the golden lamb of Atreus?

Notes on the text

BY KATE MACDONALD

1 The Shining Pyramid (1895)

pigeon-holes: old-fashioned desks contained many shelves with small partitions for filing, which resembled the roosts of domestic pigeons.

Doré: the French illustrator Gustav Doré had become famous in the UK as an engraver of atmospheric scenes with his 1861 illustrated edition of Dante's *Inferno*, followed by *Purgatorio and Paradiso* in 1868.

'far in the spiritual city': a line from Sir Galahad's poem 'The Holy Grail' in *Idylls of the King* by Alfred Lord Tennyson, describing Galahad's vision of heaven.

Monte Cristo: in Alexandre Dumas' celebrated and much serialised novel *The Count of Monte Cristo* (1844).

idol of the South Seas: presumably one of the monumental stone *moai* of Rapa Nui, formerly Easter Island.

the worm of corruption, the worm that dieth not: 'The worm of corruption' may be a paraphrase from Job 17.14, in which he complains bitterly to his friends of being abandoned by God. 'The worm dieth not' from Mark 9.44 is part of Jesus's insistence to the disciples of the reality of hell.

Achilles and the tortoise: a paradox made famous by Zeno of Elea, which misleads the reader into thinking that something is impossible because critical information (in this case, speed) has been left out.

ghastly yellow: Machen is not equating the yellow skin of his previous 'Chinaman' and Mongolian similes with supreme evil here but it isn't far off.

Edmond Dantès: the protagonist of *The Count of Monte Cristo.*

horrible Chinese oubliette: Dyson's apparent obsession with evil Chinese people may be assigned to the contemporary fashion for 'Yellow Peril' sensation fiction, which vilified Chinese communities in London's Limehouse and other dockyard quarters.

de novo: Portuguese, again.

Devil's Punch-bowl: a deep steep-sided circular valley near Hindhead in Surrey that forms a natural amphitheatre, probably due to geological collapse by erosion.

Turanian: The term Turanian, a now-obsolete nineteenth-century racial category which was originally applied to the linguistic Uralic and Altaic groups of Central Asia, was incorporated into the belief proposed by Scottish folklorist David McRitchie, the 'Turanian Pygmy Theory'. This theory, taken up by Machen and other writers of the time, suggested that the fairies or 'little people' of folklore and mythology were in fact the last remnants of a pre-Indo-European pygmy race who had been driven into the remote areas of the British Isles with the coming of the Celts.

2 Through The Veil (1911)

cattle-thieving: in common with many other border territories, the medieval Scots and English living alongside the border made a habit of stealing each other's cattle, intermarrying and fighting.

rest a wee: Scots, to take a short rest.

gang: Scots, to go.

thole, lugs: Scots, to endure, their ears.

foss: a high wall.

Valeria Victrix: the twentieth legion of the Imperial Roman Army, who worked on the construction of the Wall in AD 122–125.

beneath us: on the other side of the defensive wall that the Picts have climbed.

3 The Ape (1917)

felucca: a small wooden sailing boat, typical of Nile river traffic.

suspicious: probably fake.

wares of Manchester: the ingenuity of the British Industrial Revolution had ensured that British manufacturing could sell anything to any market, even fake Egyptian artefacts to tourists in Egypt.

sub rosa: Latin, 'under the rose', signifying a pact of secrecy.

sovereign: the standard English gold coin valued at twenty shillings, one pound sterling, accepted widely outside the UK in the nineteenth century.

boy with the ink-mirror: presumably a soothsayer, who looks into a pool of ink as a mirror to see the future.

pulling his hands apart: in the original publication in 1920 this was phrased as 'severing his hands' but was rephrased in later collections containing this story.

board-schools: organised education along English and Christian lines, imposed on the Egyptian and Islamic population.

Book of the Dead: a collection of Ancient Egyptian funerary texts, spells and devotional incantations. The example in the British Museum was discovered in 1888.

Karnak, Abydos, Hieropolis: Karnak is the site of a vast temple and tomb complex in Egypt dating from 2000 BCE; Abydos (Abdju) was one of the oldest cities of Ancient Egypt, dating from 3200 BCE, containing many tombs and temples; Hierakonpolis (Nekhen) was also an Ancient Egyptian funerary site containing important cultural and devotional artefacts.

baksheesh: originating from Persian, a generic term for a tip or charitable donation throughout the Middle East.

piastres: another generic term, for small change, used as currency in Egypt up to the mid-twentieth century as well as in many other countries.

ushapti figures: ushabti or shabti are miniature funerary figurines from Ancient Egyptian tombs, collected in modern times as art.

Parthian retreat: a feigned retreat to lure the enemy on in pursuit, with the intention of attacking suddenly when they least expect it.

4 The Next Heir (1920)

mullioned: where the panes of glass in a large window are separated vertically by pieces of carved stonework.

japanned: a European imitation of the lacquer finish on bamboo and metal items from China and Japan.

tea: in the first usage the butler means the drink, while the second the afternoon meal of sandwiches and cake is intended, with tea to drink.

tessellated: tiled in mosaic.

Lupercalia: an ancient Roman festival of purification, possibly connected to a celebration of an aspect of the Greek god Pan and the wolf. Lindsay doesn't sound as if he knows his Roman festivals very well.

farthing dip: the cheapest form of candle, not likely to give much light or last long.

jocund: lively, full of good-humour and merriment.

peg: a measure of spirits deriving from British India. Measuring out whisky by a number of finger-widths is also a traditional Indian army practice.

wether: an older sheep, often the leader of the flock.

braxy mutton: the meat of a sheep that has died from the bacterial disease braxy.

under that cover: a country-house breakfast presented a variety of hot dishes under metal covers to keep them warm.

jerrybuilding: cheap construction that doesn't last long.

scryer: one who looks into the future, or can see visions in water or another reflective surface.

styptics: pharmaceutical treatments to contract the blood vessels and stop bleeding.

5 View From A Hill (1925)

longer drink: a beer, or a drink with more volume than a cup of tea, such as cider-cup (see below).

Borgia box: the Borgia family were notorious for drawing the blood of their enemies.

park: not a public park, but the lands of the estate beyond the formal gardens, greenhouses and kitchen garden. They were maintained as property, might be grazed by stock from the home farm, but would have been kept in rougher condition than the gardens near the house.

ordnance map: the Ordnance Survey made the first scientifically measured maps of Britain, originally for military purposes.

white moving cloud: this was the era when trains were fuelled by steam.

letterpress: the text in the journal.

a little glass: a small amount of stained glass in the church worth seeing.

cider-cup: a refreshing summer drink related to punch, made with differing quantities of cider, brandy, lemons and sodawater.

cover: a section of managed woodland.

fish basket: a long soft basket traditionally made of rushes to hold a catch of fish.

in the servants' 'all: in the English class system it was not common for servants to sit and have conversations with their employers, and those that did so, even the most senior rank of servant like Patten, would be talked about with disapproval by their peers as getting above themselves.

was took: before he died.

6 Curse of the Stillborn (1926)

piqué: a woven cotton dress fabric now used for sportswear, as it absorbs sweat

pith helmet: the classic British colonial headgear worn to ward off the sun as well as insects, and to allow a lady to wear a suitable hat for the climate.

haik: a large cloak covering the head and body as an outer garment for women in North Africa, secured with a belt and pins.

wried: twisted to the side.

7 The Cure (1929)

The moon doth with delight: from William Wordsworth's *Intimations of Immortality* (1807).

8 Ho! The Merry Masons (1933)

the old Runagates Club: Buchan published a collection of clubland tales in 1928 as *The Runagates Club*, after-dinner stories told to fellow diners with a private club of semi-retired adventurers and experts as a framing device. Several characters in this story appear in that collection, and in some earlier Buchan stories.

oysters: traditionally oysters are not served when there is not an 'r' in the name of the month, ie not in the summer months when oysters are spawning and should be conserved. Oysters also spawn in April, so the rule isn't quite perfect.

Dee, Wye, Blackwater: well-known fishing rivers in Wales and southern England.

in the chair: the elected host of the club evening.

with a heart: with a heart problem.

sederunt: a Scots term for a formal ecclesiastical meeting.

trait d'union: French, a hyphen, that which joins two unconnected objects.

the courts: Leithen is a barrister, with chambers at the Inns of Court in London.

Greenbourton: an invented village name, but since Buchan lived in the Cotswolds he may have based it on a place he knew.

glen: Leithen is not Scottish, and Oxfordshire valleys are not called glens: this is Buchan's own voice creeping into his character's narration.

Marches: the border country between Scotland and England.

curtains: curtain walls, added to medieval castles to make it difficult for attackers to get in, or to protect doors and inner grounds from the weather, with towers and battlements depending on their size.

entailed: an indivisible part of a family inheritance, property that could not be sold off but had to descend to the next heir.

Vaunus: while Priapus and Nodens are known in Classical myth, Vaunus is a vengeful Roman god of Buchan's invention, about which he wrote 'The Wind in the Portico' (1928).

muniment room: the family archive, a room where estate papers, charters and other documents and records were kept.

Guy Mannering: a novel published in 1815 by Sir Walter Scott, of whom Buchan wrote a biography.

bad plumbing: a polite euphemism for sewage-related diseases such as cholera.

powdering closet: a small room off the master bedroom in which eighteenth-century gentlemen and ladies would have their hair dressed with powder, a messy business for which a separate room would be convenient. This is presumably the medieval cubby-hole Leithen mentioned earlier.

point-to-point: a horse race, originally measured by a set series of landmarks across country which its riders would have to reach in turn. In its more organised form it would contain standard obstacles such as hedges, walls, ditches, ponds and tight corners, raced on a confined course rather than across country.

Lord Rosebery: Liberal politician and a Victorian Prime Minister of Britain, of whom Buchan wrote a biography.

9 Roman Remains (1948)

credo quia impossibile: Latin, 'I believe that it is impossible'.

'everything possible to be believed is an image of truth': from William Blake's 'Proverbs of Hell', in his *The Marriage of Heaven and Hell* (1790–93).

a Chair: a professorship.

got out just in time: managed to escape the worst of Nazi persecution by escaping Germany before the Second World War.

a negligible matter: even during wartime, among the upper classes (ie those who had their own country estates), changing from day to evening clothes for dinner was a mark of good manners and an indicator of respect for class conventions.

fishing was out of the question: sunlight reflecting on water makes it impossible to see what might be moving underneath.

Missgeburt: German, a freak, something not normal.

Urmenschen, *unheimlich*: German for, respectively, primitive man, and ominous.

Operations: Breddle's military service.

11 Whitewash (1952)

The Story of San Michele: a memoir published in 1931 by the Swedish doctor Axel Münthe that relates selected episodes from his life and career as a medical man among the rich and famous, with embellishments. It became a world best-seller. He had built the Villa of San Michele on the site of ruins from the reign of the Emperor Tiberius on the island of Capri.

Tiberius: now remembered as one of the most notorious Roman emperors, son of the emperor Augustus's wife Livia, whose lurid activities during his self-imposed exile on Capri were recorded in Suetonius's *Lives of the Twelve Caesars*.

bernous: burnous, a long cloak with a hood, traditionally worn in white or beige in North Africa, and more recently incorporated into the uniform of a regiment of the French army. It gives a dashing appearance, and is usefully warm and all-enveloping.

Veni, cete, veni: Latin, literally 'come, whale, come', an invitation to the waiting shark (though not a cetacean) to come and eat.

Abi, cete, abi hinc: Latin, 'Off you go, whale, away with you'.

Norman: probably Norman Douglas, the British novelist and alleged paedophile who lived for many years on Capri, where his personal conduct and written works from the early twentieth century advocated for greater moral and sexual freedoms than were socially admissable at the time: many still are not. He died in February 1952, shortly before this story was first published.

12 The Golden Ring (1954)

a rag: archaic term for a joke.

intaglio: a method of carving into gemstones so that the design is incised into the surface.

Schliemann: Heinrich Schliemann was a pioneering amateur archaeologist who specialised in Bronze Age Greece, and is most famous for excavating the sites now agreed to be Troy and Mycenae of the *Iliad*.

Lion Gate: the largest surviving sculpted structure from the prehistoric Aegean, set at the entrance to the city of Mycenae.

spinning wool: a practice common worldwide in pre-industrial societies for which wool production was a means for women to gain income while travelling or working at other tasks. These women also have a resemblance to the Fates, who spin and cut the threads of human lives.

British Weird

Selected Short Fiction, 1893–1937

Edited by James Machin

British Weird
Selected Short Fiction,
1893–1937
Edited by James Machin

'Classic stories, but also less familiar ones' – *Washington Post*

British Weird is a new anthology of classic Weird short fiction by British writers, first published between the 1890s and the 1930s. This collection – curated by James Machin, author of Palgrave Gothic's *Weird Fiction in Britain, 1880–1939* – assembles stories to thrill, entertain, and chill. Stories that embrace the malignant qualities of structures and artefacts:

- 'Man-Size in Marble' by Edith Nesbit (1893), in which statuary walks.
- 'Randalls Round' by Eleanor Scott (1927), in which a mound should not be disturbed.
- 'N' by Arthur Machen (1934), in which a particular window gives London an entirely a new aspect.
- 'Mappa Mundi' by Mary Butts (1937), in which the streets of Paris have an alternative existence.

Includes 'Ghosties and Ghoulies', Mary Butts' ground-breaking essay from 1933 on the supernatural in modern fiction.

Machin's introduction describes the background for these excellent stories in the Weird tradition, and identifies their use of peculiarly British preoccupations in supernatural short fiction.

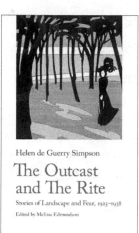

The Outcast and The Rite

Stories of Landscape and Fear, 1925–38

by Helen de Guerry Simpson

The long forgotten Australian author Helen de Guerry Simpson (1897–1940) was a prize-winning historical novelist, and wrote uncanny terror like a scalpel applied lightly to the nerves. She published many supernatural short stories before her untimely death in 1940 in London. This new edition selects the best of her unsettling writing. Featured stories about historic structures with intentions of their own include:

- 'As Much More Land', in which an Oxford undergraduate challenges a haunted bedroom to scare him.
- 'Teigne', in which a house with a curse is stripped of all its fittings.
- 'Disturbing Experience of an Elderly Lady', in which a new-made widow buys the house she has always longed for.

The Introduction is by Melissa Edmundson, senior lecturer at Clemson University, South Carolina, a leading scholar of women's Weird fiction and supernatural writing from the early twentieth century.

D K Broster

From the Abyss

Weird Fiction, 1907–1945

Edited by Melissa Edmundson

From the Abyss
Weird Fiction, 1907–1945
by D K Broster

D K Broster was one of the great British historical novelists of the twentieth century, but her Weird fiction has long been forgotten. She wrote some of the most impressive supernatural short stories to be published between the wars. Melissa Edmundson, editor of Handheld's *Women's Weird*, has curated a selection of Broster's best and most terrifying work. Stories in *From the Abyss* include these tales of particular archaeological and architectural interest:

- 'The Window', in which a deserted chateau exacts revenge when one particular window is opened.
- 'The Pavement', in which the protectress of a Roman mosaic cannot bear to let it go.
- 'Clairvoyance', in which the spirit of a vengeful Japanese swordmaster enters an adolescent girl.
- 'The Pestering', in which a cursed hidden treasure draws its victim across centuries to find it.
- 'The Taste of Pomegranates' draws two young women into the palaeolithic past.

CPSIA information can be obtained
at www.ICGtesting.com
Printed in the USA
JSHW011225250423
40785JS00004B/4